THE
FALLEN

THE
FALLEN

BEN SANDERS

HarperCollins*Publishers*

HarperCollins*Publishers*

First published in 2010
by HarperCollins*Publishers* (New Zealand) Limited
PO Box 1, Shortland Street, Auckland 1140
Reprinted 2010 (twice)

HarperCollins*Publishers*
31 View Road, Glenfield, Auckland 0627, New Zealand
25 Ryde Road, Pymble, Sydney, NSW 2073, Australia
A 53, Sector 57, Noida, UP, India
77–85 Fulham Palace Road, London W6 8JB, United Kingdom
2 Bloor Street East, 20th floor, Toronto, Ontario M4W 1A8, Canada
10 East 53rd Street, New York, NY 10022, USA

National Library of New Zealand Cataloguing-in-Publication Data

Sanders, Ben, 1989-
The fallen / Ben Sanders.
ISBN 978-1-86950-876-0
I.Title.
NZ823.3—dc 22

Cover design by Priscilla Nielsen
Cover images: gun and bullets by Joshua Sheldon/Getty Images; all other
images by shutterstock.com
Typesetting by Springfield West

Printed by Griffin Press, Australia

50gsm Bulky News used by HarperCollins*Publishers* is a natural, recyclable
product made from wood grown in sustainable plantation forests. The
manufacturing processes conform to the environmental regulations in the
country of origin, New Zealand.

This book is dedicated to my parents,
who always made me read.

■ ONE

Treverne came to slowly. Unconsciousness was a new experience, and the transition to reality was not pleasant.

His vision improved gradually; contrast returning as lines sharpened like stone etched with acid. Certainly that's how he felt, like he'd been bathed in something corrosive. Skin abraded, recollection stripped bare. His left knee ached, and when he tried to raise his hands to his face, he realized his wrists were secured at the small of his back.

He lifted his head off the carpet, and as he did there was a tacky, adhesive sound like masking tape peeling free, and from the rich coppery stench he inhaled he knew he must have been bleeding.

He worked splayed hands beneath his butt, clenched his stomach and threw himself into a sitting position. The sudden movement of his leg heralded a front of nausea, but he clenched his teeth and dropped his jaw to his chest, and after a moment it receded. He breathed deeply through his nose, and from the throb of it he knew it must be broken. Christ, where was he? The entrance hall. The sky through the glass in the front door was as black as nightmares. The glow from streetlights penetrated the fissure between the panelling and the jamb, freezing dust motes as they floated.

He listened, but the house was near silent; the only sound the rattle of breath through his broken nose. Broken nose. Jesus, that was the least of his worries. He shuffled left and his shackled hands found something wet, and the way it greased his fingers he knew it was partially congealed blood. The certainty that it was his own re-summoned the nausea, and this time he couldn't quell the need to vomit. He convulsed and bile slid from his mouth, warm across his chin, settling in his lap.

'Christ,' he said thickly.

His eyes went to the window again, cut right to the kitchen; instinctive reactions designed to search out someone to acknowledge his state, but his house was still empty, the only noise his own. His heartbeat quickened, and the sharp taste of his stomach contents met his palate a moment before they fell wetly to his lap.

Nothing, and then the light through the crack in the door changed from white to an alternating pattern of red and blue.

His heart stumbled. His stomach constricted.

He had no idea how long he had been unconscious, no idea whether cops had been called. He looked at the flashing lights again. Clearly somebody had. Shit. Talking to them would be the end of it. Talking to them would mean a report with his name and address on it. More harm than good.

He leaned his weight against the wall beside the door and extended a finger to better gauge what secured his wrists. Handcuffs, obviously. Whether he could remove them without a key would prove critical.

He rolled right, tucked his knee to his chest and used a combined sudden jerk from his shoulder and foot to get to his feet. Light in the door stronger now. He tested his bad leg hesitantly, gradually increasing the weight he entrusted to it. The pain of it tipped the floor around him, but he stayed upright. He shuffled into the kitchen, blood rolling off his chin, probed his way past the table to the cutlery drawers beneath the sink. He turned and scrabbled with his fingers for the handle of the top drawer and pulled it open, squeal of wood squeezed too tight. He arched backwards and searched unseeingly through its interior, feeling his heart leap against the material of his shirt. Through the window above the table he saw the red and blue lights outside peak in intensity, then fade again, as if the source of the glow had simply approached and moved on, unsure of the correct destination.

He dug into the far recesses, panicking that his search could prove entirely unsuccessful, until his fingers closed around the cool, rigid form of a fork. He removed it from the drawer, and, shuffling sideways, grasped the middle section with his right hand and used the first finger of his left to tap the tines cautiously. He then pushed the implement firmly against the edge of the steeled bench top, until the left-most tine was bent out at a ninety-degree angle.

Shit. Come *on*.

His attention still on the light in the door, he held the fork steady in his right hand, oriented so that the deformed tine could insert into the barrel of the lock in the left cuff. He had just sufficient movement in his right wrist to rotate the fork and incrementally manipulate the cuff's ratchet.

It works in theory. He breathed evenly to regulate his heartbeat and watched as the light rinsing the hall carpet returned to its earlier maximum intensity. He heard a car door slam, followed by muted voices, radio static carrying on the dead air. He felt the fork growing increasingly slick in his hand, and willed himself to operate faster. A blast of static, and he sensed the mechanism free. He dropped his wrist a fraction, the lock popped open, and a beat later his hand was released.

He crouched with his back against the cupboards, face cocked to the doorway, then slipped the fork into his back pocket, careful to leave the deformed tine exposed. He estimated there were perhaps two police vehicles parked outside, but clearly they were hesitating. Activity appeared to have halted. He rose unsteadily to his feet, and with his free hand took a quick inventory of the contents of his pockets. Nothing. He moved right, cautious about the stress he applied to his injured knee, his body a silhouette of crisp black as he entered the hall. He made it up the stairs to the first floor with surprisingly little difficulty. Through his bedroom window he could see a single patrol car parked at his letterbox. *Just one, then.* A faint chime as one of them tried the bell, a hushed tick as blood struck his duvet.

He crouched and removed a duffel bag from beneath his bed, hefting it onto his shoulder. He hobbled into the bathroom and drank straight from the tap. Never sweeter.

The bell sounded again, but he was confident they wouldn't attempt to enter. He felt his way back down the stairs, balance corrupt in the dark. He turned left into the kitchen, and this time it took him only a moment to free himself from the one remaining cuff. He placed the bloodied manacles and the fork soundlessly in the sink and made his way painfully back to the hall, face cut with discomfort. He figured one car, probably two cops. Not insurmountable.

He passed the stairs and followed a short corridor floored with linoleum to a door that gave out onto the rear of the property.

He felt the coolness of the night on his face as he padded down the back step and stood with his back to the rear wall of the house. He inched his way left along to the corner nearest the front door and peered out, pleased when he realized he had never known a richer darkness. He adjusted the weight of the bag, stood erect then limped for the edge of the property, cutting through the now familiar red-and-blue pulsation with as much vigour as he could summon. Light rain began to fall, and he welcomed its coolness against the injuries to his face.

He vaulted the fence, ignoring the protestations from his leg, and shuffled quickly into a neighbour's backyard. He moved hurriedly through the property, then the next, and then the one after that, before cutting left along a driveway to the street, where he hung a swift right, putting his home and the patrol car directly behind him.

He allowed himself to slow as the red-and-blue glow grew increasingly indistinct. The road curved gently as it meandered downhill, and before long he was out of sight, just another fractured glimpse of shadow more likely cast by tree than man.

There was a cluster of vehicles ahead; anonymous sedans parked bumper to bumper against the kerb, all lit yellow beneath the glare of a street lamp, lonely amidst a stretch of gloriously lush darkness. He could hear uproarious laughter and a rapid bassy thud emanating from a house opposite. Revellers oblivious to the plight of the victimized.

Five minutes' walk got him to the bottom of his street. The patrol car hadn't reappeared — curious — but he was grateful.

Directly opposite was a retail block of about ten or fifteen shops, fronted by an empty pool of asphalt parking.

Windows in the front wall spanning from footpath to rooftop. He could see himself shimmering there, waiting. He and his mirror-image self waiting to collide.

The place at the right-hand end was a pharmacy. A fire exit with a wooden ramp for disabled access jutted out from the exposed wall. The street was empty, but he checked left and right out of reflex before he crossed.

He darted around the wash of gold from a street lamp, padded across the asphalt and made his way around to the fire escape, zipping open the duffel bag as he did so, removing a large flat-head screwdriver.

The fire exit consisted of an aluminium frame panelled with glass. He used the screwdriver to punch out an opening large enough to fit his hand through, then cocked his wrist and turned the handle from the inside, freeing the lock.

He returned the screwdriver to his bag, slipped inside and closed the door gently again, the glow from outside ghostly through the glass. He was wary of alarms; motion sensors were the greatest concern. He stood still just inside the threshold and stared hard into the black for the telltale red flicker. After a long moment of fruitless vigilance he moved forward cautiously. He was in the central room of the place, a reception counter to his left with a door adjacent to it, shelving gondolas to his right, and beyond them, a door leading to the street. Another door behind the counter leading out back. Everything illuminated dully by overhead tubes.

He stepped behind the counter, multiple shadows pursuing faithfully. It was cluttered back there. Computer monitors and cushioned office chairs, folders littering the desktop and the floor. Everything alien-like in the flicker of the tubes.

He opened the door behind the counter and stepped through it to a storage area, walled on all sides with cubbyholes. There were bundles of gauze and bottles of antiseptic, boxed-for-sale blood-pressure monitors and cardboard dispensers of latex gloves, and bags of 3 ml hypodermic needles and plastic containers of labelled pills From one shelf he grabbed a bottle labelled CH_3OH, took a packet of ibuprofen from another, and then a handful of white cotton gauze and a roll of masking tape from a third.

Cradling everything awkwardly in one arm he worked the handle of the door adjacent to the desk. He shuffled his way blindly down a short corridor, opened the next door he arrived at and stepped through. He found a light switch and snapped it on; the room flashed instantly yellow and he raised a forearm against the sharp intrusion on his vision. There was a washbasin to his left, a toilet directly ahead and a refuse bin to his right. He placed everything on the floor and unbuckled his trousers, which collapsed limply at his feet. He turned to the washbasin to see a face he hardly recognized in the mirror. Lined and drawn, a portrait of a tired man. The small room amplified his stink.

There was a hole in his left ear. *Shit*. He hooked a finger behind it and eased it forward, making the missing section of skin all the more visible in the glass. He smiled, despite himself. The hole was nearly a centimetre across, ringed with a browny redness which had spread down his neck and seeped into his collar. He ran the tap, enjoying the tender coolness on his fingers then sluiced water on his face, through his hair; watched the evidence of the violence he had suffered slowly dilute and swirl towards the drain.

He wiped the water from his face then stepped back and glanced down at his knee. There was a deep vertical laceration bridging the gap between calf and thigh; not deep, but it had bled.

He gathered the gauze and the bottle, sitting down on the floor. The label CH_3OH meant little to him, other than that the *OH* indicated alcohol of some kind. He unscrewed the cap and inverted the bottle quickly over a wad of gauze. He cleansed the cut on his leg, then blotted it with more gauze. He used the masking tape to secure the last of the gauze to the aching wound. He sighed raggedly and lolled his head back against the door, calmed by the knowledge that, for now, he was safe; his injuries were less severe than first anticipated, and, despite everything, he was still breathing.

■ TWO

Like any form of employment, detection has its down-sides. Not that I'm complaining: criminal investigation is inherently recession-proof, so lack of activity is never an issue. It's the nature of the work that sometimes proves problematical. Homicide, in particular. Murder leaves a mental imprint that tends to linger. It keeps your innocence, ignorance and sense that all is right with the world firmly pinned down, and sends you home at the end of the day with creases in your brow.

Pollard called me at home about the Emma Fontaine case on a Saturday afternoon cast grey by fairly typical July weather. I was alone in the living room, stereo set to a discreet low. The window that gave onto the front lawn was open, and a chill breeze filled the curtains periodically, bringing with it the smell of recent showers.

'You're not allowed to call me on my day off,' I said, when I answered my cell.

'Sorry.' He didn't sound apologetic. 'What's that, The Verve?'

'Echo and the Bunnymen,' I said. '"Fools Like Us".'

Quiet on the line.

'Is this a social call?' I asked him.

'Purely business,' he replied. 'Someone found a body.'

I didn't answer. The clock above the bookcase on the opposite wall was showing four-twenty.

'Teenage girl,' he continued. 'Found next to a fence in Albert Park, been there maybe fifteen, twenty hours. This rent-a-cop from the university across the street was on a late lunch break, went for a stroll, happened to look in the garden, hey presto.'

'Shit.'

'That's what I said, too,' he answered.

I pinched the bridge of my nose and watched the luminescent display on the stereo on the shelf opposite my armchair clear as it found the next track. I probed the coffee table beside me for a notebook but found nothing but lampshade. 'And you're telling me this, why?'

'You're back on the hard road tomorrow. I thought

maybe you'd want to get up to speed with things as soon as possible.'

I said nothing.

'In a way you could say I'm doing you a favour,' he said. 'Like, I've got your best interests at heart.'

'Cheers,' I said. 'I'll buy you a beer sometime.'

'You going to take a look?'

'OK,' I told him.

'They're set up over the eastern side, you'll see where to go.'

The trip west into the central city was easy late on a Saturday. Traffic was thin until I reached the CBD, and the light phases seemed to be scheduled in my favour. I kept the stereo occupied with R.E.M.'s *New Adventures in Hi-Fi*. Vintage 1996.

It was nearing five when I parked my unmarked Commodore on Bowen Avenue. I signed the scene attendance log proffered by a uniformed cop, ascended the steps from Victoria Street up the hill into Albert Park, and crossed to the eastern boundary where the body had been found. The sky above was gunmetal, a slight breeze was beginning to murmur, and the leaves of the huge oaks that dot the green were beginning to click with rain.

Albert Park sprawls across the Symonds Street ridge, bridging the gap between the top of Victoria and the western side of Princes streets in the Auckland CBD. During summertime, the gardens that surround the central fountain are stunning, and with a blue sky present, it's the sort of image you'd want on a postcard. By winter, however, things are generally a little more subdued and unappealing. And dead bodies don't contribute much towards a positive atmosphere.

The crime scene, which consisted of about twenty square metres set tight against the eastern perimeter garden, had already been cordoned off with emergency tape. Scene of Crime technicians clad in overalls moved beneath a large tarpaulin erected to protect evidence; namely, a large piece of black plastic wrapped around a person-shaped lump.

The lead tech was a guy I'd met before — Mark Jameson. He was about forty, prematurely grey, with a face etched with deep crevices — to be expected if your job is looking at dead people. He turned to face me as I ducked under the tape and approached the tent. I saw a challenge form in his eyes, then vanish as I produced my badge and he recognized me.

'It's you,' he said.

'Correct. Well spotted.'

A grunt escaped his lips as he made a quick scan of the rumples in my suit, as if to check if there were items of interest hidden there. 'There are probably better ways to spend a Saturday.'

I smiled and looked around as a means of avoiding a reply. The park was close to deserted, uniformed cops its only occupants. Traffic over on Princes Street was intermittent at best. 'So, what's the story?' I said.

Jameson turned and beckoned, leading me under the shelter to where the corpse lay. It was positioned at the very edge of a flowerbed; the disturbed shrubbery nearby suggesting its original location had been slightly more concealed. I knelt on the grass beside Jameson as he used a gloved finger to pull back a flap of plastic and reveal an attractive, pale face streaked with both blood and fair wisps of hair so fine they were more akin to cobwebs than something human. There was a deep trench the approximate diameter of a crowbar forming a neat line from the crown of the girl's head to the bridge of her nose. Her eyes were open and her gaze fixed ahead of her, perpetually transfixed by the incoming blow that had surely killed her.

'We slit the bag down the side so we could get a look

at her,' he said. 'We found a driver's licence in her purse, gives her name as Emma Fontaine.'

'Jesus, what is she, sixteen?'

'Seventeen in November.'

'What do you think?' I asked.

He removed his hand and the black plastic fell back into place, obscuring the girl's face. 'Other than the laceration to the cranium, we haven't found any other injury,' he said. 'Best bet at the moment is that she took a blow to the upper face with something hard and elongated.'

'Crowbar?'

His knees popped as he stood. 'Yeah, or a tyre iron. Or piece of rebar.'

The breeze picked up suddenly, bringing with it the sound of nearby VHF chatter from the wandering cops, and further unwanted raindrops tapping audibly on top of the plastic shelter.

'The wound to the head would've bled a lot,' he said. 'But there's no evidence of any blood here.'

'OK,' I said.

'She must have been transported then, postmortem.'

I turned my head and looked up at him, one eye squinting against the wind. 'So somebody put her in a car and dumped her,' I said.

He nodded. 'There's vehicle access further along, council staff said the chain hasn't been across for three or four days.'

'Not very well concealed,' I said. 'Public area where she's likely to be found.'

He shrugged. The iron fence ahead of us marking the park's boundary produced a low, mournful whistle. 'So you're looking for a guy with an IQ of thirty-seven,' he said.

'What about time of death?' I asked.

He rocked his head from side to side and made a face. 'Lividity and rigor mortis are fairly advanced; you're looking at sometime last night, say, midnight or thereabouts.'

I nodded, then stood up and took a step back, looking left across the width of Princes Street. I could see the University Clock Tower in the near distance, partially hidden by foliage.

'Did you find anything in her pockets? Cellphone, keys, receipts, anything like that?' I asked.

'There were some odd bits and pieces in her purse. Scraps of paper that could have been itemized bills, I suppose.'

'What's she wearing?'

'Miniskirt,' Jameson said. 'Some sort of wool-lined jacket. And make-up.'

I said nothing. The plastic crackled gently under the influence of the breeze, and the park's central fountain dribbled water into its surrounding white basin with a constant audible trickle.

'She was dressed up for a night on the town,' Jameson said. 'Probably hit a few bars yesterday evening, downed a few too many drinks, things didn't pan out quite as they should have.'

I shielded my eyes against the sudden flare of a camera flash. 'I take it you've decided what happened,' I said.

Jameson ducked under the scene tape and stepped onto an aggregate path. He gave a dismissive shrug, then removed his gloves with successive rubbery snaps. They dropped to the ground like pieces of translucent skin, yellowed and pungent with sweat. 'Probably the boyfriend,' he said. 'Wanting to get in her pants.'

'You found sexual interference?'

'Not yet.'

I said nothing. There was a storm rolling in from the north, and in the distance I could see thin veins of lightning flecking the cloud gatherings.

'I'll probably have to take this one tomorrow,' I said, still turned away from him. 'Do me a favour and give me a ring in the morning, just to let me know what's happened.'

Jameson made no reply as I looked at the shrouded form of Emma Fontaine in the silence. Soon, an ambulance would arrive, and paramedics would swap the black bag for a white sheet, put her on a stretcher, and cart her off to the mortuary down on Grafton Road. I wondered what she could have done to deserve such a violent end, but as always when I asked myself that question, my subconscious churned up the same answer: nothing.

■ THREE

My house is a small, two-bedroom unit nestled beyond a rise east of Mission Bay, on the outskirts of the central city. The place has been mine for seven years. It was probably intended for a quiet elderly couple. It was also probably intended to be sold to me for about three times as much as it was. Unfortunately for the previous owner, the house's exterior cladding had leaked and subsequently rotted so a market-value sale price was never likely. As a result I was able to buy it relatively cheaply, and quickly became accustomed to the process of home improvement. It's not a particularly glamorous house, but it's the time and effort I've devoted to it over the years which has fostered my profound fondness for it.

It was dark by the time I turned into my driveway at

a little after six. I parked beneath the branches of the Norfolk pine which serves as the centrepiece of my property, walked back along the driveway to check my mail, then went to unlock my front door, pausing only when I realized the woman next door was sitting in the front porch.

I halted, mid-step, surprised by her presence and the fact she hadn't said anything. My security light blinked on and I feigned casual, using the search for my key as a distraction to avoid her gaze, speaking only when I was within a metre of her.

'Hi, Grace.'

She let the greeting hang a moment before responding. 'Hello, Sean. How are you?'

'Struggling on.'

I stepped past her and unlocked my door, flicking a switch that lit up the main hallway, then moved aside and beckoned for her to enter. She was wearing jeans and a sleeveless V-neck T-shirt, and in the chill evening air I was surprised she wasn't shivering. 'Come in, I'll put the jug on.'

Her mouth flashed a tight smile, but there was nothing in her eyes. She eased herself up, arched her back and sidled past me, slightly sheepish, as if conscious of the fact

I could construe her presence as an intrusion. She had visited before, and knew the way through to the kitchen without difficulty. I closed and locked the door, then followed after. She sat herself down at the dining table, her back to the sink along the left-hand wall, and I hit the lights and turned on the stove to warm the room. I half-filled the kettle and set it going, then scraped out a chair and sat down, looking across at my neighbour. I wasn't sure of her exact age, but picked her to be somewhere in her early thirties. She was red-haired and pale, and the skin across her nose and cheeks was dusted with tiny freckles. She was chewing at her bottom lip, and her eyes were focused on a space somewhere above my right shoulder. Her arms were white and dimpled with goose bumps.

'Do you mind if I smoke?' I asked.

Her eyes flicked quickly to my face, and she shook her head emphatically, as if surprised by my politeness. 'Go ahead,' she said.

I rolled open a cutlery drawer next to the sink, removed a cigarette from a half-finished packet and clamped it between my lips as I lit up. 'How's Matthew?' I asked.

She gave me the quick smile again, watching the tip of the cigarette smoulder lazily. 'Michael,' she corrected.

'He's great. Saturday's karate night, so he's abandoned me at home. No, he's really great, though. He's ten now, decided he's going to be a policeman.'

I smiled. 'Maybe I could take him on a ride-along.'

She laughed awkwardly. 'He'd like that.'

I drew on the cigarette to mask the quiet. I could hear the clock above the fridge ticking, and the kettle beginning to hiss as the temperature built.

'Your garden's doing well,' she said. 'Lawn's looking nice.' Her speech was stilted, hesitant.

I smiled. 'I do my best.'

'I can't seem to stay on top of mine. I never seem to have time in the evenings, and during weekends I'm just too shattered.'

I didn't know how to answer this. She chewed intently on a hangnail for a moment, then surveyed my ceiling as if looking for more cringe-worthy conversation-pushers. The ceiling had been repainted recently in a shade of pale yellow in an effort to match my twenty-year-old Kelvinator fridge. Admittedly it's not entirely appealing. It matches the linoleum though, so fits the existing decor.

'Busy at work at the moment?' she asked.

'Sort of,' I said. 'I've just cleared a couple of major cases, but I've got a few other things on the go.'

She nodded, kept at the hangnail. The kettle clicked but I didn't move to pour the drinks. I altered my posture so my face was lined up with the little patch of open space where her limp gaze was hanging, like a spurned handshake.

'What is it I can do for you, Grace?'

She raised one of the goose-bumped arms a fraction and threaded a loose strand of hair behind her ear. She glanced around the kitchen; the steel bench behind her, the old yellow fridge beside the door, the stove at the opposite end of the bench, the handmade wooden shelves below the single window. She folded her arms across her chest and took a breath that caught twice in her throat. 'I wanted to come and talk to you,' she said.

I smiled. 'Hence the reason you're here.'

'I've been having problems.'

I looked at her and said nothing. I was hungry; I hadn't eaten since twelve, and there were some instant noodles in my pantry I was looking forward to.

'Well, *a* problem,' she said.

The sky through the window above her head was a rich, impenetrable black. I waited for the clock to count to three before I asked her to elaborate. 'What sort of problem?' I asked.

While the strand of hair hadn't come loose, she re-threaded it, regardless. She reminded me of a P addict, the way her gaze couldn't pause.

'What is it I can help you with, Grace?' I asked.

There was a pause. 'There's been a man watching me,' she answered quietly. 'And I'm terrified.'

■ FOUR

I managed to retain her gaze for a half-second longer before it flitted away to another corner of the room. I removed the cigarette from my mouth and placed it carefully on the table, perpendicular to the nearest edge, so it wouldn't roll off. The ash tip was almost an inch long, curled and shrivelled, like a witch's finger.

'Explain,' I said gently.

I heard the hush of material as she crossed her legs. She took a breath that snagged inside her throat. 'About a month ago,' she said. 'Maybe three weeks. I began to notice a car out in the street. I saw it one afternoon, then the morning after, and then the day after that. Just parked at the side of the road, doing nothing.'

I got up and stepped around her, stretched across the

stove, and flicked it off at the wall. The interior light vanished like a curtained-over window. I sat back down, raised my cigarette and took a lengthy pull.

'There are cars parked on the street all the time,' I said. 'Just because you saw one in particular a few times doesn't mean there's someone watching you.'

She shook her head, and her hair freed itself from behind her ears and splayed down onto her bare shoulders. 'I went out into the front garden last week and it was there. I stood watching it, and after a moment it started up and just drove off.'

I placed the cigarette on the table again, then tapped the floor twice with my shoe. I hadn't swept up in a while, and it sounded gritty. 'What sort of car was it?' I asked.

'A red one. A BMW, I think. An older model.'

'I've never seen it.'

'You're at work all the time.'

'Have you seen the driver?'

'No.'

'So how do you know it's a man? It could be anybody.'

She made no reply. Rain was only just beginning to fall; the storm I had seen approaching earlier must have been making slow progress. Droplets of water were striking the roofing iron with dense, heavy slaps.

'Maybe it belongs to one of the neighbours,' I offered.

'I checked. It doesn't.'

'So how many times have you seen it?'

She made a face and shrugged. 'Once every couple of days for the last three weeks. Maybe ten or twelve times, I guess.'

'Just sitting out on the street, doing nothing?' I hoped I didn't sound overly sceptical.

She nodded and fixed her hair again.

'Have you called the police? If you think someone has their eye on you, they'll send someone past to check up. Did you get a licence plate?'

She didn't reply. She folded her arms firmly across her chest, causing her skin to pull taught across the tops of her shoulders. 'I gave them the licence plate,' she said. 'And they told me it didn't exist.'

I didn't answer.

'They said no such number is registered to any car, much less an old, red BMW.'

The rain on the roof increased to the point where I could no longer discern the individual impacts. The fridge hummed and the clock ticked on, oblivious. 'What do you want me to do, Grace?'

She made no reply. I saw her bottom lip quiver.

'Why would somebody be watching you?' I asked. 'Have you any idea?'

She shook her head.

'Has anything happened lately that might have provoked someone into following you?' She sniffed loudly and opened her mouth, inhaled and blinked twice. 'No.'

I did my best to sound comforting: 'Have you considered the possibility that everything's in your head? That you're getting worked up over nothing?'

She started to say something, then abandoned the thought, and instead leaned forward, resting her elbows on the table and gazed skyward, lips pursed. 'It's just, it's on my mind, and I'm worried about it. Do you know what I mean?'

I nodded.

She snatched a breath, bit her knuckle and looked at my ceiling.

'What do you want me to do, Grace?'

She said nothing. The rain stopped and started, maintaining a strict and patient rhythm. The window above her head was pebbled with thick bright droplets. The air was perfectly still, and smoke from my cigarette was tracing a razor-edge path towards the ceiling.

I smiled. 'I'm not really in a position to hang around all

day on the off-chance the car turns up. I have bills to pay.'

'I know,' she answered meekly.

'So what did you plan on having me do?' I asked.

She cupped her hands against her face, fingers tracing the contours of her nose and brow. 'I want someone to check it's OK,' she said, voice muffled because her face was still hidden. 'Just to make sure everything's all right.'

I exhaled, causing the perfect cigarette fume to deviate sideways and dissolve into nothingness.

'What do you think?' she asked. 'You're a cop. You must know someone.'

I twisted in my seat and checked the clock above the fridge. Nearing seven. I was looking forward to those noodles. I turned back to face her and steepled my fingers in front of me on the tabletop, the way I'd seen judges do in court.

'There's a guy I used to work with,' I said. 'I could probably get him to keep an eye on you for a couple of days.'

She dropped her hands to her lap and nodded, eyes on the floor beside her, as if finally she was making progress. 'Did he used to be a cop?'

I nodded. 'Before that he was an investigator in the army.'

'What does he do now?'

'He owns a security and investigations firm.'

'Is he good?'

'Extremely.'

'What's his name?'

'John Hale.'

'Is he expensive?'

'I'll call him. I reckon he'll probably do it *pro bono*.'

She brought back the quick, mouth-only smile. 'That would be great,' she answered. 'Thanks very much, Sean. I appreciate it. Thanks a lot.'

Just before seven on that damp Saturday evening, two men were clearing the passport check-in desk at Auckland International Airport.

They had touched down eighteen minutes earlier on a Qantas flight from Brisbane. One of the men was in his forties, tall and dark-skinned, with a shaven head that dropped a shade lighter above his hairline. Physically, his companion was his polar opposite: early thirties, short, heavy, with medium-length blond hair swept back into a ponytail and secured at the back of his skull with a loop of black elastic.

Despite their dissimilarities, the two men were

collectively referred to within professional circles as 'the twins'.

They had no luggage between them other than one nondescript black duffel bag, which the short blond man had taken with him inside the aircraft cabin, allowing them to bypass the wait at the baggage carousel and head straight through to the X-ray machine and then on to the immigration desk. The short blond man had entered the country on an Australian passport which looked real but wasn't, and the tall bald man had had similar success with a piece of documentation falsely identifying him as an individual who had drowned in 1969, in a boating accident off the Sydney coast.

They left the arrivals terminal without incident, and made their way through shiny darkness, full of the sounds of hissing automobile tyres and roaring turbofans, to the long-term vehicle-parking compound, stopping at a dark four-door Toyota sedan parked near the far boundary fence. The short blond man knelt beside the front right quarter panel, reached inside the wheel well and removed the keys from the dish formed by the plastic shielding protecting the suspension. He clicked the remote fob and watched the indicators flare once as the locking mechanism disengaged, then he opened the driver's door and slid inside. He waited until the tall dark man was seated beside him, then reached across the console and removed a single sheet of folded, standard white A4 paper from inside the glove compartment. He unfolded it with a precise movement of his thumb, and angled the page towards the window, reading the carefully detailed instructions it contained, twice. He then refolded the paper and passed it wordlessly to his companion, inserted the key into the ignition, started the motor, and drove towards the exit.

Later, once the rain had stopped, I sat on the front step, lit another cigarette and used my cellphone to call John Hale.

'I have a business proposition for you,' I said.

A sigh. After five, Hale doesn't like to talk business.

'My neighbour's distraught,' I said. 'She thinks some-one's watching her.'

'Who's the someone?'

'A guy in a red BMW. Apparently he's been sitting out on the street for the best part of a month.'

The sigh again, but less pointed. 'Have you seen it?'

'No.'

'Did you get a licence plate?'

'It doesn't exist.'

'How peculiar,' Hale answered.

I said nothing.

'You want me to keep an eye on things?' he asked.

'That would be swell, John. Thanks.'

I ended the call, pocketed the phone and stood up, awkward because the seat of my pants was soaked from the wet porch boards. I headed down the short concrete path that leads across my lawn to the driveway, and stood facing north and east, looking towards the road. The air was dense and replenished, sweet with an aroma drifting from the wet Norfolk pine. Cloud cover was heavy, and the sky was the same rich shade of black I had seen out of the kitchen window earlier. The lawn was saturated, and the earth beneath was making a gentle sucking noise as the moisture worked through it. I raised the half-finished cigarette to my mouth, and as I inhaled and the tip flared orange, a car parked on the near side of the street started its motor with a cold, rattling mutter, and accelerated gently away from the kerb. Its lights were off, so I was unable to make out even the general shape, much less a licence tag. I waited until the tang of its exhaust had settled, then I turned and walked back inside.

■ FIVE

The next morning, Sunday, the sky outside my kitchen window was the colour of dull steel, and there was a firm wind whipping south, sending fallen twigs and gutter debris alike scurrying across my front yard. I ate breakfast, then drove the Commodore along Tamaki Drive into town, up to the Auckland Central Police Station on the corner of Cook and Vincent Streets.

A blue plastic binder containing the case file for Emma Fontaine was sitting on my desk up at CIB. There was a yellow Post-it note attached to its cover; a request from the officer-in-charge that I speak with her as soon as I arrived that morning. I found her seated behind her desk in her office off the main detectives' suite, hands linked behind her head, a whimsical expression pasted on her face as she considered the blades of the slowly rotating fan attached to the ceiling. Her name was Claire Bennett. She was a grey-haired, no-bullshit fifty-something who'd had her finger in virtually every major investigation since before anyone could remember. Her manner, although severe and often inflexible, had the general effect of creating respect, as opposed to dislike.

I pulled up a chair from beside the filing cabinet and sat down opposite her. She dropped her gaze from the fan and looked at me without altering her expression.

'I'm putting you on the Fontaine case,' she said.

'So I gathered. Any developments overnight?'

She unlaced her hands from behind her head and leaned forward, propping her forearms on the edge of the desk. She looked ill close up; her skin pallid, the lines on her face more deeply cast. 'We found her car,' she said. 'Honda hatchback, in a parking lot behind a bar down on Customs Street. Patrol turned up a witness who claims she saw Fontaine enter the premises at around seven p.m. on Friday night.'

'Have you checked inside the vehicle?'

She nodded.

'Anything?'

She shook her head. The office was windowless, and as

a result the air seemed stale and pungent, despite the fan. 'Nothing interesting. No cellphone or handbag, no diary, no convenient list of contacts.'

'Only the one witness?' I asked.

She nodded.

'Anything from Forensics?'

Head shake. 'They haven't got to the car yet.'

'What's the next-of-kin situation?'

'She lived with the mother. She's been notified.'

'How did she take it?'

'Not well.'

I gave the mandatory respectful pause. 'So what do you want me to do?'

The phone on her desk began to ring, but she made no move to answer it. 'Keep things ticking over. Her street is being canvassed, in case the neighbours have seen anything odd. But have a chat to the witness, have a look through the bar, see if you can roust out somebody else who saw something on Friday night. Call me at midday and we'll see what's happening.'

I went back to my desk and took an enlarged print of Emma Fontaine's driver's licence photo from the case file, then called the officer in charge of the night-shift crime squad, and obtained the name and address of the woman who had identified Fontaine on Friday evening. He told me the bar the girl had been seen inside was a seedy establishment down on Customs Street East, called Heat. I knew the place well. I had been called to it on numerous occasions, and my memories of it weren't fond.

When I parked the Commodore outside at just after eight-thirty that morning, my recollections were reconfirmed. Customs Street is a mostly commercial, four-lane stretch running laterally across the bottom of town, and the quality of the real estate tends to fade the further east you head. By the time you reach the intersection with Beach Road and Anzac Ave, the high-rise office blocks full of accountancy and law firms have vanished, replaced by side roads lined with porn retailers and slightly gritty superettes and pubs. Heat was one of the latter establishments. It was located on the ground floor of a double-storey building occupying the corner site of a fairly decrepit section. The pavement outside was littered with truncated cigarettes like dead insects, whilst the area to the left of the building was a vast, undeveloped lot tufted with grass, interspersed with the twisted remains of a couple of burned-out cars and kitchen appliances. Parked either side of a navy Honda Civic hatchback near the edge of Heat's eastern wall was a marked patrol car and a tow truck.

I got out of the car and blipped the locks with the key remote, then crossed through light commuter traffic to the empty lot next door. There was no fenceline, so access wasn't a problem, but the terrain was an issue: it was lumpy with exposed metal, broken glass and Lord knows what else.

The tow truck driver stayed in his car when I reached the small grouping of vehicles, but a uniformed sergeant of about my age climbed out of the patrol car and walked around his bonnet to meet me. His posture told me he was bored, and his red eyes suggested he needed to cut back on caffeine. I badged him and introduced myself, shouting to be heard over the background wash of traffic. He didn't reciprocate.

'I thought I might end up sitting here all day,' he said.

'You still might. It's not going anywhere until Forensics has taken a look.'

He gave me an *up yours* expression, then said, 'I've already looked through it. There's nothing. If this is the car she was driving, you're shit out of luck. It's useless.'

'A lazy man would believe you,' I said. 'Do you have any gloves?'

He looked at me silently for a moment, then ducked into the patrol car and came out with a box of disposable latexes, which he tossed across the roof at me. I removed a pair and snapped them on, throwing the box back at him, harder than was really necessary. 'Is it unlocked?'

He nodded at me, then ran a hand through short brown hair which had clearly been teased into messiness with copious amounts of styling product.

'Did you find it that way, or did you open it?' I said.

'Found it that way,' he said.

'Were you the first on scene?' I asked.

He nodded a second time, then let his eyes wander past me to where traffic was backed up at the lights on the corner of Anzac Avenue. 'Got sent down here to check whether anyone had seen the girl in the park. Found this dude who reckons he saw the vic leave a blue Honda hatch in here at around half past seven, so I came and had a look, ran the plate number, and here we are.'

The tow truck driver had his radio on, and I could hear pop music, like a faint and disembodied voice, coming through his windscreen. Engine noise behind me built suddenly as the traffic lights changed to green. I stepped past the patrol car to the passenger door of the Civic and glanced in through the window, trying to ignore the lean, thirty-two-year-old face reflected back at me. The car was a baseline model, manual, fitted out with cloth and vinyl and finished in cheap matte paint and plastic hubcaps. A typical first car. But it was completely empty. There was no discarded paper on the floor, no loose items of clothing, no change in the central console. No evidence. I opened the door and checked the glove box. A Honda manual, a Ryan Adams CD, another by Pearl Jam. She'd had good taste in music.

I looked through the boot. There was a spare tyre and a standard toolkit, and that was the extent of it. I slammed the lid shut and crunched back to where the patrol guy was sitting on his bonnet. There was a breeze blowing through the lot, and he had his chin ducked against his chest to combat the chill.

I tugged my sleeve back and checked my watch: eight forty-five. 'Don't go anywhere,' I said.

The contact occupied an address north-east of the airport, in a suburb where dilapidation had taken a firm hold. The twins arrived dead on eight forty-six. They had spent the night in a noisy, substandard motel in Mangere, before rising early to prepare for their brief morning rendezvous.

The small blond man stopped the Camry outside the

address and the tall bald man slid out into the chill of the morning. He stood surveying the neighbourhood as the blond man eased the car away down the street, chased faithfully by a silver tail of exhaust.

The tall bald man quickly concluded the environment was favourable. Housing was dense but activity was minimal, hence the chance of being observed making his little visit was correspondingly minute. Not that being observed would be fatally problematic. His attire was discreet and forgettable: worn blue suit, blue sunglasses. The salesman's dress code. As if his job was pitching cut-price mortgages, or washing machines.

The target address was a run-down prefabricated yellow box structure supported on cinder blocks. It was set at the rear of a rectangular section overgrown in knee-high grass and bordered on three sides by a corrugated-iron fence the colour of dead leaves. The tall bald man felt it was a fine addition to a street characterized by chipped paint, missing fence palings, broken windows and general disrepair.

The property was unprotected from the street, so he stepped off the path and trod carefully through the front yard, feeling his trouser cuffs grow damp with dew. The longer side of the structure was oriented parallel to the street. There was a small square window at the left-hand end and a door at the right. He made another cautious survey of his surroundings before approaching the door and tapping on it twice. It was skinned with aluminium sheeting and rattled in its frame as he struck it.

His knock was answered almost immediately. The door swung back against a rusted hinge, revealing a small worn man in his sixties, clad in blue denim jeans and a red-chequered button-down shirt straining over a bulbous paunch, hair like steel wool peeking out between buttons. He wore a pair of tortoiseshell spectacles that were fractionally askew, and the cheeks beneath the lenses were flushed with hypertension. The skin above his collar was as thin and wrinkled as cured meat. The tall man knew his name was Bernard.

The tall man smiled up amicably. In his right trouser pocket he had a length of very fine, high-tensile plastic cord, fashioned by way of a small buckle into a sort of slipknot or lasso. Like a snap tie, only larger. 'Morning pick-up,' he said.

Bernard made no reply. He took a step back and turned slightly, in what the tall man interpreted as a nominal invitation to enter. The floor was lined with sheets of newspaper, and the next breath he took was lined with the odour of feline urine. The cinder-block supports meant the floor of the place was level with his mid-thigh, so he raised his foot high and stepped awkwardly inside, careful not to touch the metal doorframe.

Bernard closed the door behind him. The box was entirely open-plan. The right half housed the kitchen; there was a metal bench with a sink and taps against the far wall, topped at one end with a small gas cooker. A Formica table for two and a single chair stood in a patch of blotched orange lino. The left half was occupied by a threadbare couch and a single bed, and an old CRT television and a grey armchair with a spring penetrating through the seat lining. No sign of a bathroom. Magazines and discarded clothes, and empty bottles of Steinlager and cans of Jim Beam littered the floor. He felt something brush his inner calf and when he looked down saw an emaciated grey tabby staring up at him with eyes the colour of old men's teeth.

Bernard toed the door gently as if checking it was secure, then stepped past the tall bald man, threading around the table to a pair of cupboards beneath the sink. He dug in his pocket momentarily, removed a key attached to a split ring and knelt and inserted it into a lock in the left cupboard before swinging the door back and removing a black leather duffel bag. It was weighty, and he had to use his foot to slide it back around the table to the tall man, newspaper concertinaing in front of it.

'It's one-five for the lot,' Bernard said.

'You sourced everything OK?' the tall man asked.

Bernard adjusted his glasses. The cat padded over and nuzzled his bare toes. 'Decommissioned military and police issue,' he said. 'I cleared the serial numbers.'

The tall bald man moved closer to him, careful not to breathe too deeply; Bernard emitted an odour somewhat akin to cat food. There was a row of three windows in the opposite wall, but grime accretion had rendered them opaque. He knelt and examined the contents of the bag, then, satisfied, rose to his full height and produced the amicable smile again. It was becoming very natural. He placed his hands in his pockets.

'You take a cheque?' the tall bald man said.

Bernard adjusted his glasses. 'Yeah, I guess so.'

The cat purred.

The tall man had the cord out of his pocket and looped around Bernard's neck before he could even register what had happened.

He kicked Bernard in the groin, dropping him to the floor, then tightened the buckle viciously. Bernard's entire head pulsed bright scarlet, his eyes bulged and cracked with crimson capillaries, and his tongue protruded thick and purple between dry lips. Bernard struggled. Terror escaped his lips in the form of unintelligible grunts. The tall bald man persisted. The plastic was indented along its length so the buckle could be tightened, but not easily released. Bernard scrabbled furiously for purchase on the loop around his neck, but the tall bald man was incredibly strong. He manoeuvred himself behind the older man and forced his face to the floor, panting and hissing with exertion. The cat meowed and skittered beneath the table as the tall bald man gave one last almighty yank, the pressure from which was sufficient to rupture a vessel in Bernard's eye, misting the newspaper below his face with blood.

At length the panicked thrashing ceased. He used a thumbnail to release the catch on the buckle and the cord slipped free. He fed it back into his pocket, warm and fluid and serpentine.

He hefted the bag on one shoulder and left moments later.

■ SIX

Heat was just as I remembered it. The floor-to-ceiling windows facing the street were still fogged with grime, the exposed wooden floorboards still looked filthy as opposed to interestingly weathered, the metal tables spanning the gap between the front door and the bar at the rear were still pebbled with food scraps, and the air still reeked of a pungent cocktail of booze, nicotine and body odour.

A woman of about forty-five was seated behind the bar in back, wearing a baggy white sweat top and leaning heavily over an open newspaper. Her hair was bleached blonde with dark roots showing at her scalp, giving the impression of a shot of espresso that hadn't been stirred. She didn't glance up as I pushed open the front door, and when I sat down on one of the blistered vinyl-covered stools across from her, she made no sign she was even aware of my presence.

'I'm after the owner,' I said.

She didn't look up. She had the newspaper open to the first double-page-spread, but the way her eyes couldn't settle told me she wasn't actually reading anything. Her hair was thin and unwashed, framing her face lankly.

'You want to talk about the dead girl?' she asked, without looking up.

I didn't answer. She carefully draped the first page of the paper over the second and tamped the edge to square it, as if she was preparing the bedspread in a luxury hotel. She halved it again, then dropped it beside her on the floor, looking up at me for the first time, eyes curious.

'You a cop?' she asked.

'I am.'

She shook her head. 'He's not in. He went home an hour ago, left me to keep watch.'

The bar was made of thick, lacquered wood, the surface marred with deep crevices which could have been inflicted with the blade of a pocket knife, or even the nib of a ballpoint pen.

'Where's home?' I asked.

'Howick.' She reeled off the street address with the sort of ease that made me think she was used to telling police officers where her boss lived.

'Were you here Friday night?' I asked.

She shook her head. There was a line of beer taps against the wall behind her, two of them dripping at perfectly synchronized intervals. There was a door marked *TOIL T* and another marked *PRIVATE*. I swivelled on my stool and felt the cushion compress, hearing the air hiss out through the fractures in the fabric.

'He's already spoke to you people once already,' she said. 'He's going to be pissed off about having to do it again.'

'I'll take my chances,' I said.

Back when I had occasion to frequent the premises, Heat had been owned by a guy in his mid-forties by the name of Tyler Mitchell. He was a reedy, unhygienic-looking sort of man, with the kind of soft, white skin that had spent longer beneath the neon flicker of cheap indoor lighting than it had outdoors. More often than not, the reason I was called to his business was to investigate an offence in some way related to him, as opposed to the bar's clientele. On one occasion, a gay man had been hospitalized after he was assaulted with a barstool, an attack which left him not only sightless in one eye, but virtually toothless. I had reached the scene minutes after the triple-one call had been placed, and although my gut feeling had always been that Mitchell had dealt the blows, nothing was ever proven.

I found Mitchell in the garage of a small, slightly run-down unit, three doors along from a Korean church off Pakuranga Road in Howick, south-east of Auckland CBD. He had the roller door up, and I could see him, in bike shorts, white singlet and red padded gloves, attacking a heavy bag he had bolted to an overhead rafter. He had clearly aged; pale skin around his bristled jaw deflated and sagging, flesh on his upper arms more empty than it had been a decade ago.

There were two light-coloured sedans parked in his short concrete driveway, so he failed to see me as I pulled up at his letterbox, only noticing as I entered his garage.

He struck the bag twice more in quick succession, perspiration flicking from his forehead, then turned towards me, stripping the gloves from his hands and letting them fall to the floor.

'Have I caught you at a bad time?' I asked.

He had dense black hair greased flush against his skull, fanning out in a mullet at the back of his neck, like a duck's bill. His white singlet was darkened with moisture across the chest, and the whole room stank of sweat.

'Who are you?' he asked.

'The heat,' I said.

'The what?'

I paused. 'I'm a cop.' I removed my badge from the pocket of my suit jacket and opened the leather holder for him to see.

'It's Mitchell, right?' I asked.

He held my eyes a moment, nodded once, then said, 'Are you going to ask me new questions, or should I just repeat what I told the other guy?'

I slipped the wallet back into my pocket, then brought out the copy of Emma Fontaine's DL photo, holding it in front of his face. 'You recognize this girl?'

He kept his gaze on me and nodded without so much as a glance towards the photograph. 'She walked in around seven-thirty, eight, stayed until nine. Then she walked out again.'

I creased the photo lengthwise and pocketed it again. 'This was Friday night?'

'Uh-huh.'

'You notice what she was doing while she was in?'

'Not really,' he answered.

'Was she served?'

He grimaced and inhaled wetly through one nostril. There was a wooden bench against the right-hand wall, stacked with metal carpentry tools and little dishes of screws and nails. He kicked the gloves across the concrete floor so they were concealed beneath the bench, then pushed the heavy bag so that it began to rock gently on its restraint, like a leaden pendulum. 'I don't know,' he said.

'You don't normally pay attention to what's happening out on the floor?'

'I do, but I leave the orders to the drinks girls. I'm all the way back behind the bar, I don't have a clue what's going on.'

'That's not very good management policy.'

'It's an effective management policy.'

I looked at him without saying anything. There was an open door to the left, beyond which I could see a short, carpeted hallway. A window in the rear wall of the garage revealed a small backyard occupied by a kidney-shaped swimming pool skinned with algae. A guy of about forty reclined in a deck chair, his back to me, drinking from a bottle of Corona. Mitchell turned and followed my gaze, moving slightly to see beyond the window frame.

'You perving my brother?' he asked drily.

I ignored him. 'I'll just get you to go over that again,' I said. 'The girl came in around seven-thirty, eight, she stayed about an hour, you don't know if she had a drink.'

He nodded, then raised one hand and gripped the top edge of the bag, the bare skin of his upper arm dimpled and sagging.

'Was she with anyone?' I asked.

'I've already been through this. Someone else talked to me.'

'The case has been transferred. I have to backtrack. Was she with anyone?' I repeated.

'She came in alone.'

'You have security footage indoors?'

'Not right now. Some shithead threw a glass at the camera. Fucked it. Like, completely.'

'Can you give me a list of the people who were in there, maybe give me some descriptions, help me find another witness?'

He shrugged and picked at something on his arm with fingernails that were thick and yellow and rimmed with black.

'I don't really recall,' he said.

'You don't have any repeat customers? People who come in regularly, who maybe saw something?'

He shrugged, made no reply. His face was shining and droplets of moisture were falling from his chin and speckling the concrete at his feet, the skin across the top of his cheeks webbed with a matrix of purple veins, like stress fractures in concrete. I took a business card from my jacket pocket, stepped forward and offered it to him. He took it reluctantly, then pocketed it without bothering to read what it said.

'You look kinda familiar,' he said, his mouth curled. 'Are you an alcoholic?'

I shook my head. 'I was called to your business once when you nearly beat a man to death with a barstool.'

His eyes darkened and then faded again, almost within the same instant, but he held his tongue.

'I'll be needing the names and contact details for any staff you had rostered for Friday night,' I said. 'Please don't leave town. If you think of anything, don't hesitate to contact me.'

He considered what I had said for a moment, then turned and squared his stance, striking the bag with his right hand, as if demonstrating his strength to me, or maybe just reaffirming it for himself. The bag swayed twice before its motion was absorbed by the straps holding it.

I watched him for a moment, listening to the chime of the support ring suspending the bag, then said, 'A young girl is dead. It's a very serious matter. I suggest you start being a little more forthcoming.'

I turned and walked away without waiting for him to respond.

■ SEVEN

Y ou think he's holding something back?' Claire
Bennett asked me a moment later.

Light rain was falling, pebbling my windshield and
obscuring the view of Tyler Mitchell's garage, which was
now closed. 'Hard to say. His answers were vague, but he
didn't appear nervous. Although that could just indicate
he'd prepared a speech for me.'

She mulled this over for a beat. R.E.M. were still on the
stereo, midway through 'Leave'. A superb track, if you're
patient enough to make it through the lengthy intro.
'Can you think of a reason why he wouldn't want to be
truthful?'

'Not really,' I said.

She grunted, then ended the call. I pocketed my

cellphone, then started the car and pulled a U-turn, heading towards the motorway.

The witness address the night-shift crime squad chief had given me was listed as somewhere in Northcote, across the bridge from the central city. The witness's name was Sandra, and her home turned out to be the middle unit in a row of three single-bedroom flats in an area consisting primarily of cheap, slightly dismal state houses.

Sandra opened up more or less immediately when I knocked on her door. She was dressed immaculately in a full-length red gown that clung as if it had been sprayed on. Her hair was blonde and shoulder-length, and smelled faintly of shampoo. Her nails were long and shaded light pink. On her cheeks was a two-mil dusting of stubble, and an Adam's apple floated at the front of her throat.

'Hi,' I said brightly. 'I'm after Sandra.'

'That's me. You can call me Greg. I'm Greg at the moment.'

I flipped my badge. Casual, like I was always bumping into transvestites. 'I'm a police detective,' I said.

'Oh,' he said. 'Do come in. I've got coffee.'

'I'm kind of pushed for time,' I said. 'I've picked up an investigation from yesterday. I was given your name.'

'You're here about the girl?'

'I am.'

He glanced past me to the street, as if to check for observers.

I said, 'I was told you were in a bar called Heat, early Friday evening.' I removed the photograph of Emma Fontaine and offered it to him. He didn't take it from me, but gave it a careful look. 'Her name was Emma,' I said. 'I was told you saw her in Heat sometime after seven-thirty.'

He looked at me over the top of the photograph, and his jaws expanded fractionally, as if his teeth were clenched. A breeze caught his dress and he flattened it against his stomach.

'I was there from quarter past seven through to eleven,' he said. 'She came in at a little after seven-thirty, then headed out again about forty-five minutes later.'

'Do you know what she was doing while she was there?'

'Doing bar stuff.'

'Yeah, but did she meet with anyone, pay interest to anyone, maybe come in with anyone?'

He examined the sky briefly, as if searching for an elusive thought. 'You want coffee?' he asked.

'No thanks.'

He touched a nail and pursed his lips, then jerked his

head left and right in order to clear his hair from his eyes. 'She came in with a guy,' he said. 'Early twenties, not much hair, tattoo on one cheek.'

I paused. He ran a hand over his stubble.

'She came in with a companion?' I said.

He repeated the description.

'He was a Caucasian guy?' I asked.

He nodded.

'You're sure they were an item? They didn't just come in together by coincidence?'

He shook his head and frowned at me. I could hear the roof squealing as trees somewhere traced its cladding.

'The pair of them came in, all lovey-dovey, you know? Him with his arm round her, her whispering dirty stuff in his ear, that sort of carry-on. They went and sat at the bar, ordered drinks, then after a while the owner started chatting to the guy.'

'What did the owner look like?' I asked.

He made a face, hitched up one of the shoulders on the gown, then drummed the pink nails on the back of the open door. 'Maybe fifty, black hair in a sort of mullet do. He's owned the place for ages. Name's Terence or Terry or Troy, something like that.'

'Tyler,' I said.

He nodded. 'Yeah, that's the one.'

'He was talking to the pair of them?'

He hitched the gown again. I could smell tobacco and coffee beans from inside. 'The guy mostly.'

'You know what they were talking about?'

'I didn't catch anything.'

'You weren't close enough to overhear?'

He traced his jaw line with an index finger. 'People who run those joints like to keep friendly with certain people,' he said.

'In what sense?'

He tapped the doorframe. 'Drugs,' he said. 'Organized crime. All that sort of shit. The dealers keep the owners friendly, give them a cut of takings. It keeps everyone happy. Dealer's business isn't impeded, owners get to make a little cash under the table. You know?'

I said nothing.

He scratched his cheek, where the stubble was at its thickest. 'I've been hitting that place a lot; I've seen it happen.'

'You go there often?' I asked.

He shrugged. 'I guess you'd call me a regular.'

I said nothing.

'I'm a prostitute,' he explained, in a tone you might use

if you were telling someone you were a car salesman or an accountant. His face was giving nothing away.

I nodded. He looked at me calmly, waiting for the next question.

'And then what happened?' I asked. 'They just got up and left at eight-fifteen and that was the end of it?'

He leaned back and combed his hair with his fingers. 'Uh-huh. In more ways than one.'

I tried to look as if I didn't understand his comment. 'Thank you for your time,' I said. 'Someone will be in touch, we'll need to get a detailed description off you.'

I passed him a business card, and he accepted it and read it carefully.

'Have a good one, Detective.'

The benefit of working Sundays is there's no traffic. The trip from Northcote back across the bridge, through the CBD and east into Howick, took me twenty minutes.

Tyler Mitchell's garage door was still down, and the two light-coloured sedans I had seen earlier were still parked bumper to bumper in his concrete driveway. The sky overhead was dense with low-lying cloud the colour of gravy, and the intermittent drops falling left distinct watery rings on my windshield.

I waited for 'Electrolite' to die on the stereo, then got out of the car, locked it with the remote and walked down the driveway, knocking twice on the front door. The door was perched above a small wooden porch just to the left of the garage. It was painted sky-blue, which clashed horribly with the creamy colour scheme of the rest of the house, and was blistered like day-old sunburn. I was expecting Tyler himself to come running, but in the end it was the guy I'd seen earlier in the backyard by the pool — Tyler's brother — who answered.

'Yes?' he asked, tone neutral.

He was larger than I remembered; a fraction taller than me at just under six-foot-one, with a body made out of loose, bulky tissue which wasn't quite muscle. He had Tyler's brushed-back haircut, although his was speckled with silver. He was wearing a plain green T-shirt tucked into a pair of faded blue jeans, cinched around his waist with a thin leather belt.

I showed him my badge. 'Is Tyler in?'

'Yep.' His voice had dropped an octave.

'I'd like to have a brief chat.'

'He's sick of talking to cops,' the guy said.

I gave him sceptical: 'How do you know?'

'I'm his brother.'

'And what's your name?' I asked.

He considered me a moment before answering, trying to decide whether he was legally obligated to answer me. 'Tavis,' he replied at length.

'Tavis,' I repeated.

'It's like Travis,' he said. 'But without the "r".'

'Tavis, when I last spoke to your brother, he more or less lied through his teeth to me, so I'm not really in the mood to pussyfoot around this time. My best advice would be to let me in.'

He frowned at me and said nothing, glancing past my shoulder to where the Commodore was parked, trying to determine whether I'd come with reinforcements. The rain had become a cool mist on the back of my neck.

'I'm getting old here, Tavis,' I said. 'Make a decision.'

His lips cracked, giving me a snapshot of yellow, misaligned teeth. 'OK,' he replied.

He started to close the door. I stepped forward and grabbed him by the belt buckle, pulling him off-balance, then used the opportunity to push past him into the house. I followed a carpeted hallway past a living room and bathroom, both of which were unoccupied, down to a kitchen at the rear of the house, where Tyler Mitchell was sitting at a small wooden table, eating a sandwich. I stopped, framed by the doorway, making my final step heavier than it needed to be so he was aware of my arrival.

He looked up and raised his hands in exasperation, dropping the sandwich onto a plate in front of him. He was still wearing the white singlet, and his hands were damp and shrivelled like cured meat from his gloves. 'What the fuck? I've had enough of you guys already, get lost.'

'We need to have another talk,' I said. I pointed to a screen door that led out into the backyard. 'I suggest we take it outside.'

I sensed Tavis behind me.

'The sandwich is going to have to wait,' I said. 'Peanut butter won't spoil.'

Tyler Mitchell looked at me with the sort of distaste he probably reserved for bar patrons that vomited on his floor. There was a stainless-steel bench behind him, above which were wooden shelves holding bottles of vodka and gin and bourbon. He waited another moment, then got up out of his chair and stepped to the door, and I followed him as he pushed through it to the backyard. The recliner I had seen Tavis on earlier was still beside the pool.

Tyler stopped about two metres shy of the pool, where lawn met brick. He stood staring into its murky depths, as if that was where he kept his sense of calm. From where I stood behind him, I could see the muscle and sinew in his back writhing like snakes beneath a sheet.

'A girl died,' I said to him. 'It's a homicide. Feeding people bullshit during the course of the inquiry is unacceptable. I'm going to run the questions I asked by you again, and I'm going to get you to think about the answers a little more carefully.'

He paused. 'Fine, but do it from back there. The stink of your self-righteousness is going to make me puke.'

I grabbed him from behind by the shoulders and thrust hard, at the same time stepping forward and trapping his feet with the back of my right ankle so he fell forward, striking the tiled border of the pool with a slap that shot the breath out of him, as if he'd been sat on. The green skin of algae coating the pool was oscillating under the breeze and the gentle rain, and I resisted the urge to dunk his face in it. Behind me to the left, I could see Tavis framed in the door to the kitchen, hesitating.

'Fontaine came in with a friend,' I said. 'A guy in his twenties. You were talking to him. I want to know who he is.'

He shook his head and squirmed. He looked pathetic, but I didn't pity him. All I had needed from him was his honesty, and if he couldn't grant me that, then he'd get no sympathy.

'He had a tattoo on his face,' I prompted.

He rolled onto his back and moaned. 'Yeah, yeah,' he said. 'Shit . . .'

'Who was he?' I asked. Tavis still hadn't moved.

'I don't . . .' He rolled onto his shoulder and coughed once and hawked phlegm onto the tiles. There were pieces of bread from his sandwich smeared around his gums. 'I don't know.'

'You talked to him for forty-five minutes,' I said. 'If your memory's that bad you need to consider cutting back on the alcohol.'

'No, dickhead, I don't know his name.'

'But the description's right?'

He nodded, head scraping the tiles. 'White guy, twenties, skinhead.'

'What about the tattoo?'

'It's a swastika. Next to his left eye.'

I turned and looked towards the kitchen again. Tavis was still there. The neighbouring homes were hidden by a corrugated-iron fence, which had started out as grey but had rusted back to an orangey-red. 'What is he, some sort of Nazi or something?'

He shrugged.

'And what were you talking to him for?' I asked. 'Planning your next Klan meeting?'

'No.'

'What for, then?'

He said nothing, and I slapped his stomach with the back of my hand. He swatted ineffectually at me, then moaned and coughed up more phlegm.

'Drugs?' I asked.

He rolled onto his back and draped his arm across his forehead, as if shielding himself from some immense brightness. 'He's been known to deal,' he said.

'So who is he?' I asked.

'I told you, I don't *know* his fuckin' name. He comes in a couple of times a week, normally a Friday or Saturday, hangs around, then pisses off to God-knows-where. I don't know anything about him, I swear.'

'You don't know his name?'

'No, man.'

'Anything else about him that's particularly memorable?'

He pinched the skin between his eyes and grimaced, as if in pain. 'Wait,' he said.

He began to cough gently, freeing moisture from

his chest, gathering it in his mouth. He parted his lips fractionally, as if preparing to say something, then levered himself up off the ground and spat into my face. I felt the warmth of his saliva strike my skin, coating my nose, my eyebrows, my cheeks, in an obscene web. It began to drip even as it hit me, as if the sheer force of his malice and his vulgarity had given it life. I grabbed him by the front of his shirt, dragged him backwards and tossed him into the pool, the film of filth coating it fracturing like a dropped biscuit. I rose and used my sleeve to wipe the wetness from my face, then walked towards the house, my feet squelching faintly on the damp lawn. Tavis was still standing in the doorway, blocking my exit.

'Fancy a swim?' I asked.

He stepped back inside the kitchen and I moved past him, heading towards the hallway.

■ EIGHT

Swift evacuation is a necessity following perpetration of a violent crime, and by eleven a.m. the twins were well clear of the CBD, arriving at an address on Sandringham Road, west of Mount Eden.

The address corresponded to a white, single-storey structure nestled behind a red brick wall, which offered a nominal degree of privacy despite the proximity to the street. The short man stopped the dark Toyota sedan outside and shut off the engine, then both men climbed out and stood together for a moment on the footpath, the breeze filling their coats, as they observed the immediate neighbourhood. Satisfied they weren't being watched, they pushed through a wooden gate in the brick wall, crossed a small barbecue patio, and approached the plain, wooden front door, set above a low step, and bordered on one side by a strip of frosted glass. The tall man positioned himself so that his bulk obstructed the view of the door from the street, while the short man placed a pleasant expression on his face and pressed the electric bell, twice.

There was a subdued, high-pitched chime from within the house, and then, after a brief pause, the door was pulled open to reveal a small delicate man in his early thirties, wearing a green bathrobe and a pair of leather boat shoes. He didn't offer a greeting, just arched his eyebrows in a wordless enquiry, his brow wrinkling like ripples in a pool.

The short man maintained his expression of tranquil pleasantry for a moment longer, feeling the touch of the wind against the nape of his neck, and hearing the ebb and flow of the traffic on the street behind, then he turned swiftly, pulled his fist back and struck the man in the green bathrobe hard in the solar plexus, so that his breath escaped him in a sudden involuntary rush, and he crumpled forwards, overcome by pain.

The short man delivered a second, equally agonizing, blow to his victim's throat, before moving quietly into the entry hall of the house, waiting as the tall man stepped in after him and pulled the door closed against the latch.

My afternoon was occupied by a two-hour case meeting held in a conference theatre set aside as the Fontaine situation room, followed by a thirty-minute battle home through six-o'clock traffic along Tamaki Drive. I had a compilation CD in the player; *I'm Your Fan: The Songs of Leonard Cohen*. The John Cale cover of 'Hallelujah' is superb. The magic of the original Cohen recording has been preserved perfectly: beautiful piano backing, vocals good enough to put a quiver in your lip.

The Norfolk pine was an inky silhouette against a purple horizon when I swung into the driveway, my headlamps cutting twin golden streaks across the street-facing wall of my house. The air through my window was cool and replenished, and in the silence after I shut down the engine I could hear pooled rainwater dripping from the garage guttering onto the lawn. I locked the car, walked back and cleared the mail, then headed inside just as my cellphone rang. It was John Hale.

'I'm a hundred metres shy of your place, looking south,' he said.

'I didn't realize you were still on shift.'

I heard his breath on the line, rhythmic and unhurried. 'That car's here. Red BMW. Tinted windows, so I can't see the driver.'

I moved back to the entry hall, cracked open the front door and peered out into the blackness, the air cold on my face. The pavement was marked at discrete intervals with glowing streetlights, although I couldn't see a red BMW.

'I can't see it,' I said. 'How long has it been here?'

'Thirty minutes.'

'I'll be with you in a moment,' I said.

I ended the call, pulling the door closed against the jamb, then trod through to the bedroom and exchanged my suit for black jeans and a cotton sweater. I transferred my badge to my pocket, took a black torch from beneath the bed and pocketed that too, then headed back down the hall to the kitchen and let myself out the back door. I padded across damp grass, vaulted the wooden fence marking the beginning of the adjacent property, skirted the edge of a deck, and headed towards the next section.

Lights were burning behind virtually every window in the houses I passed, but nobody saw me as I cut through their empty yards. At the fifth address I came to, I scrambled over a waist-high hedge, then jogged down a right-of-way out to the street. Hale's pitch-black '79 Ford Escort was sitting directly in front of a parked rubbish truck, equidistant from the two nearest street lamps. The bulk of the truck was sufficient that, in the dim light, anybody looking at the Escort front-on would probably fail to see it.

I pulled the passenger door open, sunk down into the seat and glanced at Hale. He was clad in jeans and jacket; his standard surveillance attire. Light through his window touched the tips of his short hair, greyed twenty years ahead of schedule. The stereo had been on, but he flicked the knob to mute it, a tune sounding suspiciously like The Cure's 'Maybe Someday' fading to nothing.

'How's your day been?' I asked.

I heard the material of his jacket heave. 'So-so,' he said. 'You?'

'I chucked a guy in a swimming pool.'

He said nothing. I closed the door, gently.

'I didn't say you had to sit out here all day,' I said.

He shrugged.

'Where's the car?' I asked.

He leaned forward and pointed up the street through his windshield, which was fogged. I squinted in the direction he was indicating, and, after a moment, was able to make out the form of a small, low-slung sedan on the opposite side of the street parked in a similar manner to Hale, in front of a hulking SUV. Though I had failed to see it earlier, it couldn't have been twenty metres from my letterbox.

'You reckon it's been here thirty minutes?' I asked.

'More or less. It came up from the beach, parked across the street, hasn't moved since.'

'Does he know you're here?'

'Nobody knows I'm here, but he might have seen you.'

As if in confirmation, the headlights on said vehicle flared to full-beam and the engine started with a cold stutter of exhaust, the sound carrying easily in the evening silence. The driver paused momentarily, then swung the car in a U-turn across the width of the street and accelerated north, back in the direction the vehicle had appeared from.

Hale leaned back in his seat, hand hovering over the ignition, head twisted towards me. The dim light accentuated the contour of his jaw, making his lean face seem almost spectral. I could see the glow of the receding tail-lights in the whites of his eyes.

'What do you think?' I said. 'Follow, or pull back and call the cops?'

'We *are* the cops.'

'I am. You only used to be.'

He turned back to the windshield.

'Leave your lights off,' I said quietly.

He twisted the key in reply, the motor shuddering to life. The '79 Escort was only a 1300 cc capacity, so Hale had supercharged it to overcome any potential power deficiencies. He dropped the brake and took us away from the kerb. He floored the pedal and the car responded with a flick of the tach and a jolt that pressed me back into the seat. He pushed it to eighty, slipping through quiet suburban stretches shiny with recent rainfall, then picked up the glow of the BMW at the turn onto Tamaki Drive. He eased off the gas, falling back a fraction as the other car indicated left and turned west towards town. He pegged the brakes and idled at the Give Way sign until there was a four-car cushion between us and the BMW, then took off again.

He kept us fifty metres back, the speedo only just nudging sixty-five, elbow propped on the sill, wind and the smell of the sea fluttering in through his open window like he was out for a Sunday-night cruise. Not once did he draw closer than twenty metres to the red sedan, and even as the traffic built through the restaurant stretch east of town, he managed to keep our quarry in sight.

'How far are you prepared to go?' he asked.

I was silent a moment, considering whether there was a

double meaning to his question, or whether the ambiguity I was hearing was false. *How far are you prepared to go?*

'Just don't lose it,' I replied.

The BMW remained westbound on Quay Street through Mechanics Bay; passing a skyline dominated by stacks of cargo containers and skeletal arrangements of cranes. It indicated, eased into the far lane, hung a left and turned south onto the bus-only stretch of Queen Street. We were three cars back, stuck behind two taxis and a minivan full of Asian tourists. Hale floored it to overtake them, squealing the tyres on the corner, only just making the turn before the light flicked over to red.

'Just like the good ol' days,' I said.

'You weren't as good a driver,' Hale replied.

I said nothing. The BMW turned left at Customs Street and we followed it, trailing as it passed Heat on the right-hand side of the street, then up the hill onto Anzac Ave. Traffic became more scarce; there were no other vehicles between us and the car ahead, and Hale had to hang back to stay inconspicuous.

'You think he's seen us?'

'I'm pretty discreet,' Hale said.

We cruised up onto Symonds Street, threading through low-density traffic along the eastern edge of the university campus, past the renovated sixty- and seventy-year homes now housing the music and arts departments, and the human-sciences building further along. The neighbourhood hadn't changed much in the twelve or so years since I'd been in attendance.

The BMW held a constant, restrained pace all the way, slowing for lights, never displaying any sign it was aware of being followed. But as it reached the intersection with Grafton Road, it braked sharply, tail-lights flaring, rear wheels scrambling briefly against the slickness of the road, then turned right up Alfred Street.

Hale toed the brake and the whole front of the car wallowed under the loss of speed, but we were going too fast to take the turn, and shot past.

'Jesus, John, he must've seen us. Turn around.'

He hesitated, checking his mirrors, foot hovering over the brake, preparing to swing back, but in the end he just hit the gas again and the tyres hissed, and the throaty burble of the little motor shot up the scale to an urgent whine, which disappeared as he changed gear.

'I'll come around the block, link up with him on Princes Street.'

I twisted in my seat in an effort to catch a glimpse of the BMW, but the only trace of it was a faint tinge of red against the south wall of the General Library. Hale kept the pedal pinned somewhere in the region of the front-end suspension, and the features either side of us were reduced to a phosphorescent blur as the speedo crept up past ninety, then one hundred, then one hundred and twenty. I found myself gripping the edge of the seat squab, stomach clenched with the realization that I might be on the verge of becoming another road statistic, but Hale's face was empty. He still had his window open, elbow propped on the sill, driving with one thumb hooked through the rim of the wheel. He pulled out across a double yellow line to overtake a truck, dropped down a gear, causing the engine to howl in protest, then turned right onto Wellesley Street, blasted it again for a stretch, then made another right-hand turn onto Princes Street, where Alfred connects through from Symonds.

I placed my hands in my lap and tried to relax. My palms were damp and I could feel my pulse leaping in my neck. 'He would've turned back towards the waterfront,' I said. 'Obvious direction to head, if he was trying to lose someone, back the way he came.'

Hale turned his head and looked at me; one second, two. The speedo was reading one hundred. 'You look a little scared,' he noted.

'No, John, I'm dandy.'

His mouth fish-hooked at one end. Albert Park and the location where Emma Fontaine had been found flicked past on the left, and then the back end of the library on the right. No sign of the red car.

'Do you think it's more likely he tried to get some distance on us, or that he was focused on hiding?'

Hale touched the brake. We slowed to ninety. 'Why?'

'If it was distance he wanted, he would've stayed with Princes Street all the way to the docks, otherwise he might've turned.' Hale considered this. The cartilage in his jaw pulsed and the stitching in his jacket creaked as he freed the tension in his neck. We slowed to seventy, then sixty. Fifty. I could feel the seatbelt biting my shoulder. Hale pumped the clutch and threw us down a gear, then swung the wheel hard, turning us onto Bowen Avenue. He opened the throttle again and sent us careening down the hill towards the intersection with Victoria Street.

'You're losing your touch, John. We've lost him.'

Hale said nothing.

The BMW was thirty metres ahead of us, idling patiently at a red light.

▪ NINE

Once again, the BMW gave no indication it was aware of being followed. We pursued it north through the CBD onto Quay Street, where it turned left along the waterfront. It took Lower Hobson Street up to Fanshawe then rolled west, and for a moment we thought it was going to link up onto State Highway One, until it made a right, bouncing hard over the raised median strip, and pulled into the Caltex station opposite Victoria Park.

Hale slowed and jolted us up onto the footpath across the street, positioning us with a view of the station forecourt, then shut the engine. The BMW made an almost nonchalant loop of the pumping bays, tyres tracing a crisp, damp path across the concrete, then came to a halt tight against the far perimeter fence and killed its lights. There was a moment's pause, then the driver's door opened and a man I hadn't seen for ten years climbed out and stood blinking and smiling in the artificial light, before heading inside the service station building.

The man's name was Lionel Moss. The last time I had seen him had been in court in September 2001. Moss had been facing assault charges relating to an incident in July of the previous year, when he stabbed and robbed a thirty-six-year-old woman in a parking complex in central Auckland.

Moss was an interesting character. He spent the first ten years of his life in a foster home, and then, for one reason or another, the next ten years with no home at all. His police record dated back to the age of fourteen with a minor drug-possession charge. Six months down the track he broke into the home of a pensioner and stole a television and two hundred dollars from the drawer of a bedside table. At the age of seventeen he entered the premier division of criminality when he and three other young men ordered a takeaway pizza, lay in wait for the delivery man, then assaulted him with lengths of four-by-two.

At the age of twenty-five, jobless and desperate for money to buy drugs, he had driven into a parking garage at the eastern end of Victoria Street in central Auckland late one evening, and stabbed and robbed the woman as she was getting into her car.

John Hale and I had helped serve his arrest warrant. We found him living in a trailer home with four other people in the long-term section of a camping ground in Avondale. When Hale cuffed him, Moss told him to make the cuffs tight because the female officer with us looked like a Jew and he had a good mind to stuff his fingers in her eyes.

His defence for the stabbing had revolved around the concept that his judgement had been impaired by use of class-A drugs. The prosecution didn't buy it though, and pushed for attempted murder. The media had loved it. Moss was a drug-using degenerate with long hair and bad skin; his female victim was an upstanding solo mum no longer able to work due to the trauma she had suffered. The pictures had made for good contrast when run side-by-side above the fold.

The jury didn't run with attempted murder, but Moss still got prison time. Clearly his sentence had now reached its conclusion.

'We could keep following him and then shoot him when he gets home,' Hale said.

'Effective, but probably not advisable.'

Hale folded his arms across his chest, the material of his jacket creaking tight against the swell of his shoulders. Traffic through the window to his right was gradual, and the pillared section of the motorway that swung in over the western edge of the park was topped with white light streaming south.

'I thought he was in prison,' I said.

He shrugged, kept his eyes across the street. 'Stabbing someone won't keep you locked up for very long. That's why shootings are such good punishment. They tend to be permanent.'

'They also tend to be frowned upon. Give me another option.'

He unfolded his arms and gripped the bottom of the wheel with both hands. 'Scaring sometimes works,' he said. 'We're a pretty formidable pair.'

In my peripheral vision, I saw Lionel Moss exit the front of the service station and head back towards his car. Ten years ago he had made the front pages and the six o'clock news, but none of the three customers refuelling paid him any heed. He had purchased something from inside, an object encased in thin plastic packaging, which he was struggling to open. He used his teeth to get at whatever it was, then dumped the plastic in a waste bin, slipping the object into his pocket.

'What do you want to do, Sean?' Hale asked.

I made no reply, just kept my eyes on Moss as he made towards his car. Physically he didn't appear to have changed since I had last seen him: His hair was shoulder-length and streaked prematurely with grey; his tall frame lean, almost to the point of appearing underfed. He was wearing faded cotton pants and a hooded sweatshirt which hung loose over his narrow shoulders, and his face was inclined towards the ground, his eyes seemingly downcast, making him look furtive, sheepish even. I opened my door and put a foot out onto the concrete outside.

'Front or back?' I asked.

'I'll take the front,' Hale said.

We slid out of the car and closed our doors just enough to catch, then jogged diagonally through the traffic towards the Caltex station. The forecourt was well-lit from overhead, and the two women and one man who were pumping gas didn't seem to find Hale or me particularly suspicious.

We threaded in between the pumps, treading tip-toed

in order to minimize the sound we made, then slowed to allow Moss to reach his vehicle. He approached the driver's side, using a key from his pocket to unlock the door then slid in. We quickened our pace, Hale making for the front passenger side, me for the back right, directly behind Moss. We reached the car simultaneously, pulled the doors wide and threw ourselves inside. Moss was in the process of turning the key. He glanced up in surprise, but then relaxed and smiled faintly to himself, as if he had somehow anticipated our arrival. He started to say something, then stopped as I reached around the front of his seat and jammed my forearm across his throat.

'Hi, Lionel,' I said.

In the rear-view mirror I saw his eyes pan left to Hale, then focus in on my own. His pupils were dilated and the whites surrounding them were flecked with tiny red veins, like fork lightning. He didn't attempt to resist my grip. The muscles in his neck were flaccid, and his expression was more akin to curiosity than outrage or even apprehension. He dropped his right hand from the ignition and I sensed him link his fingers in his lap.

'Lucky you have tinted windows,' I said. 'Else we couldn't do this.'

His eyelids contracted fractionally, as if acknowledging

the irony, and I saw his cheek flutter in a half-smile.

'I picked you up on Tamaki Drive,' he said. 'I was wondering when I might be so lucky as to experience a face-to-face encounter.'

Hale smiled to himself and said nothing.

'To what do I owe the pleasure, gentlemen?' Moss said. His voice was calm; a perfect monotone.

'Take a guess,' I said. 'I think you know the answer.'

He shook his head and produced the expression of irony a second time. 'No,' he said, 'I'm afraid I really don't.'

'You're watching my neighbour,' I said.

Moss's eyes held mine in the rear-view mirror. The skin on his forehead creased upwards and his tongue ran out along his lips, as if remembering a sweet residue. 'What gave you that idea?' he said.

'You were parked across the street from her home. For three weeks.'

He licked his lips again, smiled and looked across at Hale, as if searching for somebody to share his apparent bemusement with. I felt his Adam's apple throb against my arm. 'I know you two,' he said. 'You arrested me that time.' His eyes drifted momentarily and then found mine again. 'You've changed,' he said.

'Excuse me?' I said.

He shrugged against the grip of my arm. 'I bet you didn't used to assault people for sitting in a parked car.'

'Don't preach to me about right and wrong,' I said.

'Oh, but I can,' he said, and he reached up to his neckline, removing from beneath his sweater a cross suspended on a fine gold chain. 'I'm a Christian now.'

'Adopting religion doesn't change you,' I said.

He laughed softly at my comment and dropped the chain back out of sight. 'Only kidding,' he said. '"Nature art my goddess," to quote Lear. It makes a nice pendant.'

Hale stirred in his seat. There were still customers in the forecourt, although none were focused in our direction. Moss inclined his head towards Hale.

'And you had Dirty Harry here playing lookout,' he said. 'Seems to me like an unjustified waste of time.'

He moved slightly against my grip and I sensed his hand make towards his pocket.

'Keep still,' Hale said.

Moss's eyes flashed yellow as they turned towards him. They narrowed in a sneer, but he held still. 'I think I liked being in prison better,' he said. 'Less arseholes like yourselves.'

'How long have you been out?' I asked.

'Long enough to realize freedom doesn't cut it.'

'You liked it better inside?'

'To an extent. It cultured me. I kicked the P, took up Christianity instead. And I started reading John Steinbeck. You ever sampled his work?'

'*Cannery Row* was a good yarn,' I said. 'But *The Grapes of Wrath* is the one that stays with me.'

He chuckled dryly. 'I love a well-read man.'

'Whatever,' I said. 'I see you around again, I'm going to do something to you.'

He smiled to himself. 'Kinky.'

'People like you need to be flushed away and forgotten.'

'I'm gratified.'

'Don't go near her again,' I said. 'Understand?'

His response feigned innocence, but the amused perk of his mouth told a different tale. 'I'm not quite sure who this woman is that I'm supposed to stay clear of,' he said.

'So stay away from people in general.'

He gave a drawn-out sigh. 'You guys are losing the knack,' he said. 'You nearly lost me.'

'Nearly being the operative word,' Hale said. 'All we had to do was follow the scent of shit on the wind.'

'I'm offended,' Moss said. Then, addressing me, 'Officer, if you'd kindly remove your arm, I'd like to be on my way.'

'Not just yet,' I said. 'We're not quite done.'

He smiled at me in the mirror. His teeth were even and white, an inexplicable contradiction to the impression of ill-hygiene the rest of him displayed. '*I* am,' he said coolly.

And with that he twisted suddenly, way quicker than I could ever have anticipated, thrust into his left pocket, and removed a plastic-handled box cutter, which he arced, blade extended, towards Hale's throat. I was in no position to react, but Hale was much faster than me, and he countered effortlessly. He viced his forearms either side of Moss's wrist, jerked once and cleaved the bones in Moss's arm, even before it had finished its short trajectory.

The box cutter clattered to the floor of the car, and Moss collapsed against the steering wheel, face convulsing with pain, skin paling with shock.

'Have a stroke,' Hale said. He pushed open his door, swivelled on the seat and stepped back outside, then ducked his head back in to address me.

'Let's go,' he said. 'I don't want to leave the car sitting for too long.'

Hale beat me to the car. He slid into the driver's seat, set the engine going and pulled us out onto Fanshawe Street even before I had my door closed.

'He's right,' I said. 'We're losing the knack.'

Hale shifted gear and dabbed the brake, then glanced at me as we slowed for a light.

'He bought the knife as soon as he arrived,' I said. 'I saw, but I didn't figure what it was.'

Hale shrugged.

'You didn't have to break his arm,' I said.

He shrugged again.

'It kind of elevates what we just did from a casual warning to premeditated aggravated assault.'

'It was self-defence. He had a knife.'

I shook my head. 'You didn't have to hurt him so badly,' I said. 'You're better than that.'

The light went green. We moved forward.

'If you'd been in the front you'd be dead now,' Hale said. 'You're slower than me.'

I turned in my seat and looked at him, waiting for him to elaborate, but he kept silent for the rest of the journey.

■ TEN

The twins stayed at the address on Sandringham Road until well after sundown. The tall bald man drove the car to a less conspicuous location, and then the pair of them moved their captive into the bath, brought in a set of knives from the kitchen and began asking questions. By eight o'clock in the evening, however, they had yet to receive a satisfactory response to any of their queries, so the short blond man moved to the living room and used his cellphone to place a brief call.

'He doesn't know where he is,' he said.

'Are you sure?'

'He's fairly adamant, and we have been persuasive.'

'How long have you worked on him?'

'Maybe seven or eight hours. He hasn't said a thing.

And it's not because he doesn't want to.'

'Shit.'

'So what do you want us to do?'

The response was a long time coming. 'OK, if you're sure, get rid of him and I'll call you in the morning.'

'All right,' the short man said.

He ended the call and walked back through the house to find his partner.

Hale and I drove back to my place to find my neighbour Grace sitting on my front step, just as I had found her on Saturday evening: elbows on knees, hands clasped, clearly distressed. I led her inside to the kitchen and Hale put the jug on, then the three of us sat down at the table.

'What's up?' I asked.

She bit her lower lip. 'I saw that car again,' she said. 'The red one I was telling you about.'

'So did we,' I replied.

'We dealt to it,' Hale said.

Grace made no reply, and just looked at Hale with an expression of mild surprise as if she had only just noticed his presence.

'This is John Hale,' I said. 'The guy I told you about. We used to work together.'

Grace nodded, adjusted her posture while righting a loose strand of hair, and gripped her hands tighter. I got up and took a pack of cigarettes from a drawer next to the sink, lit one, then sat back down again.

'So who was he?' she asked timidly.

'Just a guy.'

'One man?'

'Yeah, but you shouldn't have any more trouble from him.'

She looked at me, then at Hale, then back to me, her expression blank. She probably thought we'd slit his throat and dumped him in a river.

'What did you do?' she asked.

I tried to think of a suitable euphemism, but Hale beat me off the mark. 'We broke his arm,' he said.

Grace nodded to herself and looked down at the floor, as if that was the sort of answer she had been expecting. The jug clicked. Hale got up and politely enquired how she took her coffee. The consummate gentleman. She asked for it black, which he probably admired. Hale can't keep coffee down unless it's twitch-inducingly sweet. He bustled in the sudden awkward quiet then distributed the mugs wordlessly, reclaiming his seat.

'Thank you,' Grace said.

I didn't think it was for the coffee. She took a sip then placed the cup on the table in front of her, watching the steam forming at the surface of the liquid before it rose and melted away into the air.

'What's troubling you?' I asked.

She did the triple-glance thing again: me, Hale, me. She leaned back in her chair and exhaled sharply, then combed her fingers through her hair and screwed her palms into her eyes.

'It's just . . .' her voice fractured and disappeared. 'I'm sorry. I've just been so stressed lately, with work, and worrying about that guy, you know.'

I took a pull of my cigarette, swilled the fumes then turned and blew them towards the hallway. Hale coughed. It sounded forced.

'I kept waking at night, you know, hearing noises, convinced the guy in the car was trying to break in. Michael's noticed and so he's worried about me, but I couldn't say anything to him . . .' She fell silent again and just sat for a moment, watching the steam. At length she shook her head quickly then wiped her eyes with the back of her hand, and whispered, 'Oh, shit. Sorry, I shouldn't get all emotional like this. Look, I'm going all teary-eyed.'

'It's OK. Just pretend it's my cigarette.'

Her mouth flickered into the beginning of what I thought might become a smile, but it didn't quite get there.

'What if he comes back?' she said. 'What if you haven't scared him off for good? What if it's like, you know, made it worse?'

'He won't come back,' I said. 'He's got a broken arm.'

A spark of satisfaction on her lips. She watched the steam above her cup for a second longer, then looked up at the clock and pulled her feet up onto the chair, tucking her heels in against her butt, chin floating above her knees.

'Don't fret,' I said. 'Just relax.'

She didn't look at me. 'Easy for you to say,' she said. 'You don't have anything to worry about.'

'Only lung cancer,' Hale said.

'You don't have to worry about a kid,' she continued, 'you've got no dependants, you don't have money issues.'

Silence in the little kitchen for a long time. My cigarette was only a quarter gone, but I stubbed it out on the table and threw the dead butt in the sink.

'Take a holiday,' Hale said.

She pulled her attention from the clock and looked at

him. 'I work,' she said. 'So I can't. You can't just decide on a vacation. Doesn't quite work like that.'

'Where do you work?' Hale said.

'Hospital in Greenlane. I'm a research nurse.'

'It's winter,' Hale said. 'Maybe you caught the 'flu. Maybe you need a week off.'

'Maybe you caught swine flu,' I said. 'And need six weeks off.'

She shook her head wearily, leaned forward and raised her cup to her lips, taking a tentative sip. 'I have a child,' she said. 'I can't abandon him.'

'He can stay with Sean,' Hale said.

She took some more coffee, then glanced between the pair of us, eyebrows raised.

'Would that be OK?'

'It'd be fine,' I said.

She looked hesitant. 'He has school.'

'I used to skip school all the time,' I said. 'And I turned out spiffingly.'

She chewed a nail, attention on the floor, weighing her options in her head. There were deep bruise-coloured hollows beneath her eyes. 'Where would I go?' she said quietly.

'Book yourself into a hotel,' I said.

'Where?'

'Anywhere you like. Take a break, relax, chill out, whatever. Take a week off, and when you come back everything will have blown over. I'll even get the bill for you.'

'Oh, I couldn't let you do that.'

'Sure you could.'

She went teary-eyed. I gave her my best comforting wink.

She cleared her eyes and her mouth twitched to a smile — this time it didn't fade.

'My mother lives in Whangarei,' she said. 'I can stay with her. Michael might want to come, too.'

'If he doesn't it's no trouble, he's more than welcome to keep me company.'

'So when should I go?' she said.

'Tomorrow morning,' I said. 'Pack your bag, drive away. Just for a couple of days.'

'And Michael can stay with you?' she asked. 'He's only ten, what about when you're at work?'

'Hale might baby-sit.'

I glanced in Hale's direction but caught him mid-sip, and he offered no feedback.

She began to perk up a bit. Fingers setting a rhythm

against the tabletop. The sky outside was clearer than when she had last visited, and the blackness was pin-pricked with white stars like fragments of cracked glass. She took a final sip from her cup, set it back down on the table, smiled at both of us in turn, then stood up, with apparently renewed vigour.

'Thank you, boys,' she said. 'You've been a great help.'

Her perfume remained even after she'd gone.

■ ELEVEN

Grace's son Michael turned up on my front step the next morning at seven sharp, with a large-looking bag and an eager expression on his face. He was bigger than I remembered. He had his mother's slight build and light skin, and I guessed his curly dark hair was a genetic hand-me-down from his father. He was standing too close to the door and had to cant his neck right back in order to see me when I opened up for him.

'I didn't want to go on holiday, so Mum says I have to stay with you,' he said.

'Super.'

He grinned. His smile was a doozie: all crooked gaps. Some lucky orthodontist was going to have a challenge on their hands. He dropped the bag, dug into his trouser pocket and came out with a sealed envelope.

'Mum says to give this to you. Money to pay for me, or something.'

'Keep it. Buy yourself a DVD.'

He didn't argue.

'Come in,' I said. 'Shoes clean?'

He picked up the bag and trampled past, depositing half the lawn in my entry hall. I led him through to the spare bedroom and let him dump his stuff, then gave him the grand tour. Everything seemed to meet with his approval, except for the living room.

'Where's the telly?' he asked.

'I don't have one.'

He gave me a look suggesting he certainly hoped I was kidding. He looked at the couch along the far wall, then the bookcase opposite my armchair, then the Lundia shelving holding my stereo and music collection. I repeated my last statement for emphasis. His jaw dropped a fraction.

'Do a puzzle,' I said. 'I have to go to work. A friend of mine's on the way to keep an eye on you.'

'When's he getting here?'

'In about two minutes.'

'Is he cool?'

'He used to be in the army, and he plays a mean game of Scrabble.'

Michael nodded sagely. 'OK,' he said. 'See you later on, then.'

I left the house and drove along Tamaki Drive through whispering grey drizzle to the station at Cook and Vincent Streets. I signed in at the shift office and took the stairs up to my desk at CIB, only to find a large balding man in his forties already seated behind it. He had his hands linked behind his head and was facing the adjacent wall, so he didn't see me approach. I stole a chair from a nearby desk and sat down opposite him.

'Help you?' I asked.

The guy swivelled to face me slowly, as if I represented some great intrusion, hands cradling the curve of stomach that swelled above his beltline. He paused momentarily, as if trying to focus on the hush of background conversation, then said, 'I need to talk to you, I hope you'll excuse me.'

I smiled. 'I guess I'm going to have to.'

He looked at me blandly. 'Do you give lip to everyone, or just your superiors?'

'Just people I find sitting behind my desk.'

He traced his belt buckle with his index fingers and looked at me quietly. 'I don't think we've met,' he said.

'You're probably right. I leave a pretty distinct first impression.'

He didn't find that amusing. His hair was very thin, brushed vigorously straight back over a scabby crown, accentuating a growing widow's peak. He had a moustache that reminded me of a not-quite-done bird's nest and a skin tone strangely akin to corned beef left on the boil too long.

I smiled. 'Sean Devereaux.' I leaned forward and offered my hand.

The guy in my chair didn't take it. He gazed up at me with an expression suggesting he would have enjoyed pushing me down a flight of stairs. 'My name is Detective Inspector Alan Nielsen. I'm officer in charge of Manukau CIB Drug Intelligence Unit.'

I took my hand back. 'Good title.'

The corners of the moustache raised self-indulgently. He leaned forward suddenly and picked up a manila envelope off the desk in front of me, inverting it so that a single sheet of paper fell free into his lap. It looked like a photograph, black-and-white. He raised it and inspected it briefly, with interest that I supposed was meant to appear genuine, then reached across the desk and handed it to me. The sheet contained a single X-ray image of a human arm. The arm was broken just above the wrist. The X-ray had taken a good image, and the fracture was starkly obvious.

Nielsen picked up a pen from my desk and creaked his bulk forward on the chair, tapping the top of the photograph twice.

'Know what this is?' he said.

'It's my blue ballpoint.'

'No, dickhead. The photograph.'

'It looks like an X-ray of a broken arm.'

He flicked me under the nose with the pen, then leaned back in my chair and probed the corner of the moustache with a grey tongue threaded with purple veins.

'Look familiar to you?' he asked.

'Should it?'

'I'd expect so, seeing as though you inflicted it.'

I spun the photograph back onto the desk. It skipped off my copy of the Fontaine file and landed on the floor next to Nielsen. He didn't move to pick it up.

'Lionel Moss is a registered drug informant,' he said. 'He tells us things about bad people who make bad chemicals to sell to even badder people. And now he has a broken arm.'

'I'm sure you have a splendid reason for telling me all this,' I said.

The corners of his moustache jumped and his eyes receded fractionally into the folds of fat cresting his cheeks. 'Yesterday evening Moss was pursued by two men in a black sedan through central Auckland, to a petrol station on Fanshawe Street. After Mr Moss made a purchase at said station, he got back into his car, where-upon the two men who had been following him also entered his vehicle, before threatening him and eventually breaking his left arm.'

I said nothing.

'The licence plate on the sedan comes back to a guy named John Hale,' Nielsen said.

I just looked at him.

'I'm told the pair of you go together like pigs and shit. Which I guess is convenient, given the descriptions provided by Moss fit the two of you perfectly.'

I waited a moment before offering a response. 'I take it he didn't give you the unabridged story, then?'

He smirked.

'Moss was watching my neighbour,' I said. 'He's a

111

predator. He went to prison because he stabbed a woman and nearly killed her. I think you can see why the lady who lives next door to me was quite upset to find him keeping an eye on her from across the street.'

Nielsen's eyes came back out of their folds. 'You saw him watching your neighbour?'

'He was parked out front of her house.'

'I wasn't aware sitting in a car was a crime.'

'It is if you've been to prison.'

Nielsen paused. 'Did you see him in person?'

'After we'd been following him.'

'Where did you start following him?'

'From my house.'

'He said you picked him up at the top of Vic Street.'

'We lost him momentarily, then found him again, yeah.'

Nielsen smirked to himself and threaded his hands under his belly again as if some central question about the nature of the situation had just been made clear to him. 'How do you know you found the same car?' he said.

'Licence plates. They've been around a while, I expect your car probably has them.'

Nielsen shook his head. 'Nothing you might say can justify the broken arm,' he said. 'That's assault.'

'It was self-defence. We got into his car in order to warn him off, and he pulled a knife on Hale.'

Nielsen just looked at me.

'Get out of my chair, please,' I said. 'You're going to crush the springs.'

He didn't move for a beat. Then he unclasped his hands from beneath his stomach and levelled a finger at me, across the desk. 'I don't mind your vigilante Batman-and-Robin superhero crap if I don't have to hear about it,' he said. 'But when you start screwing with my work, it becomes another issue, and I get really pissed off.'

'I'll bear it in mind,' I said. 'Next time you want to come visit, ring in advance, so I'll know which direction to fart in.'

He didn't reply to that. He gathered together the photograph and the manila envelope, creaked himself forward then got up and walked past me towards the door, fanning me with his funk as he moved.

I went into Claire Bennett's office and found her seated behind her desk, looking at the door.

'Who was that?' she asked.

'Who was who?'

'Front desk told me you had a visitor.'

I shrugged and pulled up the chair from beside her filing cabinet and sat down across from her. 'Some arsehole.'

'I see.'

'Drugs cop called Nielsen,' I said. 'Angry because one of his informants got hurt.'

She pursed her lips. 'I see,' she repeated.

'You know him?'

She nodded once, leaned forward to square up a stack of files and raised her eyebrows. 'What happened to the informant?' she asked.

'Me and John Hale.'

She said nothing.

'It was a guy named Lionel Moss,' I said. 'Ring a bell?'

'Mmm-hmm.'

'He had his eye on the lady next door to me. Hale and I sorted it out.'

Bennett's mouth twitched as she slumped back into her chair and shook her head. 'You're thick, sometimes,' she said.

'I didn't come in here with the intention of getting a telling-off, if that's OK.'

She shot her chair forward and dug in the stack of files on her desk, keeping her eyes on my face. She removed the blue case folder for the Fontaine homicide and tossed it into my lap. I didn't open it.

'Fontaine's mother's address is listed in the persons-of-interest list,' she said. 'She's already been interviewed, but you might be able to find something extra. The house was searched yesterday and she could be a little tender from that, so take it easy.'

I thumbed the file. 'Have you found Emma's friend?'

'Friend?'

'The guy with her in Heat.'

She shook her head. 'Not yet. Something'll turn up though. It always does.'

I went back to my desk and called Hale.

'What are you up to?' I asked.

'Getting into some Scrabble. Is commonest a word?'

'No.'

'What about addressal? Or urbanness?'

'No,' I said. 'I just met a guy named Alan Nielsen. Know him?'

'No.'

'He's on to me about Moss,' I said. 'He says he's an informant.'

His breath on the line. 'What do you want me to do?'

'Nothing really. If you can dig up some dirt on Mr Nielsen it might be beneficial. If you can work it in with your day job.'

He laughed.

'Have a nice day,' I said. 'Try urbaneness, that's a word.'

The information gathered on Emma Fontaine made for ordinary reading. Sixteen years old, no siblings, no father. No police record, had not been known to associate with people who dabbled in criminality. Quit school at the end of the previous year and enrolled in a design course at AUT. She left home at around midday on Friday and simply never came back.

Her address was in Epsom, about ten minutes south of central Auckland. I checked out my Commodore and took the motorway down to the exit ramp next to the Remuera train station, then turned right at the overpass and headed into the suburbs, Radiohead's OK Computer set to a rousing middle volume. I pictured the Fontaine house as a huge stately affair surrounded by tall hedges and ornate cast-iron fences, and I was more or less correct.

The home was a slightly off-white, two-storeyed structure with a pitched tile roof and huge square wooden window frames, a basalt driveway and a stone chimney dribbling grey smoke towards the overcast skyline. It was on a side street branching off the main road towards Mount Eden, and was relatively secluded, even on a Monday. It blended in well with the general impression of affluence Epsom exudes.

There was no gate, so I crunched up the drive towards the house and parked behind a dark-blue VW Beetle. The driveway expanded into a bulbous turning circle just before the house, in the middle of which was an island of green grass stacked with bouquets of flowers and cards decorated with pink ribbon. There were more flowers placed at the bases of the windows, and along the stone paving slabs bridging the gap between the grass island and the front of the house. Most of the cards were still in their envelopes.

I got out of the car and approached the house. The air was cold and carried the scent of wood smoke, damp pine, and perfumed paper from the flowers. The front door was a dark piece of stained oak that looked as if it belonged on a seventeenth-century naval vessel. It was slightly chipped and worn and had a huge ornate iron knocker which rang about as subtly as a passing train when I dropped it. There was a brief silence, and then the sound of padded footsteps. The door was pulled back to reveal a tall, dark-haired woman somewhere in her mid-forties, with the kind of strained, beaten expression people only get when a child has been murdered.

'Mrs Fontaine?' I asked.

She nodded and managed to conjure a smile. I flipped my badge open for her and identified myself.

'If it's not too much of a bother right now, I was hoping to speak to you about your daughter.'

She gave me the smile again, but a slightly weaker version, as if it needed to be rejuvenated before further use. She leaned out a fraction and looked at the Commodore, as if she was worried I had dinged the edge of the turning circle or traded paint with the 'dub.

'Come in,' she said simply. She was wearing a long, silken gown that could have been the exact shade of her car outside. I thought it would have been more appropriate for an Oscars after-party than something for knocking around the house in.

She shut the door after me then stepped past with a swish of silk, leading the way through the house. The interior was as impressive as the exterior. The carpet pile was thick and every second surface seemed to be made from polished mahogany, with the smell of warm baking drifting through from somewhere. Homely. She led me through to a small living room near the rear of the house, where a pair of leather couches faced each other across a low glass coffee table. There was an assortment of magazines and a couple of books on the table, and when she saw them, Elizabeth Fontaine hurriedly gathered them up and dropped them out of sight behind one of the couches, before turning to me apologetically.

'I'm sorry it's such a mess, it's just I've been so overrun lately.'

'It's understandable, don't worry about it.'

She cupped her lower face with her hands, closed her eyes and exhaled deeply, and I sat down and set about making myself comfortable as a means of affording her some decency. After a moment, she dropped down opposite me and brought out the smile for the third time. It was back to full-strength.

'I know it's been very hard for you lately,' I said, 'I know it must be irritating having to put up with us all the time.'

She laughed politely, but it was far from genuine. Something caught in her throat, and she coughed, but managed to stifle it before it became a sob. Her dress was cut off across the shoulders and I could see the tension in the tops of her arms from clasping her hands in her lap too tightly. She closed her eyes and took a deep breath, releasing it slowly and straightening her posture.

'Do you live here alone, ma'am?' I asked.

'Yes, I do.'

'The last time you saw Emma was around midday on Friday, is that correct?'

She nodded.

'Did she voice her intentions for the evening to you, ma'am?'

Elizabeth Fontaine arched her back slightly and took another deep breath. Her features were thin and elongated, giving her face an almost regal aspect. 'She was vague,' she said. 'She told me she was going to a friend's house. A girl a few streets over. I spoke with her mother yesterday; I'm told Emma was there until five.'

'There was nobody with her?'

'No.'

'And nobody knew where she was going?'

She shook her head. The leather covering the sofa was extremely supple, and creaked even as she moved her neck.

'Did Emma have a boyfriend?' I asked.

'No, definitely not.'

'Any male friends at all that you know of?'

Her lips parted a fraction and then closed. 'No.'

'She hadn't mentioned having trouble with anybody lately?'

'No,' she repeated flatly.

Silence as she sat there and watched me, face drawn and miserable.

'I know how you must feel, ma'am.'

'Why, has a member of your family been recently murdered?'

She took my silence as a *no*.

'Then don't try to speculate about what I'm going through. It serves more as an insult than a comfort,' she said calmly.

She smiled at me, and this time her mouth stretched right the way back to her molars. She dipped her head and threaded her hair behind her ears, looked up at me, the smile still at maximum wattage, and said, 'To make things easier for you, I'll give you the basics: My daughter was a lovely, special child. She had lots of friends, and not many enemies. She was, in short, Detective, my special little angel.'

She stopped and pursed her lips and looked away from me towards the door.

'Sorry, I didn't intend to cause offence.'

'Yes, I know you didn't. Neither did the men who came and asked questions yesterday. And neither did the men who came and asked questions the night before that. And neither did the others who visited for three hours yesterday and searched through my home as if it were nothing more than a piece of evidence.'

I said nothing.

'What I would like,' she continued shakily, 'is for some-one to tell me why some fucked-up lunatic has taken my daughter away. And I'd also like to know why none of you seem to understand just how devastating it is to me that she's gone.'

I said nothing. She stood up then, slowly and precisely, feigning normality, perhaps, and walked out of the room, leaving me sitting alone on the couch, unsure of what to do next.

▪ TWELVE

At approximately six a.m. the twins' instructions had undergone a minor, though highly significant, modification in the form of a single phone call. The short man had answered the call on his mobile whilst staring out at the dull predawn from the window of their motel room, before relaying what he had been told to his partner.

They had moved to carry out their altered itinerary immediately, and were located as their employer had specified before the first rays of the sun had crested the edge of the harbour behind them.

Two-and-a-half hours after receiving the initial call, the short man used his cellphone to deliver a brief update.

'The woman's gone,' he said into the phone. 'She drove away at quarter to seven.'

'Where to?'

'We don't know, we didn't follow. You said she doesn't leave for work until later, so we don't know where she's headed.'

'What about the boy?'

'He's still there.'

'In the house?'

'No, next door. At the detective's place. He's got a babysitter there. Guy in a black sedan, looks like some shitty old Escort.'

The phone hushed with static for a moment before the reply came. 'Hang in there,' the voice said. 'Call me if there are further developments.'

Elizabeth Fontaine vanished to some far-off corner of the house, and I didn't attempt to follow her. I guessed the layout of the house was as straightforward as bedrooms and bathroom upstairs, and everything else down, so I headed up in search of Emma's room.

The stairs were made of pieces of golden, polished timber, which looked new but were probably much older judging by how my movement was accompanied by several audible squeaks. The walls were off-white, adorned with foggy photographs in elaborate brass frames. The subjects were all people, although I didn't see anyone who resembled either Emma Fontaine or her mother.

On the upstairs floor there was a carpeted landing with a corridor, and open doors branching off each side. Emma's bedroom was the last room I came to, the final door in the corridor. It was a large, square space with a window facing north towards the road, and another facing west towards the neighbouring property. The carpet was cream and the walls were a slightly peculiar combination of more cream with dull pastels in places. There was a single bed against the west window and a desk beneath the north one, with a girl in her early twenties sitting in a swivel chair next to it going through a stack of exercise books balanced in her lap. She didn't see me enter. She had her chin ducked to her chest, trapping the tops of the books as she lifted them, inspecting their covers one by one.

'Hello,' I said.

She lifted her head and looked at me, so the stack of books she had been sorting through slapped into her lap. She lifted them with an effort that made her grin, wheeled herself forward and dropped them onto the corner of the desk. She stood up and came towards me, offering her hand. I took it. Her hand was soft and yielded slightly under my grip. She had the sort of build she would probably like to describe as plump, but which I would describe as heavyset. She was wearing faded blue jeans and a red fleece jacket lined with sheepskin to ward off the chill.

'Ruth Morgan,' she said. 'Pleased to meet you.'

'Sean Devereaux.' She gave my hand back.

'Are you a cop?'

'Yes indeed.'

'I was Emma's tutor,' she explained.

'For design?'

She looked at me strangely. 'No, for maths.'

I moved past her, towards the bed. The room was immaculate; the bedspread crisp, items on the desk ordered neatly, the shoes beside the dresser against the left-hand wall in a tight sequential line of three pairs.

'I thought she'd left school?'

'She has. Or had. Yeah. Elizabeth wanted her to keep up with stuff, though.'

I nodded.

'So what are you here for?' she asked.

I glanced at her. 'Cop stuff.'

'Are you, like, a detective or something?'

'Yup.'

'That's pretty cool.'

'I think so.'

I heard the cylinder in the chair hiss as she let herself down again.

'Always thought it would be pretty neat being a cop,' she said.

'Really?'

'Uh-huh.'

'I can give you a taste of what it's like by asking you a few questions, if you want.'

She said nothing. 'People asked me questions yesterday.'

'You know the family well?' I asked.

I saw her shrug, heard her twist from side to side on the chair. 'It's not really a family. Just Liz now.'

'I know, but before that.'

'My mother's friends with Liz. So yeah, I guess you could say I know them fairly well.'

'So tell me about Emma,' I said.

She waited a moment. 'Shouldn't you like, show me your badge or something?'

I showed her my badge. I held it out at arm's length so she could see it, and she arched forward in the seat, reading the word *DETECTIVE* written beneath the police crest.

'So tell me about her,' I said.

'Emma?' she said.

I nodded. There were posters on the wall: close-up shots of young men and women with their hair arranged in various degrees of extravagance. I pocketed my badge. On the desk there was a large hemispherical paperweight beside the stack of exercise books, a glass ballerina, frozen mid-curtsey, trapped in its centre. I picked it up off the desk and inverted it, watching as little flakes of white confetti were roused from the bottom, falling slowly through whatever it was that constituted the atmosphere of that little sealed-off world.

'She was OK, I guess. I tutored her twice a week for eight months and found her to be tolerable.'

A smattering of rain against the north window shook the wooden frame. 'Tolerable?' I asked.

She shrugged. 'Yeah. She was OK, like I said. But . . .' she glanced around as if in fear of being overheard. 'You know how people can be sort of, upper class?'

I nodded and tipped the snow globe back the other way. The ballerina was proportioned perfectly. I wondered how they made her. Was there a special machine for carving thousands of little glass figures, or was she etched by hand?

'I always kind of got the feeling that, even though it was me helping her, she thought she was somehow better than me. And everyone else.'

'Were you friends?'

She made a face and draped her hand over the stack of books, like an absent-minded gesture of affection. 'I suppose I would've liked to be.' She laughed. 'I don't think I was really her cup of tea.'

I smiled. 'So what are you when you're not a tutor?'

'Nothing at the moment. I did my degree in operations research. Optimizing processes in businesses and things. Not much of that going at the moment. So I help Elizabeth with stuff. And tutor Emma.'

'Why did she want tutoring?'

'She didn't. Her mother did. In the event Em wanted to do something worthwhile one day. Liz's words.'

'She have a boyfriend?' I asked.

'Emma?'

I nodded.

She looked at me without saying anything for a moment, then swivelled the chair a fraction, leaning back and linked her fingers behind her head. 'Haven't you already asked Liz that?'

'Yes. Now I'm asking you.'

She was quiet. 'No, she didn't.'

'Liz said Emma had lots of friends,' I said.

A grimace. 'She had a few. But those few had a lot of friends, so I guess, yeah, by association, Emma had a lot of people she was friendly with.'

'Emma ever tell you she was upset with any of them, if there'd been any conflict?'

She smiled. 'You don't know girls very well, do you?' she said.

'Not especially.' The window rattled again.

She shook her head and chuckled softly to herself, as if I had somehow managed to skip one of the most fundamental aspects of my education. 'Girls are catty,' she said. 'There was something going on every week.'

I stepped towards her and put the paperweight back down on the desk.

'So what was the most recent?' I asked.

She made a face. 'The details escape me. You'd have to talk to her friends.'

'Elizabeth told me Emma was at a friend's house the evening she died,' I said.

She nodded. 'Carrie Jordan's. She lives a couple of streets over.'

There were drawers in the desk; two, at the right hand

end, one above the other. I opened them one at a time and sifted through their contents. Stationery: pens, pencils, loose bits of paper with quadratic equations scrawled across them. I went through the dressing table beside the bed, but turned up nothing other than clothing. There was a wardrobe opposite the bed, but it was unexciting in terms of what it yielded: more garments.

'What are you looking for?' Ruth said.

'I don't know,' I lied.

She went quiet as if she were aware of my dishonesty. I turned and gave her a wink as I walked out of the room.

I found Elizabeth Fontaine in the downstairs kitchen. She was removing a tray of biscuits from an oven large enough to spit-roast an elephant. Odd behaviour following a murder. You see it sometimes. People find comfort by clinging to the familiar, mundane things.

'What can I do for you, Detective?' she said, without looking at me.

'Did Emma take anything with her on Friday when she left the house?' I asked.

She placed the tray down on a wooden chopping block, slipping her hands free of lilac-coloured oven mitts. She reached forward and broke a segment off one of the biscuits, placed it in her mouth and chewed with pursed lips and raised eyebrows. 'Probably.'

'Probably?'

She made the whirling motion with her fingers I had seen her do earlier. 'Well, I guess she took everything she would normally take.'

'Handbag, cellphone, keys, purse, that sort of thing?'

She nodded, then prised the remainder of the biscuit free of the tray and popped it in her mouth, chewing slowly. 'Why?' she asked.

'We didn't find anything like that in her car, and they're definitely not in her room.'

She just chewed, her expression suggesting that even if she had an answer, it would be beneath her to offer it. There was a line of windows above the stovetop which gave out onto a backyard full of tall, lush greenery.

'Her tutor told me Emma visited a friend named Carrie Jordan the afternoon before she passed away,' I said. 'She might have left something with her?'

'I doubt it.'

'Perhaps you could give me the address anyway.'

She did so.

'Enjoy the biscuits, ma'am.'

■ THIRTEEN

The short walk to the car left me freezing cold and peppered with light drizzle. July for you.

Carrie Jordan's home was located two minutes west of the southern motorway. It was a building of similar grand proportions to the Fontaine palace, with the added luxury of a metal gate. Fortunately, it was standing open, enabling me to turn in off the road and drive up to the house. Where the Fontaines' home radiated classiness with its expansive wood-framed windows and brick chimney, Carrie Jordan's was just plain unappealing. It was constructed of glass and concrete. There were too many hard angles. Everything was either parallel or perpendicular. The door was metal and had a digital combination lock.

I got out of the car, walked to the door and pressed

the buzzer. I had to push it three times before I got a response. Eventually a small compact woman, whose physique reminded me of a bag of walnuts, opened up. She wasn't smiling. I showed her my badge.

'She's not here,' the woman said. I could hear a television playing somewhere.

'Who's not here?'

'Carrie. So no, you can't talk to her.'

'That's a pity. Where is she, ma'am?'

'Where do you think?'

'I couldn't hope to guess.'

'School,' she said.

'What school is that, ma'am?'

She gave me the name of some private, upmarket institution she'd either made up or I simply hadn't heard of.

'What time does she normally get in?'

She rolled her eyes, as if my presence was a real burden to her. 'Not until about ten o'clock. She has polo until nine; she's really not going to be in any state to answer questions today.'

She took the business card I passed her without thanks, and I sensed her eyeing me suspiciously as I walked back towards the car.

'Can we expect the pleasure of your company tomorrow?' she asked.

'You betcha,' I said.

She closed the door firmly.

My afternoon between three-thirty and four was occupied by a press conference. It was a pointless exercise. In the absence of progress in a tangible sense, the media need something alternative to chew on and distribute to hungry consumers: theories of crime perpetration, 'persons of interest', local sightings of aberrantly oriented individuals. Aside from the standard promise of unrelenting determination and consummate thoroughness, we gave them nothing of the sort. But they didn't seem too disappointed. They took photographs and jostled for prime microphone positioning. A sound bite's a sound bite.

I drove home along Tamaki Drive at a little after six o'clock, through shiny blackness and dense traffic, typical of July evenings. Hale's Escort was sitting idle beneath the Norfolk pine when I pulled into the driveway. I left the car in the garage then headed inside to find the pair of them playing snakes and ladders at the kitchen table.

'Score?' I asked.

'Two–one,' Michael said.

'To who?'

'Me.'

I dumped the contents of my pockets at Hale's elbow and went to the fridge. Depressingly desolate. I took the second-to-last Heineken from a six-pack that had been intact that morning and popped the top with an opener from the cutlery drawer, then leaned back against the bench and took a welcome pull. There were three empties in a neat row on the floor beside Hale.

'Eventful day?' I said.

Hale rolled the dice. 'Like you wouldn't believe.'

'Sarcasm is the lowest form of wit.'

He moved his counter along four squares, hit the business-end of a snake and dropped down a row. 'Someone from a legalize-cocaine political party called. They're sending a collector around later this evening because I told them you wanted to make a donation.'

'Oh, goody.'

I didn't think Hale was particularly enthused by the game.

'Nothing out of the ordinary, though?' I enquired.

'Nothing out of the ordinary.'

From their vantage point across the street, the twins saw

the Commodore pull into the driveway and come to a stop in the garage. The short man watched the red flare of the tail-lights disappear into the gloom, then he removed his cellphone and pressed three on speed-dial.

'Status update,' he said, when the employer answered.

'Developments?'

'The detective's just come home, dinner's probably coming out of the oven.'

The employer allowed himself a quiet chuckle. 'What's the neighbourhood like?'

'Quiet. It's cold, people have their curtains drawn.'

'So who's home?'

'All three of them.'

'You want to do anything tonight?'

'What do you think?'

The employer paused. 'The baby-sitter's hard-case. I pulled his file, he's done a bit of everything. Army, two years duty with Diplomatic Protection.'

The short man didn't feel those credentials were insurmountable, but chose not to voice this. 'And what about the detective?'

'He's no pushover either. He's been in strife for breach of protocol, but CIB seems to love him.'

The short man said nothing and watched his breath

condense against the windshield in front of him, blurring the street lights on the road ahead.

'It's your choice,' the employer said. 'All I ask is that you don't leave it too late.'

A day of board games with John Halc had proved taxing for Michael. He was knackered. I had him in bed in the spare room by eight o'clock.

'Your house is cool,' he said, when I flicked out his light.

'I know,' I said. 'It's because I made it.'

'You didn't make it.'

'How do you know?'

He rolled over and slapped the base of the bed; an old divan I'd picked up in an inorganic collection a few years back. 'You're pretty cool, too,' he said.

'Well, shucks.'

He gave me a look like he was expecting some reciprocating gesture, so I said, 'You're pretty neato as well, I guess.'

He beamed. 'You have lots and lots of music in your lounge,' he said.

'Yeah, I like music.'

He kicked his toes beneath the blankets, considered the new bedspread topography. 'Do you have a favourite song?'

I leaned against the doorframe. '"Rockin' in the Free World" by Neil Young would be up there,' I replied. '"Walk Unafraid" by R.E.M., maybe. They keep you pointing forward.'

'Who's R.E.M.?'

'Arguably one of the greatest bands ever. They've been around for yonks.'

He squirmed his head on the pillow. 'How long's yonks?'

I thought about that. 'I guess, almost since the time I was born.'

A quiet beat of contemplation. 'That's ages,' he concluded.

'It is.'

He looked at me quietly for a short moment. 'Thanks for letting me stay in your house, Sean. I like it here.'

I smiled at him. 'No problem, kiddo.'

■ FOURTEEN

Hale was gone by eight-thirty. I cracked a bottle of Taylors 2007 Merlot, put on The Phoenix Foundation, flicked the lights off and sat down in my armchair. That to me epitomizes relaxation. A glass in one hand, a bottle in the other. Stimulation for the ears, but none for the feet. The darkness is a key ingredient, too. Loss of sight helps underline the acoustic subtleties. Although, depending on how much of said bottle you wish to consume, it could be safer to leave the lights on, if only very low.

It was a chill night, and the sky visible through the living-room window was black and starless. I wondered how many others sat alone in dark living rooms with bottles at hand. A thought to ponder: did they consider themselves the fortunate or the unfortunate of this universe?

I let the Phoenix boys run to midway, then traded them for an old Lucinda Williams CD I'd forgotten I even owned. Musically, they were a nice contrast: alternative rock versus a more traditional, country vibe from Lucinda. Balance is everything. With this in mind, I went to the kitchen and lit a cigarette to complement the wine.

My cell fluttered against the kitchen tabletop, caller ID: John Hale.

'Sometimes you just can't get enough of me,' I said when I answered.

He grunted. Humour doesn't sit well with him after a long day. 'You ever hear of a guy named Burke Donald?'

I trapped the phone between ear and shoulder and topped up my glass. 'No.'

'Drugs guy at Manukau CIB. He and Alan Nielsen earned some newspaper time about three years ago after a job went pear-shaped.'

'Doesn't ring a bell.'

'*Herald* archives had an old story on it, some sort of transport stuff-up. Central city, they were moving a cache of P out of a place on Beach Road. Someone on a bike with a gun pulled up alongside on Quay Street, told them to pop the boot, got clean away with everything they were carrying.'

I remembered the case vaguely, although I hadn't been directly involved so was unclear on the details. I consumed some more smoke and alcohol.

'You found this out on the ride home?' I said.

'I called in a favour,' he said. 'The favour called me back about eleven minutes ago.'

Eleven minutes. Mr Precision. I moved through to the hallway to escape Lucinda, made a right into the bathroom and flicked on the light, shielding my eyes against the sudden yellow onslaught. 'Who was in the car?' I asked.

'Four of them, I think. Nielsen, Donald, one unknown, and a guy called Leon Ross. Remember him?'

I nestled the Taylors bottle behind the bathroom tap. 'Yeah, I know the guy.'

Ross had been attached to Auckland CIB. Back in 2000. I remembered he'd helped us out with the original Lionel Moss situation. I knew him reasonably well. I had some more wine. Warm on the way down, but not overpoweringly so. Restrained, but you were still aware it was wine.

'And what do you think?' I asked him.

A long hushed pause. 'Nothing. I have no opinion. You wanted background on Nielsen, that's what I found.'

I swilled my drink, puffed my cigarette. The smoke rose and formed a blue skein against the ceiling. 'How specific were the details?'

'Not very. It was a one-column follow-up story.'

I said nothing for a moment and looked at myself in the mirror above the basin. Not a cheerful image. I was wearing a grey suit which could have been scavenged from a clothing bin, the fold of my blue shirt collar was showing white with fray. I try to keep my hair on the back foot with a short cut, but messiness still prevailed. There was a three-centimetre-long lick of white scar above my left eye, courtesy of a suspect ultimately less agreeable than my twenty-two-year-old self had anticipated. My stubble had grown out to two or three mils. Delightful. I would have made a good subject for an Edward Hopper painting. *Portrait of the Detective*. Or just *The Unfortunate*.

'You still there?' he said.

'Yeah, sorry. I'll look into it,' I said.

'Professional curiosity?'

I shut the light off to save me from myself. 'I guess so. That and the fact that Alan Nielsen pissed me off to the extent I want to rake up some dirt on him.'

Hush for a short moment, like he was digesting my response. 'I'll catch you tomorrow,' he said.

The employer called back at nine o'clock. The short man answered.

'What's happening?' the employer said.

'The baby-sitter left.'

'OK. You're still at the detective's place?'

'Yeah. The lights are off, I think he's gone to bed.'

The employer exhaled slowly. 'Leave him be,' he said. 'Lull them into a false sense of security. There's always tomorrow.'

■ FIFTEEN

The weather the next morning was pleasant for July; the wind still, the air mild, but the presence of cloud cover suggesting rain wasn't too far away.

When I reached my desk at a little after seven-fifteen, I dialled Pollard at police communications.

'How's this for a joke,' he said once I'd identified myself. 'How do you tell the difference between a journalist and a cop?'

'Please tell.'

He paused for effect. 'Journalists have less paperwork.'

'That's absolute gold, Pollard. I'll remember that one.'

He said nothing. Perhaps he sensed the sarcasm.

'I need a number for a guy called Leon Ross,' I said.

'Leon Ross, Leon Ross. Rossy-rossy-rossy. Detective?'

145

'Far as I'm aware.'

Keys tapping, then he reeled me off a number. I thanked him, hung up and punched in the number. Leon Ross answered with his name on the third ring.

'Leon, it's Sean Devereaux.'

An extended pause while his memory kicked in. 'Shit, man, it's been far too long.' His voice was husky and abrasive, like he was on the mend from laryngitis.

'Definitely.'

'What can I do for you?' he asked.

'I want to have a chat.'

'Oh, yes?'

'About a guy called Alan Nielsen.'

Quiet on his end for a spell. I could hear traffic noises; an early morning motorway commute. He laughed humourlessly. 'I'm kinda stretched right now, but there's a bar at the bottom of Queen, corner of Quay, called Traffic,' he said. 'You know it?'

'I do.'

'Is six o'clock too early for you?'

'Six sounds splendid.'

'Bring your wallet,' he replied, and hung up.

Standard covert-operation doctrine called for extreme

caution in regard to temporary accommodation. Lengthy stays were to be avoided. The trick was to keep moving. Therefore, Monday evening had called for a motel swap. They'd found one in Manukau, off Great South Road. The staff seemed inattentive, which was always a bonus. Being ignored is incredibly advantageous when engaged in illegal activity.

Tuesday morning, the tall man had ducked across the road at six-thirty for pancakes, and they were through them by the time their employer called for the daily briefing at seven sharp. The duration was far briefer than usual.

'What's happening?' the employer said.

'We're finishing breakfast,' the short man said, taking a sip of milk from the glass he was holding. 'We're heading over to the detective's place now.'

'You'll proceed with things tonight?'

'Absolutely,' the short man said, then ended the call and took another sip of milk.

At seven-thirty I logged out my car and drove south on State Highway One through dense early-morning traffic, and was parked at the kerb twenty metres shy of Carrie Jordan's home by quarter to eight in the morning.

The severe concrete edifices forming the house's structure looked even more grotesque in the early light, with the smoke drifting free of the twin chimney pipes breaking the roofline giving the whole place a slightly Gothic aspect. Certainly it was the ugliest house on the street. The architecture of the surrounding homes was mostly elegant despite its grandiosity. In general it looked the sort of neighbourhood where lawyers or financial consultants or orthopaedic surgeons lived. Not Lord Sauron's wife.

Foot traffic on the street was minimal. Human movement was confined to up-market Mercedes and Audi sedans reversing out of driveways before turning towards the motorway. At a little before eight, a black Bentley only slightly smaller than the *QEII* nosed out from beyond the line of the Jordan's cast-iron fence and drove past, paying me no attention whatsoever. I had Neil Young's *Chrome Dreams II* playing. 'Ordinary People' is a great track. Eighteen minutes of rambling electric guitar and hard vocals. Classic Young.

As it turned out, Carrie Jordan was the first person I saw all morning who actually used the footpath. She turned right out of her front gate at a little after eight, heading straight towards me wearing a green skirt and woollen blazer I assumed constituted her school uniform, with a scarf wrapped around her neck. Her red hair was pulled back into a ponytail which bounced against the back of her neck as she walked, and a leather satchel hung from one shoulder.

I opened my door and got out so that I was visible to her as she approached. My movement startled her slightly, and she slowed, patting non-existent pockets in her skirt.

'Carrie Jordan?' I asked.

She frowned, almost imperceptibly. 'Yes?'

'Sorry,' I said. 'Didn't mean to startle you.'

'I'm not startled.'

She had her mother's brisk, matter-of-fact tone. I opened my badge wallet and raised it for her to see. 'I was hoping you might have a minute to talk to me about Emma.'

She looked hesitant. 'My bus leaves at half past.' Even the upper classes are confined to public transport at times.

'It'll only take a minute.'

She surveyed my face with undisguised curiosity. 'You left skid marks on our driveway,' she said. 'My mother's really annoyed — she's going to have to pay someone to come and scrub them off.'

I gave a little frown which I hoped looked genuine. She scuffed one of her shoes against the ground then turned and glanced back over her shoulder towards the concrete fortress. 'My mother said I don't have to talk to you anymore,' she said.

'I'll only take a minute,' I said. 'I'd really appreciate it.'

Carrie Jordan gave a little sigh which I guessed meant *well, in that case*. She glanced over her shoulder again, then looked at me, taking a step towards the car.

'Get in,' I said. 'It's cold.'

She moved towards the passenger door, slightly unsure of herself. She looked about fifteen. She would have had the *stranger-danger* talk many times by now and was probably hearing echoes of advice to scarper promptly. I showed her the badge a second time to emphasize my good intentions, then got into the driver's seat and closed the door. A moment later Carrie Jordan climbed in beside me, clearly satisfied I wasn't about to kidnap her.

'I've never been in a police car,' she confided.

'They're like regular cars,' I said. 'Except they have a two-way radio.'

She smiled shyly and looked away from me.

'Emma's mother told me that Emma was at your place the afternoon before she died. Is that correct?'

Carrie Jordan nodded, her face turned towards the window. 'I was having a party sort-of-thing. Bunch of friends round. I told Emma to drop by.'

'You remember what her behaviour was like?' I asked.

She twisted in her seat and inspected the radio scanner before responding. 'Antisocial.'

The speed of her reply made me think she'd probably been through this already. 'Antisocial?'

'Yeah, like she wasn't saying anything, seemed kinda depressed, wasn't interacting with anyone, just sat by herself and texted on her phone.'

Another car cruised slowly past: Mercedes coupé, a woman in her early thirties behind the wheel.

'Texting who?'

She shrugged and slapped the material of the satchel and looked in the direction of her home. 'I have no idea.'

'Boyfriend?'

She shook her head, ponytail flapping. Outside, the wind rose suddenly and the trees lining the roadside swayed and then settled. I wondered if she was uncomfortable talking to me about her dead friend. She didn't look too distraught. Maybe she was the resilient type.

'She didn't have a boyfriend,' she said.

'Certain?'

'Yeah. Far as I know. What's this music we're listening to?'

'"Spirit Road", Neil Young. When did the antisocial attitude begin?'

A shrug. 'Dunno. She started getting weird a couple of months ago, I guess.'

'You don't know why?'

Her satchel beeped once and she pulled it across onto her knee, delving inside to remove a cellphone, then thumbed in a quick message and hit send. Five seconds, tops.

'I really need to catch my bus,' she said.

'Emma ever tell you she felt threatened by anyone, had any problems with boys at all?'

She shook her head.

'Her tutor told me there might have been an issue with her friends, that there was a disagreement of some sort, you know anything about that?'

She turned and frowned. 'No, why?'

'Forget it. Did she have her handbag with her when she turned up at your place on Friday?'

She adjusted the bag strap against her shoulder absent-mindedly and faced the window again. Thinking. 'I guess so, yeah, she probably did. She always kept her purse and shit in there. Why?'

'I haven't found her keys or her cellphone.'

Carrie Jordan gave the little sigh again and ducked her head forwards to check we weren't being observed from afar. 'She has a little black imitation leather handbag she takes with her. For her purse and keys and diary. She had it with her when she came in, had it with her when she left.'

'She had a diary?'

She gave me an expression that seemed to mean *doesn't everyone?* I looked at her a moment, then reached inside my coat pocket, removed a business card and passed it to her across the central console.

'Hang on to that,' I said. 'Call me if you think of anything. You'd better go now or you'll miss your ride.'

She didn't need further prompting. She opened the door and got out into the chill without so much as a farewell.

■ SIXTEEN

I drove back east two blocks and parked in Elizabeth Fontaine's driveway behind her blue VW Beetle then went and rang the doorbell. Ruth answered. She was wearing an apron with a feather duster tucked into the front pocket.

'Hello again,' she said tiredly.

I smiled. 'You've been promoted.'

'What?'

I shook my head dismissively. 'Is Ms Fontaine in?'

She took a step back and made a slow quarter-turn, making up her mind whether to let me in or not. 'She's not her best today,' she warned.

'Neither am I,' I said.

She kept her eyes with me, surveying my face

quizzically, then removed the duster from the pocket, dabbed at the wall and said nothing.

'It's kind of urgent,' I said.

She gave the wall another gentle poke, then turned fully so my path into the house wasn't obstructed, and said, 'She's up in Emma's room.'

I moved past her, taking the polished wooden staircase up to the second level. The door to Emma's bedroom was standing open. I went in and found Elizabeth Fontaine seated at the desk, hands clasped in her lap, staring out through the window into the middle distance with an expression suggesting she'd just been lobotomized. My shoes were hushed by the carpet pile and I said nothing as I entered, but she picked up on my arrival nonetheless.

'I'm sorry about yesterday,' she said, without turning to face me.

I took another tentative step into the room. The little glass paperweight with the ballerina was as I had left it, and the stack of exercise books was resting on the corner of the desk as well.

'You don't need to apologize,' I said.

She shook her head, but her eyes didn't move. 'The job you people do is underappreciated at the best of times,' she said formally. She took a breath, still facing the window. 'Stress tends to misalign your frame of reference, muddle your perspective on things. Do you ever find that, Detective?'

'Yes, ma'am, absolutely. All the time.'

She smiled faintly but there was no emotion to it. She had ditched the ball-gown in favour of jeans and a woollen jersey.

'What can I do for you today, Detective?'

I fell mute for a second, gripped by the awful sensation of not being able to remember why I had come in the first place. Finally I said, 'Were you aware Emma kept a diary?'

If she was considering the question, her expression betrayed no evidence of it. Downstairs a vacuum whirred into action and furniture was dragged reluctantly across a wooden floor. 'If she did, I don't think I ever noticed,' she said at length.

'OK,' I said.

'Why do you ask?' Voice soft as dust.

'I spoke to one of Emma's friends. She said Emma might have had something of that nature.'

'Carrie,' she said. 'Yes, she's a good girl.'

'You know her well?'

'Well enough to know she wasn't the one who murdered my daughter, if that's what you were asking.'

'No, ma'am, I wasn't asking that at all.'

'But you were attempting to gain my opinion of her so you could eventually infer as much for yourself, weren't you?'

I said nothing to that. I stepped forward and removed the topmost exercise book from the stack on the corner of the desk and flipped through it. It was mostly empty. Towards the back there were notes on *The Fat Man* by Maurice Gee and several pages on Salinger's *The Catcher in the Rye*. Her handwriting had a deft, efficient look to it, as if she utilized it often.

Arguably, Salinger's work is not so much a novel of personal growth, but an in-depth commentary on the extent to which people wish to be viewed as an individual amidst a society which seems to thrive on the need for conformity.

I thumbed through the remainder of the pages in the hope of finding a telephone number, a scrawled name, a street address for a friend, but turned up nothing.

'Do you think about death much, Detective?' she asked.

I put the book down on the table and picked up the

one below it. Her hands were still in her lap, the bulk of her attention still out in the front yard.

'No,' I said simply.

'I find that difficult to believe. You investigate murders for a job.'

I looked at the side of her face and felt the pages of the book with my fingers. 'I try and keep my distance,' I said. 'I think that's the key.'

She nodded solemnly, as if this was the answer she had been expecting. 'I think you're right,' she said. 'It's funny, though. You manage so well to keep it out of conscious thought, until one day it just steps in front of you and spits in your face.'

I focused my attention on the book in my hands. It looked to be about a year old, maybe Year 10 history. She had studied the American Revolution. There was stuff about the Boston Massacre and the Battle of Bunker Hill and the Sons of Liberty.

'Do you have a family?' she asked suddenly.

I glanced up. 'No, both my parents died when I was very young.'

'No brothers or sisters?'

'Not that I'm aware of.'

'So you lived in foster care?' She accentuated the final

two words slightly, as if referring to something deplorable.

'Yes, ma'am.'

She nodded slowly to herself, as if carefully considering what I'd said and storing it away for later use. 'How did you get into this, then? This job, I mean.'

I shrugged. 'I was told my father was a cop; I guess the job was kind of hereditary, if you know what I mean.'

She said nothing.

'Are you OK, ma'am?' I asked.

'I'm struggling, to be honest,' she said.

I put the book back down on the desk. The vacuum sucked on.

'What are you doing up here?' I asked quietly.

She took a moment to reply. 'I'm remembering. This is where she used to sit, this is where her energy is, I'm trying to bask in that energy so I can remember.'

She licked her lips and straightened one leg fractionally, then returned it to its original position.

'Please leave now, Detective,' she said. 'I need some time alone. I'll inform you immediately if I locate a diary. Have a nice day.'

I said nothing and turned and left the room. I didn't see the point in offering her the same sentiment.

■ SEVENTEEN

headed back east and got on the motorway, then turned north towards town in traffic only slightly thinner than peak density. The city ahead looked dull-grey and subdued under the weak winter sun. My cellphone rang, caller: Claire Bennett.

'I'm at a homicide on Fort Street,' she said when I picked up. 'I need you to come take a look.'

'What's happened?' I said.

'It's the *who* I thought you might be interested in,' she replied.

I said nothing.

'The victim is your friend Lionel Moss.'

Silence for a hundred metres.

'Landlord found him dead in the entry hall of his flat,'

she said. 'Two rounds through his forehead.'

I said nothing.

'You still there?' she asked.

I trapped the phone under my ear with my shoulder and held the wheel with both hands. 'What's the address?'

'Corner Fort Lane and Fort Street.' She gave me the number. 'I'll see you there in ten.'

It was closer to five.

Fort Street is located near the northern edge of town, branching east off Queen Street, eight hundred metres south of the harbour. Lionel Moss's address corresponded to a moderately run-down two-storey building more or less directly opposite the community police station at the corner of Jean Batten Place. The lower floor of the building was jointly occupied by a kebab place and a TAB outlet. I left the Commodore on a yellow line behind an ambulance along from the police station and crossed the road to the kebab place, where Claire Bennett was standing, apparently waiting for me.

'Forensics hasn't turned up yet, but I'll take you up to have a look,' she said.

'When was he found?'

'About thirty minutes ago. He'd been late on his rent,

landlord went up to claim it, but Moss doesn't answer the door, so the guy goes in anyway, finds Moss dead on his back, shot in the head.'

I said nothing and watched a Big Mac carton float towards me along the bitumen path. There was a loose queue of men in orange vests and hard hats waiting for food, and I could smell beer and steam, cigarette smoke and vegetable fat on the wind. There was a construction site on the lot directly opposite where a rivet gun squealed repeatedly. Across the mouth of Fort Lane was a small convenience store, outside of which a man in a reflective vest and hard hat sat at a metal table eating a meat pie.

Moss's place was bordered on the left by low-rise buildings that ran right the way west to Queen Street. There was an iron fire escape clinging to the brickwork on the eastern wall facing Fort Lane, which would potentially aid somebody in going in or out unnoticed.

'Let's go have a look,' I said.

She led me up a carpeted staircase to the right of the kebab place, to a tiny landing with plain wooden doors set into the left- and right-hand walls. The door on the right was ajar by an inch and had police tape stretched across it, gun-stapled into the framing either side. A uniformed woman officer was standing guard, her expression grim in a determined effort to ward off the curious.

Bennett took disposable gloves and a pair of plastic shoe-protectors from her pocket and snapped them on, tossing me a second pair of each. She pushed the door back against its hinges, bent low under the tape and stepped inside. I would have followed, but there wasn't enough room. An object which I could only assume to be the corpse of Lionel Moss was lying shrouded beneath a sheet, occupying the bulk of the entrance-area floor space.

Bennett found a vacant section of carpet, knelt and pinched the edge of the sheet, lifting it so I could see Moss's face. It was nothing I hadn't seen before: eyes focused sightlessly towards the ceiling, mouth ajar, skin bloodless. He had been shot twice in the head at close range; two neat red holes the diameter of a pencil punched into the bone above the eyes, ringed by a light dusting of burnt powder. The bullets had been low-calibre, not more than .22s. The back of his head was intact, so clearly the rounds hadn't made an exit. Quite common with low-powered ammunition: the forehead robs a lot of the bullet's momentum, deforms it so it can't penetrate the back of the skull. So it just burrows into the brain cavity and lets soft cranial matter leach its kinetic energy. The postmortem can be off-putting. Think meat in a blender. On high.

'Anybody hear anything?' I asked.

Bennett replaced the sheet and shook her head. 'Weapon must have been silenced.'

'You find shell casings?'

'Nope.'

I stepped over the corpse and moved past her into the flat. The entry hall opened into the living room. There was a couch and a television topped with a VCR and rabbit ears, a cheap coffee table, and an armchair. A stove and a square wooden table with seating for one stood on the far side of the room. A window to the left gave out over the alleyway. I guessed the bedroom and bathroom to be situated either side of the entry hall. There was a half-finished meal of canned spaghetti on a metal tray resting on the sofa, making the place stink of tomato sauce. I was puzzled momentarily by the fact that the far wall appeared to be flickering, until I realized the television was turned on.

'Do we have a time of death?' I asked.

'The medics thought maybe eleven o'clock yesterday evening.'

I looked at the spaghetti. 'He must have had a late dinner.'

Bennett said nothing. I crossed the room and checked the contents of the stove, but it was empty and looked as if it had been for a lengthy period of time. The joinery around the taps above the sink was ringed with rust spots and the wallpaper was mildewed. The lino made a sticky sound as I shifted my weight, as if moisture had managed to invade beneath that, too.

Moss's bedroom was located to the right of the entry hall. Nothing extravagant: a single bed, a low table with a lamp, a dresser. The cross on the thin chain he had produced for me during our brief encounter was resting curled on his pillow. Maybe if he'd been wearing it he might have been saved. Above the bed, pinned to the wall about fifty centimetres over the headboard, was a plain sheet of A4 paper, oriented landscape, with a single line of text printed across it: *'For all have sinned and fall short of the glory of God.' — Romans, 3:23'*. I wondered briefly whether Lionel Moss considered himself worthy in God's eyes, or whether it was simply an assertion he saw as applicable to the rest of us. If the former were true, he'd certainly been put wrong.

I went back into the living room and found Bennett

watching a soundless rerun of Oprah Winfrey talking to Cormac McCarthy.

'What do you reckon?' I asked.

She was quiet a moment, eyes still with the television. 'I read his book *The Road*. Didn't like it much.'

'I was meaning this.'

She glanced at me, and gave a shrug that could have meant she didn't know or didn't care. 'He was eating dinner, someone knocked at the door, he got up and answered and got shot twice in the head, game over.'

'Anything been taken?'

'There's a wallet in his hip pocket. I don't know what else there is in here to steal, other than the television, and it's still here.'

I nodded at her and didn't reply. The spaghetti sauce on his dinner plate was blood-red.

Moss's home was photographed by a Scene of Crime team by two o'clock that afternoon, and Forensics was quick enough with their procedures to allow his corpse to be removed by about that time, too. I remained at the scene for the rest of the afternoon. I spoke to the occupant of the room across the hall, and the kebab guy on the ground floor, but neither of them yielded any information that Bennett hadn't already been able to elicit before I arrived.

At ten to six that evening I left the car in a parking garage at the western end of Customs Street and walked along past West Plaza to Britomart, then turned north on Queen Street to Quay.

Traffic is a bar situated in the north-western corner of the ground floor of an undistinguished low-rise block across the street from the ferry terminal at Freemans Bay. The Queen/Quay intersection has become something of a commuter chokepoint, especially from four to six on a weekday, so it's not difficult to see how the establishment came up with its name. I waited at the kerb until the red light made braving the traffic only moderately life-threatening, then crossed the street at a jog.

I saw Leon Ross before he had a chance to notice me. He was seated outside, despite the sharp chill, at a table tight against the bar's west-facing wall, protected from general footpath chaos by a low canvas screen. I hadn't seen him in close to four years, and he appeared to have gained weight; my memory of him and the man I was seeing now were not in agreement. He was heavier around the neck, the swell of his stomach more pronounced. A flush to his cheeks despite the temperature. His hair, which he'd always maintained in a state of intentionally stylish unkemptness, was now just unintentionally unkempt. He was wearing a pale grey suit that wasn't cheap, but was too roomy to do him any favours. His attention was diagonally across the street, on the tan bulk of the ferry building, and he glanced up, surprised, as I stepped around the canvas divider and scraped out a steel chair opposite him, my back to the evening rush.

His face cracked into an easy smile that shrunk his eyes and he leaned across the table and offered a hand. I took it. His skin was cool and clammy from the tall glass of lager he'd been nursing. I figured him for forty, maybe forty-one, now.

'When was the last time you and I sank a quiet one?' he asked.

'Too long ago.'

The smile grew and I let him have his hand back. 'I ordered for you already,' he said.

'Heineken?'

'Of course.'

He leaned back in his chair, a shadow of amusement around his mouth, eyes wandering with the red-and-white lights that passed across his face. 'How are you, Sean?' he said.

'I'm doing OK. Yourself?'

His gaze went across the street. 'Yeah, you know.'

I looked past him, through the window into the interior of the place. At this hour, all patrons wore suits: affluent corporate types fitting in a quick one before home. 'What are you doing with yourself these days?' I asked him.

He turned back to me, a wry glint in his eye, as if his source of income had become notably more devious since I'd last seen him. He touched a hand to his neck, spreading his shirt collar as if what little warmth there was rising off the pavement was getting to him. 'Battling organized crime,' he said.

I smiled. 'It looks like it's getting the better of you.'

There was a pang of hurt around his mouth for a fraction of a second, but it vacated quickly. He grinned at me then raised his glass and took a hard pull. 'They're beating us,' he said simply.

The street behind was loud with the shudder of buses pulling free of the station at Queen and Customs. 'Beating you, Leon? Surely not.'

He nodded, an image of seriousness despite my attempt at levity. He paused as a girl in a black apron set a tall glass of amber liquid down in front of me. 'Crime is an enterprise,' he said. 'It's structured, it's organized.

It's orchestrated by people with intelligence and social standing.'

I tasted the beer, kept my eyes on him across the top of the glass. 'It always has been,' I said. 'Capone owned Chicago in the 'thirties.'

'Chicago's on the other side of the world. Crime in this country seventy or eighty years ago was an individual action, bank robberies, assaults, you know? Opportunistic, spontaneous crime.'

'And what is it now?'

He folded his arms and shook his head. 'We closed this case yesterday, an Asian triad was using the Sky City VIP lounge as a base to organize drug distribution. A fucking casino lounge as an office! Can you believe that? They were conducting deals in the parking lot. How fucking arrogant is that?'

I said nothing. Foot traffic on the path behind me was constant, the neon advertising boards in the bus shelters back towards Britomart glowed garishly at the corner of my vision.

'The industry's been reinvented,' he said dryly. 'Major criminals drive Bentleys and own property in Parnell and walk their kids to Sunday school.'

I laughed, but he didn't join me.

'What'd you want to know about Alan Nielsen?' he said.

I shrugged and took a hit off my beer. 'Whatever.'

'Whatever,' he repeated. 'He giving you grief?'

'He did a bit, yeah.'

His eyebrows flicked skywards. A truck powered south behind me, and I waited for the diesel fumes to subside before I spoke. 'I had a go at an informant of his. He didn't like it, and he made me well aware he wasn't impressed.'

He looked into the surface of his beer as if he could see his reflection hanging there in the foam.

'I wanted to ask you about an incident a while back,' I said. 'You and he were moving a drug cache, but it got pinched . . .'

He let that hang between us for a long moment before responding: 'It wasn't drugs we were moving,' he said. Still looking at the beer.

'What was it?'

He looked up. The air smelt of petrol fumes and cigarette smoke. 'Why are you interested?'

I shrugged and he took a slug off his beer. I did the same.

'It wasn't drugs we were moving,' he repeated. 'It was cash.'

'How much?'

He made a face. 'Two million, give or take.'

'Good heavens,' I said.

He linked his fingers around his beer glass. 'It was a gang-related case,' he said. 'There was a Japanese guy we had our eye on, suspected he was acting as a distribution manager for a larger offshore establishment. He was, and we got him. He had this place down on Beach Road, in the Scene Apartments, that he used as a storage point for money and firearms. We moved the guns out during the course of a day, planned to move the cash out early evening.'

'Just you and Nielsen?'

He shook his head. 'Two others. Guy called Burke Donald, and another called Mike Harris. Donald still works for Nielsen, Mike Harris fell down his front steps six months ago and broke his neck.'

I said nothing. He shrugged, tightened his grip on the glass. 'It was a Thursday, we wanted to wait for the rush hour to finish, so we headed out about seven in the evening. Nielsen was driving, Donald was beside him in the passenger seat, Harris and I were in back.'

'And what happened?'

He took a mouthful of his drink and looked towards

the ferry building again. 'Nielsen wanted to take a longer route around the edge of town, in case we were being followed.'

'Turned out you were?'

He nodded. 'We caught a red light at the corner of Quay and Albert Streets. Two guys on a bike pulled up alongside. One had a shotgun. He persuaded Nielsen to open the boot, other guy hopped off, went round and nabbed the bag with the cash, and they were off.'

'Nielsen just opened the boot for them?'

He shook his head. 'That's the thing. He didn't. He did his best to keep it closed. Except the guy broke my window with the butt of the gun, shoved the end in my mouth and said he was going to blow my head off.'

He fell silent and just watched the traffic for a moment or two, back and forth, like a game of tennis.

'I've never been so scared in all my life,' he said. 'I actually wet myself. I was certain I'd run to the end of the line, fucking Nielsen wouldn't pop the boot, Harris is screaming at him to do it, he just sits there, like he's waiting for the light to change. Jesus . . .'

He finished his drink.

'I went home that night and cried. First time in fourteen years, swear to God. I get to work two days later, Nielsen's having me on about staining his back seat.'

I looked at him. 'You're not a fan of his, then?'

'The guy's an arsehole, without question. He was my supervising officer when I was still probationary CIB. That was fifteen years ago, shit, he was terrifying even then. We picked up this guy one night, him and a mate of his'd robbed a gas station down South Auckland. Guy was a real piece-of-shit drug addict, charges for indecent assault, you know the story. We picked him up from his home, cuffed him, put him in the car. Nielsen stayed in the back with him, I was driving. We were cruising past this park in Mangere, and there was this toilet block across the far side, and Nielsen sees it and tells me to stop.'

I looked at him and frowned. 'OK.'

'Yeah, that's what I said, too. But I did, and Nielsen opened the door and dragged this guy out onto the grass. I didn't know what the hell to do, so I followed. Anyway, this guy's still handcuffed, and Nielsen throws me a torch and makes me light the way to this block of loos. Nielsen hauls the guy in there and chucks him on the ground.'

He raised his glass to his lips and tipped it vertically to catch the last drops of foam.

'Anyway, Nielsen pulls this ballpoint pen out of his pocket, holds the guy's head with one hand, and starts pushing the end of the pen up the guy's nose with the other. The guy's screaming and carrying on, begging not to get brained. Nielsen says if the guy doesn't tell him where his mate is, the other guy who helped with the robbery, he'd push it right the way up. And man, this guy was singing like a bloody choirboy, I swear to God.'

'He told him?'

'Oh, yeah. We take him back to the car, Nielsen says to me, if I ever mention it to anyone, he'll do the same to me, except he'll pick a different hole, if you know what I mean.'

I nodded.

'So yeah,' he said. 'As far as Alan Nielsen's concerned, I wouldn't piss on the man if he was burning to death.'

I finished my beer and looked away towards the sky above the ferry building. The ambient city light was too strong to allow the stars to show, and the air up there was black like spilled dye.

■ EIGHTEEN

At six-thirty-one, the short man pressed three on his speed-dial and waited patiently until the employer answered.

'We had to move,' he said. 'The baby-sitter's like a fuckin' hawk. We were worried we were going to get made.'

'The guy in the Escort?' the employer said.

'Yeah.'

'But you're nearby?'

'Yeah, we're close.'

The employer was silent, and the short man could tell from the complete absence of sound on the line that the employer was holding his breath. 'So do it tonight,' he said at length. 'Is that going to be a problem?'

The short man assured him it wouldn't be. 'What about the other two?' he added.

'You'll have to kill them,' the employer said. 'There's no alternative.'

The short man nodded once to himself then bade his employer farewell, placing the phone back in his lap.

It was well dark by the time I arrived home. The rear windshield of Hale's Escort was pebbled with water and the wind was firm enough that the top of the Norfolk pine was oscillating a little more violently than was preferable. Winter for you.

I locked the car and headed inside to the kitchen to find the pair of them playing cards at the table.

'Hale taught me Scum,' Michael said. There was thirty bucks' worth of ten-dollar notes stacked on the table in front of him.

'That was nice of him. Where'd the money come from?'

'I won it from John.'

I looked at him blankly.

'He said he'd give me ten dollars if I could beat him. And I beat him three times.'

He beamed and tamped the edges of the bills together.

Two days in my home and his morals were already crumbling.

'I'm sure your mother will be thrilled,' I said. 'Scram. I need to have a chat to John.'

He released his breath pointedly and made a face at me, then claimed his winnings and headed for his room, bare feet slapping the lino.

I looked at Hale. He stared back benignly.

'I can see the appeal of gambling,' he said. 'I figured I'd recoup my loss after the second game. Didn't pan out, and the third game didn't end too well, either.'

'Clearly. The moths in your wallet must have enjoyed the fresh air. Have you ever parted with thirty bucks all at once?'

'Not for a while. It's pretty exhilarating, though.'

I stepped to the sink and ran the water and took a mouthful straight from the tap.

'Lionel Moss is dead,' I said.

Hale didn't answer. He placed his hands palms-down on the table and inclined his fingers one by one, as if searching for accumulated dirt.

'A penny for your thoughts?' I asked.

He shrugged. 'I'm not complaining.' He bit a hangnail off his thumb, then said, 'How?'

'He answered his door yesterday evening and somebody shot him in the head.'

'Pistol?'

'Yup.'

'Witnesses?'

'Not a one.'

'Anyone hear anything?'

'Gun was silenced.'

He paused. 'Point-two-two?'

'Two rounds above the eyes.'

'You think it's a coincidence?'

'What do you mean?'

'We have our little chat with him, then he gets shot.'

I looked at him and leaned against the doorframe, which creaked under the applied pressure. 'How could it not be a coincidence?'

'Maybe Moss wasn't acting independently. Someone might have placed him on your street. As soon as he gets made, he becomes a liability, they have to get rid of him.'

'Why would anyone want him watching my neighbour?'

'I don't know. I think there'd be a lot of people around who'd want him keeping an eye on you, though.'

I didn't reply. He dropped his cards on the table then squared them, placing them on top of the rest of the deck.

'How's the kid been?' I said.

He smiled. 'Fine. He had a headache earlier but he seems to have recovered well enough.'

'Has his mother called?'

He nodded. 'I ranked her at eight out of ten for cheerfulness.'

I went to the fridge and inspected the contents briefly. The only thing of nutritional merit seemed to be milk. A quick inspection of the bench top and cutlery drawers told me I was out of cigarettes. I took a swig of milk straight out of the bottle, then sat down opposite Hale.

'I had a chat with Leon Ross,' I said. 'You had your facts askew slightly.'

He just looked at me.

'It wasn't drugs they were transporting. It was cash. Two million bucks' worth.'

He nodded. 'And what happened?'

I shrugged. 'More or less exactly what you told me. Money was being transported out of a place on Beach Road. Four guys in the car, Nielsen driving. They left the address early evening on a Thursday, were ambushed when Nielsen stopped at a red light on Quay Street.'

Michael re-entered the room.

'Go play in your room,' I said. 'Grown-ups are talking.'

He made a face, but didn't complain. Maybe Hale had been teaching him the fundamentals of respect.

'And what do you think?' Hale said.

'Ross told me the gun was pointed in through *his* window.'

'So?'

'So Ross was the back-seat passenger. You want to stop a car from going anywhere, you point the gun at the driver.'

'Maybe it was a convenience issue. Maybe his window was open.'

I shook my head. 'Ross said the guy smashed it.'

'So what does that mean?'

I shrugged. 'It's an anomaly. And Ross told me Nielsen was an arsehole.' I related the toilet block story, Nielsen's reaction to Ross's loss of bladder control.

Hale pondered this silently for a brief moment. 'It only appears anomalous because it's not in perfect accordance with what you think is logical.'

I didn't answer for a beat. The floor beneath the lino was thin wood panelling which offered little insulation, and the room was freezing.

'I don't know,' I said. 'Something doesn't ring true for me.'

■ NINETEEN

There was tinned spaghetti in the pantry, but I wasn't feeling particularly game for it after visiting Lionel Moss. We had an omelette instead. Hale managed to salvage some bacon and tomatoes from the depths of the fridge, and the result wasn't altogether that bad. We sat eating in the living room; me in the armchair, Michael on the couch opposite with Hale beside him, fiddling with the tuning wheel on my radio in an attempt to catch some evening news.

'Why don't you have a telly?' Michael said.

'I read books.'

'Why can't you read books *and* have a telly?'

'I like books better.'

'Can I have one of your CDs?'

182

'No.'

'Why not?'

'Because they're mine.'

Hale gave up on his quest to stay in touch with the world and flicked the radio off. My cellphone fluttered in my pocket with an incoming call and I answered it, despite the unfamiliar number displayed.

'Detective, I'm very sorry to bother you at this time. It's Elizabeth Fontaine speaking.'

'Hold on a moment, ma'am.'

I transferred my plate to the floor, got up and walked through to the kitchen where I sat down. The air outside was frigid; the window above the sink was webbed with condensation.

'What can I do for you?' I said.

Silence at her end. Outside I heard something boom on the roof of one of the cars.

'I think I may have found her diary.'

I didn't say anything in case she'd been planning on expanding her sudden revelation, but she didn't.

'Where was it?' I asked.

'Well, after we spoke, I started thinking about if she *did* have a diary, where would she put it? So I searched through her room. I found it in her desk, in one of the drawers.'

'Are you at home now, ma'am?'

'Yes, yes I am.'

'Would it be all right if I stopped by now?'

She seemed to consider that. I heard a muffled shuffling sound as if she'd manoeuvred the phone in order to check her watch. 'Yes, I think that would be fine.'

'I'll be there in fifteen minutes.'

The twins saw the tail-lights on the Commodore flare, then the reverse lights switch on as the car backed out onto the street. The cabin of their dark Toyota was momentarily floodlit as the vehicle passed them, but it was far too short an interval for anybody to have seen them. Much less to remember them.

The short man turned to his companion and nodded once, then raised his cellphone and pressed three on speed-dial.

'The detective just left,' he said. 'It's just the baby-sitter and the boy.'

'What time is it?' the employer asked.

'Just after six-thirty.'

'Give it another thirty minutes,' the employer said. 'You want to be well clear of the rush hour.'

The end of rush-hour traffic made travel across town frustrating, but once I reached the motorway the congestion vanished, which meant my pre-journey estimation of fifteen minutes was more or less dead-on.

I parked on the far side of the turning circle, next to the front door. My headlights revealed Elizabeth Fontaine still hadn't had the courage to walk outside and gather the flowers left for her: many of them were still heaped over the grass island at the top of the driveway, others propped against the front wall of the house, torn and dishevelled by the wind and rain.

I shut the power, got out and locked the car, and approached the front door and knocked. Elizabeth Fontaine answered, with a wide smile that looked fake, but I knew was an important step along the road back to normalcy.

'Come in,' she said. 'I left it upstairs. Don't worry about your shoes.'

I stepped past her and paused a moment while she closed the door behind me, then allowed her to lead me through the entry hall and up the panelled staircase to Emma's bedroom at the end of the upstairs-floor landing. Her door had been left ajar and the interior light was on, spilling a warm golden beam out onto the carpet in front.

Elizabeth Fontaine slipped sideways through the gap, seemingly reluctant to disturb the door, so I made myself as skinny as possible and followed suit. What I assumed to be the diary was resting closed in the centre of the desk against the right-hand wall. It struck me as the sort of thing a teenage girl might like. It was bound in fluffy pink fabric for a start, with a fluffy pink pen attached, secured to the central binding by a length of fluffy pink string.

'You found it in the desk?' I asked.

She moved into the centre of the room and gazed around in reminiscence for a moment, then nodded, almost imperceptibly. 'Bottom drawer.'

I stepped forward, pulled out the chair beneath the desk and sat down. The book had a scent to it, some kind of perfume.

'There are names,' she said behind me. 'I don't know how important it might be to you, I thought I'd best let you know.'

I said nothing. The diary was secured down the left-hand side by a helical length of wire. There were sinewy strips of paper trapped inside, as if pages had been torn free from the book at one stage. I turned the cover and looked at the first page at the same moment as I heard the door behind me close and Elizabeth Fontaine tread away down the corridor.

My first conclusion was that Elizabeth Fontaine had been wrong. It wasn't a diary. It was a book a girl had recorded daily ponderings in, but not in the sense that it was an account of her day-to-day life. At first glance the book appeared to be a collection of observations. They ranged from the superficial (*Abby Leland looks like a slut with all the rings she wears*) to the slightly more emotional (*I'm going to murder Chloe if she ever comes near me again*). The book had been carefully organized into four apparent sections. Section One consisted of random personal opinions: on everything from Hollywood to slightly more mundane fast-food outlet quality. Section Two was a hate list. Section Three was a love list. Section Four was personal contacts. Unfortunately she'd been unhelpfully unspecific when compiling this last section. The extent of the information listed for one particular person went no further than a first name and a phone number. *Kelly, Carrie, Suze, Morgan, Blake, Mum*, the list went on. Some names were accompanied by both a home and a cell number, but most were just a cell.

I turned to Section Three. The love list. It looked as if it had been initiated several years earlier. The writing on the pages towards the front was scribbled and inexact, then the pen strokes became more distinct and refined as time seemingly went on. There were photographs. Girls at the beach, girls at school socials, girls in ball-gowns, girls at birthday parties, girls with boys. I saw a lot of recurring faces. Carrie Jordan cropped up several times.

The next series of shots were ones featuring Emma herself. I recognized her from the driver's licence photo. These images were more natural though, less forced, giving insight into her personality. And the personality I saw was a nice one. Emma Fontaine had been a happy, smiley child: an aspect of her persona that a bleached mortuary shot or a driver's licence image could never hope to convey.

On the last page was another photo, by the looks of it a cheap digital print. I reckoned it to be three months old, based on nothing other than the whiteness of the paper. It featured Emma sitting on a couch beside a boy of about her age with a shaved head, maybe a few years older. The wall behind them was painted white cinderblock, like somebody's basement, or garage, or rumpus room. Emma was wearing jeans and a hooded jumper. So was the guy beside her. Someone had drawn a stylized heart shape around the image with a pink felt-tip pen.

I pushed the diary away from me and leaned back in the chair, staring up at the ceiling. I could hear raindrops speckling the window. I closed my eyes and thought back to my meeting with Tyler Mitchell, the owner of Heat.

Who was he?

White guy, twenties, skinhead.

The last person to be seen with Emma Fontaine while she was still breathing, was a young, bald Caucasian man.

Eureka.

I picked the book up off the desk and headed downstairs.

■ TWENTY

As a general rule John Hale didn't like children. He didn't like their disobedience, didn't like their neediness, didn't like their backchat. Which made the fact that he found the child entrusted to his care quite endearing all the more unusual.

He watched the boy take milk from the fridge and drink straight from the bottle, mimicking what Devereaux had done earlier. He replaced the cap carefully and returned the bottle to the receptacle in the door, then sat down at the table, looking up at him.

'I got a real bad headache,' he said.

'Do you?' Hale said. He hoped he sounded sympathetic.

'Mum normally gives me Paradol.'

'You mean Panadol?'

'Yeah.'

'Sean doesn't have any.'

'Can you go get some?'

'From where?'

'Anywhere. Lots of places have it.'

Silence.

'Please.'

Pleading. Hale hated pleading. He looked up at the window. Black as hell's conscience. The house was like a cocoon.

'Please, John.'

Hale took a step back and glanced towards the door. 'Hop into bed while I'm gone. I'm going to lock you in.'

I found her downstairs in the kitchen, gazing out through a window above the bench. Shadows from swaying branches in the yard played across her face, pulling it in and out of darkness. I opened the diary and offered her the photo.

'Have you ever seen this boy before?' I asked.

The majority of her weight was forward on her hands, which were braced palms-forward against the edge of the bench. I could see thin purple veins threading the underside of her wrists. She looked at the photograph and shook her head. 'No.'

'You're sure?'

'Absolutely.'

She turned back to the window, her eyes tracking movements which were either entirely random or non-existent. 'Why is he important?' she asked.

I was quiet a beat. 'Emma was seen with someone fitting his description,' I said. 'I was hoping you might be familiar with him, possibly have seen him.'

She said nothing for a moment. Then, 'Have you ever lost a loved one, Detective?'

'Not in many, many years, ma'am.'

She nodded, apparently musing over my response. 'Come and stand here, Detective, look at the view.'

A slightly bizarre request, but nonetheless I stepped forward and stood beside her as she gazed out of the window. The view consisted of an immaculately kept backyard of tall pine trees surrounding a tight, crisp lawn with a simple stone water feature encircled by a white concrete path. The path branched off to the left, heading towards the trees where a seat, formed from two smooth planks of timber placed perpendicularly, sat atop a large boulder. Everything was tinged soft yellow by discreet outdoor lighting placed along the lawn's perimeter.

'I like to imagine she sits there,' she said. 'On that

bench. I think that's a good place for her. During winter it's warm in the mornings with the sun, and in summer, there's nice shade from the trees. She used to like sitting there.'

I didn't say anything. I couldn't form a suitable response.

'Do you know what sort of wood that seat is, Detective?'

I shook my head. I honestly didn't.

'Neither do I. It has a smooth, grey kind of texture. Like ash. I like to think of it as ashwood. I like to picture my little girl sitting there at the end of ashwood road. Like nothing evil has fallen on her like it has, and nothing ever will.'

I remained mute and looked out at the gathering dusk. I could understand her wish. I think it's probably a fairly standard desire that a loved one be allowed to spend eternity in comfort. Certainly it was a request I could relate to. I stood with her another moment, then I walked away and left her in the company of her memories.

Hale's trip totalled twenty minutes, ten of which were spent waiting in a queue at a late-night pharmacy, and two spent engaging in polite conversation with the woman behind the counter.

He turned back into the driveway at a little after seven. Rain was falling and he could hear the chatter of it against the leaves in the front yard, underpinned by the constant thrum against the roof of his car. He dabbed the brake as the full beams lit the interior of the garage, and brought the Escort to a halt.

There was a tap at his window.

Dull, subtle in tone, but created by something too dense to be falling foliage or a branch whisked up by the breeze. Hale turned his head and came face-to-face with the end of a shotgun.

The ability to come out of a tight situation alive is heavily dependent upon the human capacity for quick decision-making. The gun was a sawn-off pump-action. He wasn't sure of the model, but the barrel-width told him it was probably a twelve-gauge. The car was still in gear. The Escort had a good clutch. Hale figured if he gunned the car forward he might escape with nothing more than a smashed rear window. However, the success or failure of that particular exit route was very much reliant on how quick the person in control of the gun reacted. Hale figured this particular guy would be fairly swift. He looked the part, if nothing else. He was maybe five-five, but wide, like a ship's deckhand, with blond hair slicked back into a ponytail. His face was whipped with water and parched from the cold, and it looked like it had sighted down the business-end of a large-bore shotgun on more than one occasion. He was standing side-on to the car, the gun in his left hand, his right hand held up level with his head, thumb and forefinger producing a repeated twisting motion.

Turn the engine off.

Hale had a Colt .45 pistol under his seat. He was fifty to sixty per cent certain he could get the guy with a headshot through the door. But fifty to sixty per cent certain left a very large margin of error. Plus he didn't want to get blood on the car. Plus he didn't know where the boy was. Knowing the location of non-combatants was a must. Hale wasn't prepared to take any violent counter-measures under those sorts of conditions. He kept his eyes on the blond guy with the gun and leaned forward and twisted the ignition off, feeling the motor shudder once and quit, and heard the noise of the wind and the falling rain increase to fill its absence.

The guy with the shotgun took a step back and beckoned with his free hand. *Out of the car.*

Hale popped the handle, swung the door and swivelled in his seat, levering himself up and out. The air was immensely cold; like inhaling through a bag filled with ice. He felt the rain slick against his hair and shoulders, then used his heel to knock the door closed, eying the man in front of him.

'I thought I paid that last parking ticket.'

'Funny guy.'

The man was speaking softly. He didn't want the neighbours to hear. Hale looked around. The property was shielded to the east by planting. Michael's home to the west was unoccupied, and the street was empty. He looked at the house. Either there was someone else inside with the kid, or he was already dead. Needless to say, he hoped it was the former of the two scenarios.

'If the boy's hurt, I'll kill you.'

The blond guy's mouth formed a laugh and his throat pulsed in apparent amusement, but no sound came.

'I could scream,' Hale said.

'I could kill you. You know what sort of damage this thing can do?'

'I'm going to find out when I jam it up your arse and pull the trigger.'

The blond man said nothing. His knuckles were white where he was gripping the pistol stock on the gun, and his face was pale from the cold, but he wasn't panicked.

He had done this sort of thing before. He had shaved that morning and the shadow of his beard was just beginning to reveal itself again. He had used some sort of scented aftershave, and Hale could smell it, faint on the leaden air. Hale didn't consider the blond man too great a threat. Again, the greatest issue lay in the fact that he didn't know where the boy was, and until he did, he wasn't in a position to do anything except what he was told.

The blond man took a step back to lessen the angle on the gun, and said, 'Walk towards the house.'

His voice was a peculiarity. No accent. Either the result of practice or constant exposure to different inflections. Hale stared him in the face a second longer just to spite him then walked towards the front door. He was wearing a denim jacket and jeans and he could tell simply by the weight of them that he was close to soaked. He stepped up onto the small porch, feeling the boards creak beneath his weight, fumbling blindly because the security light had been turned off, before he opened the door and allowed the blond man to use his weapon to guide him along to the kitchen.

The boy was hog-tied on the kitchen table. His wrists and ankles had been bound behind him with lengths of fishing wire, and his mouth was gagged with a plain strip of white cloth. He was lying on his side, and the skin beneath his eyes was crusted with salt deposits. He was being watched over by a dark, bald guy who was standing with his butt propped against the edge of the bench. He must have been close to six-foot-four, maybe six-foot-five. Not bulky, just a huge compilation of hard, square angles crammed into a blue two-piece suit.

Hale shuffled over to the far side of the room so he was standing at the head of the table and the blond man with the gun stood just inside the door, the gun held down along his thigh. Outside the wind gusted and tree branches screeched against the roofing iron.

The boy let out a moan which was stifled by the fabric and died in his throat as a watery choke. The blond man looked down at him and smiled, then took a step to his right and lined up the barrel of the sawn-off on Hale's nose. His eyes were devoid of colour, as was his face of emotion.

'Who are you?' he asked.

'Hale,' said Hale.

'You know what's happening here?' the blond man said.

The bald guy snuffled a laugh and shook his head to himself. Hale said nothing. The barrel of the shotgun had been modified crudely; the leading edge was roughened with saw marks. 'We're taking kiddo with us, do you have a problem with that?'

Hale said nothing. The gun was beyond grabbing distance. If the blond guy pulled the trigger, Hale would lose most of his head.

'I'll take that as a no,' the blond guy replied. 'As much as we'd like to take you, too, we really can't, so you're going to have to stay here.'

He took a step forward and used the snubbed barrel to push back the collar of Hale's jacket and check for weapons. The jacket slipped off his shoulder and Hale spread his arms fractionally to let it fall all the way to the floor. The T-shirt beneath was striated laterally from his abdominal muscles. The rain had made the cotton cling to his shoulders like a second skin. Standing there soaking he looked like some wild creature, a Neanderthal being from another time.

'You hit the gym a lot?' the blond man said, his tone conversational.

Hale said nothing. The blond man moved to the other side of the room and placed the sawn-off gently on the silvered finish of the bench top, with almost loving precision. His top half was wrapped in a black nylon warm-up jacket, and he unzipped it from the neck and reached inside to remove a straight-edged filleting knife. He held it up to the single bulb suspended from the ceiling, as if checking the uniformity of the steel, then ran the ball of his thumb along the sharpened edge and began nodding solemnly, as if considering a non-existent reply Hale had offered. The man in the blue suit smiled.

The blond man glanced at Hale and took a step towards the boy, still immobile on the table. He took hold of the boy's skull with his free hand, then very gently ran the point of the knife under the boy's left eye.

'I could cut it out,' he whispered. 'Imagine that.'

Silence in the room. Even the child was quiet, his eyes tight shut against the cruelty. Hale glanced down and saw his own heart pulsating against his shirt, and the blond man looked his way and smiled, as if the palpitations were visible to him too. He held still a moment, perhaps basking in the tension he was responsible for, then dribbled the end of the knife under the boy's nose for a moment, fascinated by the terror he was inflicting, then threw his head back and produced the muted laugh again. He lowered his head and looked at Hale, wiping an imaginary tear from his cheek.

'No,' he whispered, 'I wouldn't do that, would I?'

He moved closer; began massaging the knife with his thumb again. He smiled.

'We'll treat him right and proper,' he said. 'We promise.'

Hale said nothing. The top of the blond guy's head was gleaming with water.

'What's it like?' the guy said. 'To know you're circling the plughole? Does it terrify you? Are you desperately running through all the things you should have done but never got around to?'

Hale said nothing. The shotgun was unattended, but the big guy was too close to it. Nothing Hale could do. They were going to kill him, then they were going to kill Devereaux and take the boy.

'You don't look that worried,' the blond man said. 'I like that. Good trait to mention in your epitaph.'

At the very same instant that Hale caught the guy's aftershave again, the knife reversed itself in the blond man's hand and came scything downwards, the point leading, Hale's stomach its target.

Hale caught it on the way in.

He grabbed the guy's wrist in both hands and moved sideways and let the guy's own momentum carry him down. The knife twisted free and Hale lashed out with his foot, striking his opponent's kidneys, dropping him to the floor. He clasped his hands around the guy's head and smashed upwards with his knee, the sound of the man's nose breaking still in his ears even as the bald guy was upon him. He caught Hale from behind, who felt the blows rain down on him; his back, his head, his shoulders. He twisted like a boxer and shielded his face with his forearms, backing away towards the corridor, desperate to divert the man from the boy. He danced right and parried a straight left, then caught a massive roundhouse blow on the ear which shook his vision. The punches were landing constantly, and the guy was incredibly strong. He was leaner than Hale, but he had an immense height and reach advantage.

Hale skipped backwards, tripped and took a straight right in the centre of his chest so hard it made his heart stumble in its rhythm. He dodged left and then right, using the walls to thrust himself, feeling knuckles hard as beaten copper crash against the top of his head and arms and torso. He threw himself sideways, exploding the catch on a doorway, emerging into the bathroom. He was scared, and the realization of this panicked him further. He was accustomed to physical encounters with people altogether less able than himself; people who were younger, more apprehensive, not men of equal skill and strength. He felt himself losing control, slipping beyond the point where he had influence.

He backed up against the toilet cistern and raised his arms again. His nose was bleeding, his arms were aching from the blows he had defended himself against, and his head was pulsing. The bald guy paused in the doorway, then rushed forwards. Hale tried to dodge sideways, but was caught in a tackle, tumbling into the bathtub, metal rings pinging as the shower curtain tore free of its support pole and draped them like lovers beneath a sheet.

Hale struggled. He had often heard that drowning was the worst way to go, and that suffocation came in at a close second, but images of slowly dying, the shower curtain wrapped about his neck, caused a surge of adrenaline that made his entire body buck and lash out with renewed vigour, striking against anything it came in contact with.

He tried to regain his footing and felt hands closing around his throat; strong hands, callused hands, hands used to subduing things that did not wish to be subdued. He tossed his head from side to side, desperate for air, for anything save the mildew-tainted smell of the curtain. He threw a blind left hook that connected with something he thought was an ear, then reached up and tugged with all his strength so that the last of the support rings pinged free and the damp material draped the pair of them completely.

He rolled sideways, the edge of the bath biting his hip, smothering the curtain as best he could around the man's head, throwing his shoulders to rid the grasp of the hands around his throat. He jerked upwards with his knee and felt it connect with something yielding, and the tension around his neck released altogether. He clenched his stomach and felt his feet contact the floor, levering himself up so that he was now crouched above the bald man, who, sensing the shift in advantage, began to flail wildly. Bunched fists flew backwards and cracked the tile work surrounding the bath, while his feet seemed to be governed completely independent of one another, like a parody of a man attempting to run in two directions at the same time.

Hale observed the spectacle with a somewhat detached curiosity as he held the man down and slowly robbed him of his breath. He waited until the convulsions in the bald man's blue-clad limbs had ceased completely, then he got up and walked back to the kitchen to free the boy.

▪ TWENTY-ONE

I used Elizabeth Fontaine's fax machine to send a copy of the photograph I had discovered in Emma's diary through to the night-shift crime squad at Auckland Central, then drove home.

Hale's Escort wasn't alone in the driveway. There were two marked patrol cars and an ambulance parked behind it, doors open, blue-and-reds popping. They looked as if they'd arrived somewhat frantically.

I left the Commodore parked on the road then ran up the drive, panicking that I was going to find someone dead. The front door was slightly ajar, and I pushed through it to the hallway and headed to the kitchen. Hale stepped out of the door to the living room and blocked my path. His nose was bleeding, his arms were beginning to come up in a series of bruises, and his left ear was bright red.

'Shit, what happened to you?' I said.

'People tried to take the boy.'

'Holy shit . . .'

I pushed past him and saw a compact blond man dressed in a black tracksuit lying in the foetal position beside the kitchen table. Two female officers and a paramedic were crouched beside him, checking his vitals, and there was a sawn-off shotgun resting on the bench top beside the sink. I turned around and backtracked to the bathroom, where a tall bald guy in a blue suit lay prone on the tiles, surrounded by a similar cluster of worried-looking emergency officers. I sensed Hale enter the room behind me and I turned and looked at him. His expression was placid, his arms were loose at his side, his breathing quiet. Light was filtering in through the front door, periodically illuminating the right side of his face.

I tried to say something, but my mind was forming questions faster than my voice box could produce them, so in the end I just shrugged and looked at the ceiling.

'They were going to take the boy,' Hale said.

'Are they still alive?'

'They're not conscious yet. I kneed the blond guy in the face. I nearly asphyxiated his friend with your shower curtain.'

'Christ,' I said.

He didn't answer.

'Are you OK?' I asked.

Hale didn't reply. I looked at him a moment longer then shrugged again, pushed past him and moved out into the corridor to the kitchen. The paramedics were still tending to the guy on the floor and didn't acknowledge my arrival. Michael saw me, though. He was standing framed in the entry to the kitchen, a blanket wrapped around his shoulders. His hair was dishevelled and his eyes ringed with deep purple, and his jaw was clenched so tight I could see the muscles in his cheeks protruding.

'I'm going to call your mother,' I said.

I got Hale to give me the full, unabridged version, then relayed an appropriately censored edition to Michael's mother. Obviously she was distraught. She cried into the phone and I sat patiently on the couch in the living room, repeating over and over that he was OK.

At length the sobbing subsided to the point where she

could articulate full sentences: 'He's only a *child*. Why would someone do that?'

'I don't know, Grace.'

'Holy Christ. God, I've got to get home.'

'No, stay where you are. He's absolutely fine, I promise. Look, if you want I can come and pick you up tomorrow morning.'

I didn't want her driving tonight. Late-night white-knuckle journeys following receipt of bad news are a proven crash recipe.

She sniffed. 'No, no don't, it's fine.' She was probably chewing her nails.

'Grace, calm down.'

'I *can't*, my son was almost *kidnapped*.'

'He's safe with us,' I said.

I didn't take her silence to mean she believed me.

'Why would someone want to take him?' she asked at length.

I said nothing for a moment. 'I don't know,' I said. 'When you get back we'll talk about it.'

Her breath on the line. 'Put my son on now, please.'

I walked out to the ambulance where they were giving the boy a full physical and passed him my cell. He took it without a word and as soon as he'd pressed it to his ear, the tears welled. I stood out on the driveway a moment, just to make sure I could still feel the coldness of the air, then headed through to the living room, lay down on the couch and closed my eyes. Across the hall I could hear one of the paramedics running the bath. I went to sleep and dreamed about being chased through woods by hooded creatures with knives, and of men whose guiding principle in life was violence.

They only let me sleep an hour because the cops had questions: Where was the boy's mother? Did I have prior suspicions that such an event could occur? How old was he? What was his blood type? Did he have a history of mental illness? Was he diabetic? Was he asthmatic? Was he epileptic?

A night-shift CIB unit was sent out. The lead investigator was a guy I didn't know. I figured he must have been a temporary sent up from South Auckland to cover. He spoke to Hale for nearly an hour, and to me for what seemed like twice as long. He told me the two men had not yet regained consciousness, and if they didn't, they might have to go as far as pushing charges.

'It was self-defence,' I said.

The CIB guy looked like he'd been around the block

a few times. He looked like he knew the point at which self-defence became almost-murder. 'It was excessive,' he answered. 'The smaller guy has multiple injuries. His face looks like it got hit by a train.'

'He should look on the bright side. He's still alive.'

The guy looked at me grimly. 'I'm putting a unit at the end of your street,' he said. 'Keep an eye on things for the next couple of days. Ideally we should relocate you all.'

'I'll think about it.'

He said nothing and gave me the grim look again.

They wanted to admit the boy to hospital, but Michael categorically refused. He insisted he wanted to stay with Hale and me. Had I not been so tired, I might have been more flattered.

By one o'clock in the morning everybody was satisfied they'd collected every piece of information that could prove pertinent at some later stage, and left us in blissful peace. They requested Hale accompany them back to Central for further questioning, and he agreed without too much protestation.

Sleep came to me reluctantly for the remainder of the morning. I rose at seven and showered and went through to the kitchen to find Michael seated at the table. There were red rings around his wrists where he'd been bound. His face was gaunt and colourless and his mouth was nothing more than a straight edge.

'You OK?' I said.

He didn't answer. The sky out of the kitchen window was deep grey. 'Where's John?' he said at length.

'He had to go and talk to the police,' I replied.

He looked up at me. 'The man said he was going to cut out my eye.'

I started to say something, then stopped when I realized he hadn't finished.

'Then he said he was only joking. How come he would make a joke about something like that?'

I said nothing and just stood and watched as he sat and tried to make sense of the world. Sometimes people's perception of violence doesn't develop beyond a state of glorious ignorance. It didn't strike me as right that this little boy's should be made so irreversibly stark so soon in life.

I pulled out a chair opposite him and sat down. He couldn't meet my eyes.

'I promise I'll keep you safe,' I said. 'By any means necessary. OK?'

He glanced at me quickly. 'And my mum, too?'

'And your mum, too.'

He nodded and gazed back at me and gave a tiny, thin smile, then leaned back in his chair, but he didn't look particularly reassured.

■ TWENTY-TWO

Hale turned up at eight o'clock that morning. I met him as he turned into the driveway; the concrete like ice beneath my bare feet. I moved around the bonnet to the driver's side and ducked my head in his open window.

'Where did you get to?' I asked.

'I found a set of car keys on the blond guy, but I didn't find the car.'

I reached up and flicked water off his roof. 'Our frame of reference was wrong from the start,' I said. 'I thought it was the mother being targeted, it was the kid all along.'

He said nothing, as if he'd already reached that conclusion.

'I think Lionel Moss was the first line of attack,' I said. 'We busted him, so he was replaced by the two guys who visited last night.'

He twisted the ignition off and collapsed back against his seat, squint lines cut into the skin around his eyes from lack of sleep. There was a marked patrol car fifty metres away, diagonally across the street, its windows opaque in the early light.

'So what's the motive?' he said.

'I don't know, you first.'

His jaw slackened and his breath released as a long sigh. 'Child abduction, could be a parental feud, could be someone wanting to gain leverage over the family.'

I nodded and said nothing. The rims of his nostrils were crusted with blood, and his hair was dusted with dew from driving with the window down. The wind shifted the Norfolk pine, which dropped a load of settled moisture on my head.

'You have much experience with this sort of thing?' I asked at length.

'No. Do you?'

'No.'

He thrummed his fingers against the top of the wheel. There was a gun resting on the passenger seat beside him, and he leaned across and transferred it to the glove box.

'Where's the boy's father?'

'I don't know, they're separated.'

'So check him out would be my recommendation.'

I looked at him a moment longer, but he had nothing further to add, so I turned away and went inside to the living room, taking my cell to call Grace.

'Can you tell me about his father?' I asked, once she'd picked up.

She didn't reply for a moment.

'We don't see him very often,' she answered at length. 'We split a few years ago. Michael was only seven.'

'Where is he?'

'North Shore, just over the bridge.' She gave me the address.

'What does he do?'

'He used to be an accountant. Then he was actually a cop. Now I think he does scaffolding. Like construction work, I guess. He's had problems.'

'Name?'

'Elliot Treverne.'

'You ever had any trouble with him?'

The pause again, like she was considering the

implications of the question. 'Why are you asking me this?' she asked.

I pretended I hadn't heard her and ended the call, then turned the phone off so she couldn't ring me back.

Elliot Treverne lived in a street just up from a semi-industrial stretch of Archers Road in Glenfield, called Chequers Avenue. The road was curving and narrow and lined with cars and wheelie bins, but fortunately the only available space I could find was just shy of Treverne's driveway.

His house was a two-level mustard-coloured weatherboard place dusted over with a light skin of green mildew, set at a shallow angle to the street. An unhealthy looking knee-high hedge was the only barrier to the street. His mailbox was stuffed full of bills and the front lawn would have benefited from a mow two or three weeks back.

The driveway led down to a single garage, next to which was a small square of decking cluttered with several potted plants and the shrouded form of a barbecue. The front door, panelled with frosted glass, stood above a single concrete step, immediately right of the deck.

Nobody answered when I rang the bell. I tapped gently against the glass, rattling the frame noisily, but no one came running. The deck was accessed from the house via a ranch slider, and I could see inside into an empty living room. A window set into a door in the wall of the garage revealed a plum-coloured Pajero SUV, beyond which was a bench supporting a variety of gardening tools, and what appeared to be an acetylene cutting-torch.

A search of the rear of his property revealed a small patio area with some cheap outdoor seating, a clothes-line, and a cloud of fruit flies gathered around a plastic scraps-bin. The wooden skirting bordering his back door had been bitten into beside the lock tongue, as if some-one had tried to lever it open. The exposed wood looked raw and fresh.

I found his spare key beneath the base of the fourth plant pot I lifted. It was attached to a split ring that held one other key, which I guessed granted access to the garage. The lock on the front door was stiff, but I freed it eventually. It opened into a small entry alcove. From where I was standing I could see left into the living room, and right through an open door into the kitchen. A washing machine was visible in the room behind the lounge, and there was a set of stairs directly ahead.

The carpet was brown, but the bloodstains were still obvious. A cluster of dark, oily splotches lay just inside the door, with a tail that led off to the right, into the kitchen. The tail turned a dirty red as it crossed the threshold onto the kitchen linoleum. I followed it as it streaked past a dining table for four, over to a kitchen sink, where the stains suddenly grew larger in diameter. In the sink itself was a fork, with one of the tines bent ninety degrees, and a pair of bloodied handcuffs.

I walked back into the entry hall and called North Shore police on my cell, identifying myself when a young man answered. He transferred me to someone else. The someone-else was away from their desk, so my call was automatically kicked over to a female sergeant who gave her name as McKay. I identified myself a second time.

'I'm at an address on Chequers Ave, Glenfield,' I said. 'I've found blood.'

She paused. 'What did you say your name was, again?'

'Sean Devereaux.'

'What are you doing in Chequers Ave, Glenfield, Mr Devereaux?'

'Looking for someone, but at this stage I've only come across their bodily fluids.'

The pause again. 'Describe the scene please,' she said.

'I'm downstairs, there's blood in the entry hall and in the kitchen.'

'How much?'

'Maybe a pint.'

'Is the house occupied?'

'I don't think so.'

'You don't think so,' she repeated.

I glanced into the laundry, then the living room. 'I haven't secured the scene.'

'What's the exact address?'

I gave it to her.

'Wait for me out on the street,' she said. 'Answer your phone.'

'OK,' I said, and hung up.

I stepped through the entry hall and started up the stairs. On the second level I found a bathroom, a study, a bedroom and another bathroom. All unoccupied. The medicine cabinet in the second bathroom was almost empty, except for a couple of tabs of tramadol. The basin was misted with blood. I found traces of blood on the quilt in the master bedroom and a couple of lonely splotches on the carpet, although they were almost impossible to spot.

In the study there was a chair and a desk occupied by a laptop computer and a cordless telephone and numerous sheaves of paper: bank statements, mostly. Hitting redial on the phone got me a Domino's Pizza outlet. The laptop was missing both its power cord and its battery, and wouldn't turn on.

I went back downstairs and walked outside, leaving the front door open behind me. I replaced the key beneath the pot where I had found it and called Claire Bennett on her cell.

'I heard you had some drama yesterday,' she said when she answered.

'Yeah. Sort of.'

'You OK?'

'Yeah, I'm fine, I need you to file a missing-persons report for me.'

Quiet on the phone for a beat. 'Name?' she asked.

'Elliot Treverne.'

Office sounds from her end: a chair moving on casters, drawers opening. 'Who is he?'

'Father of the kid I'm currently baby-sitting. I thought I'd better pay him a visit, seeing as though his child was nearly abducted, but his home's empty and there's blood all over the carpet.'

Sound of pen against paper. 'You sure he's genuinely gone?'

'Well, I don't know, but he left a pair of handcuffs in his kitchen sink.'

'Shit, have you called somebody?'

'Yes.'

'So what are you thinking?'

I fell quiet. 'I don't know at this stage.'

Two marked patrol cars turned into Elliot Treverne's property at nine fifty-eight and stopped just short of the garage. Two guys in their mid-twenties got out of the first car and clomped through the front door into the house as if the concept of crime-scene contamination was merely a disproved myth.

The woman called McKay climbed out of the driver's seat of the second car. I knew it was her because she walked straight up to where I was sitting on the corner of the deck and said, 'I told you to wait on the street.'

'It's rubbish collection day, I could have been run over.'

She looked down at me and smiled a thin smile. She must have been fifty. Heavy, with brown hair I thought was probably dyed. The creases in her uniform pants were so crisp you'd draw blood if you touched them. 'Oh,' she said dryly. 'You're funny.'

'Oh,' I said back. 'You're a grump.'

'Did you have a warrant to enter the house?'

'No, I had his spare key.'

She looked away and the thin dry smile faded slightly, replaced by a brief ray of genuine amusement. She stepped away and stood with her hands in her pockets, the corners of her eyes crinkled despite the fact the sky above was the colour of an iron cooking pot.

A minute later the two cops who had entered the house re-emerged and conducted a brief, hushed conversation with McKay, before climbing back into their car. I still hadn't relinquished my place on the deck. McKay approached me again, her hands still in her pockets, the corners of her eyes still wrinkled up.

'Apparently he bled a lot,' she said.

'It would seem so.'

'If he's missing, my guys are thinking kidnapping,' she said.

I shook my head. 'They wouldn't have left the handcuffs behind. There's a lot of blood by the door, I think someone knocked him around and cuffed him. When they left he crawled through to the kitchen and freed himself.'

'And then flew away on his magic carpet?'

'There're traces of blood upstairs. I think he gathered some stuff together and then got out of Dodge.'

'Got out of Dodge?'

'Yes. If you haven't heard that one you should read more James Lee Burke.'

She looked at me a moment. 'You're wonderfully insightful.'

'I'm also quite handsome and quick-witted.'

'Mmm, quite. What are you doing here, you just turn up on a whim?'

'Someone tried to abduct his son last night. I thought I'd better pop round and let him know.'

Queries materialized behind her eyes and her brow constricted. She glanced at the front door and clucked her tongue.

'I like you, sonny,' she said. 'Take a drive with me, I think we need to have a chat.'

I followed her north on State Highway One to the North Shore headquarters on Constellation, in beside the bus station. She occupied a corner office with a view of the motorway streaking north. It was a small space, cluttered with her desk and piles of loose paper, bulletin boards and black-and-white headshots of sullen-looking men with not much hair.

She sat down behind her desk. There was no other available seating, so I leaned against the doorframe.

'We had a callout to that address Thursday two weeks back,' she said.

I said nothing. She fished through drifts of paper on her desk, held up a sheet of printed A4.

'A neighbour called it in, said she'd heard, and I quote, "sounds not dissimilar to that of a ferocious beating" coming from the house we were just at.'

'OK,' I said. 'And someone was sent out?'

She replaced the page on her desk, arranging it precisely despite the clutter. The window framing the motorway was open a crack and a breeze was trickling inside.

'A car was dispatched, but the house showed no signs of disturbance. Officers knocked on the door, nobody answered. So they took a statement from the neighbour, and left.'

'OK,' I said again.

She leaned forward in her seat and dug her thumbs beneath the shoulder-straps of her stab vest and shifted the weight. 'There's a group of shops at the bottom of his street,' she said. 'We passed them on the way out.'

I paused. 'Ten or fifteen places, parking lot out front.'

She nodded. 'Our guys received the initial one-one-one callout from the neighbour at eleven fifty-six p.m. on the Thursday. Twelve twenty-nine a.m. Friday, the alarm system in the pharmacy at the southern end of those shops sent out an alert. Security contractor went for a drive-by to check it out, found the place broken into.'

She rolled a drawer open and removed a thin plastic folder. She flipped it open on the desk and I stepped forward to inspect it. The folder contained a standard incident report pertaining to the police callout to the pharmacy, followed by photographs of a glass-panelled door that had been smashed, evidential shots of blood smears on a light switch, what was probably a medicine cupboard, a stainless-steel tap, a sink, a vinyl floor-tile, and, finally, a desk drawer.

I flipped back to the front.

'No arrest,' I said. 'They didn't find anyone?'

She shook her head. 'There's a security camera parked on a lamppost at the intersection a hundred metres further down the street. Sixty cars passed in full view of it between the hours of twelve midnight and six a.m. on the Friday. That's as far as we've got. We don't have any witnesses.'

I flipped to the back and found the document she was referring to. Sixty licence-plate numbers, sixty vehicle makes, sixty names, sixty phone numbers, sixty time stamps.

I freed the page from its plastic protector. 'Can I keep this?' I asked. 'It might be useful at some stage.'

She winked at me. 'Photocopier's just outside the door. It's twenty cents a page.'

■ TWENTY-THREE

I filled Hale in on the drive back south towards the bridge. 'People don't come round to your house and make you bleed unless you're in real deep shit,' he said sagely.

'Yeah, I gathered that. Abandoning your home to break into a pharmacy is a sure indicator of trouble.'

'Come home quick,' he said. 'You've got visitors.'

'Are they after a donation?'

'No, even worse.'

I was home shortly after eleven. My visitors had arrived in style, in a dark-green Jaguar XJ6 saloon, which they'd left parked in my driveway, blocking the garage. The plate number read *BGUNIT*. Either through sheer carelessness or intention, they had succeeded in inflicting a crisp semi-circle of muddy tread mark into my front lawn.

I walked inside and found Alan Nielsen and a man of similar age and physical dimensions seated at my kitchen table. I stopped in the doorway. Hale was leaning against the edge of the bench top, his arms folded. Nielsen was at the far end of the table, facing the door, with the second guy sitting to his right, his back to Hale.

'Couldn't you keep them out?' I said.

'Goodness knows I tried,' Hale answered.

I smiled. 'Sorry,' I said to the pair of them. 'I'm happy with my current church, thank you.'

Neither of them laughed. Their presence made my kitchen feel poky.

'What can I do for you, gentlemen?' I said.

Nielsen glanced once at his companion and cast his eyes over Hale, then smoothed the front of his suit jacket over his chest. 'I hope you've got time for a brief chat,' he said.

'Shucks,' I said. 'Always.' I moved into the room. 'Who's your friend?'

Nielsen feigned mild shock, remembering his manners. 'This is Detective Sergeant Burke Donald, a colleague of mine.'

Donald nodded at me. His cheeks were rosy and

bloated, as if they were padded with cotton wool. His moustache was a perfect rectangle floating on his lip.

I sat down opposite Nielsen and smiled. He leaned back in his chair, the movement of his bulk creaking the supports. He looked around the room with undisguised interest, as if taken by the quaintness of the place, and then glanced at Hale.

'Who's your friend?' he said, the question directed at me. Touché.

'This is John Hale,' I said. 'I employ him as general help.'

They glanced at each other. I thought Donald looked unsettled, not liking Hale being out of sight.

'To what do I owe the pleasure?'

Nielsen leaned forward, creaking the chair again, and laced sausage fingers in front of him on the table. He could have been a board chairman, about to deliver a disciplinary ruling. Donald just stared at me. From the wrong side of an interview table, the two of them could probably be construed as fairly intimidating. 'You're aware Lionel Moss is dead?' he said.

'I attended the scene yesterday.'

'Shot twice in the head, close-range, small-calibre pistol.'

He was calmer than he had been during our previous encounter. There was a confidence to his speech which had been buried beneath blind irritation last time we'd spoken, and he enunciated each word slowly and precisely, as if he was almost enjoying the process of talking.

'That's what I gathered,' I said.

Outside the wind gusted and dumped water out of the pine onto the driveway. I hoped they'd left a window open on the Jag. Hale unfolded his arms, dug his hands into his pockets and gazed serenely at the back of Donald's head.

'Obviously you're aware,' Nielsen said, 'the evening before he was murdered, Mr Moss was committed to an emergency room for treatment due to injuries inflicted by the pair of you.'

I leaned forward and gave him my best remembering face. 'Do you know what? I think we might have gone through this already, when you visited me on Monday morning.'

Donald gave a little shrug of the shoulders which could have been a subtle smirk. I looked at him. 'Do you ever say anything, or do you just sit there and ride the other guy's bandwagon?'

Nielsen creaked his chair again and said nothing, as if inviting Donald to retaliate. Donald said, 'Do either of you have an alibi for the evening Moss was killed?' He spoke with the classic twenty-years-of-smoking croak. Something to look forward to.

'No,' I said.

Donald spread his hands and he and Nielsen exchanged the little glance again. Nielsen raised his sausage fingers, and, smoothing the front of his jacket, pulled something out of his moustache, saying, 'I'll lay it out for you plain and simple, in case the fundamentals of what's going on here have eluded you.'

'Go for it.'

'Sunday night, Lionel Moss ends up with a broken arm, courtesy of you two. Twenty-four hours later, he takes two in the head. A day-and-a-half after that, we turn up here to check in on the guys who delivered the first lot of injuries, and discover you're not all that keen to tell us your recent whereabouts, and your little sidekick has a nose rimmed with blood and knuckles swollen like fucking walnuts.'

I looked at Donald. 'Did he rehearse that, or did he just nail it, first time?'

Neither of them found that amusing.

'Can I ask you something?' I said.

Nielsen creaked his chair again. 'Shoot,' he said. 'No pun intended.'

'Moss had convictions for assault. Why are you so eager to come to his rescue?'

'He's a drug informant, we tend to take care of them. We have to. You have no idea of the risks some of these guys take.'

I kept my expression dead-pan. 'This is me being sympathetic, I promise.'

Donald said, 'You're a funny guy, Devereaux.'

'You're not. I think you're a prick.'

Silence in the room for a very long time. The fridge and the clock carried on with their respective thrum-tick, oblivious to the tension.

'That's no way to address a senior officer,' Nielsen said.

'He's not a senior officer,' I answered. 'And in my house I'll speak to the Queen like that, if I want to.'

Donald seemed to find that somewhat amusing. Nielsen didn't. He reached into an inside pocket on his jacket and came out with a plastic zip-lock bag packed with cotton swab-sticks. 'You seem very sure of your innocence,' he said. 'And you're entitled to, don't get me wrong. But of course an innocent man wouldn't object to

232

having his hands swabbed for gunpowder traces, would he?'

I held his gaze for a three-count. There was nothing there. It was like gazing down into a rock pool expecting to see the bottom and instead being met with your own reflection.

'Cordite residue doesn't hang around that long,' I said.

'We'll just take some saliva, then.'

'What, you think we spat in his entry hall? Hawked one up and left it in the sink? No, thanks.'

'So you object, then?'

'Yup. You try and swab me and I'll bury that entire bag down your throat.'

Hale liked that. He smiled and freed his hands from his pockets then folded his arms again. Nielsen dropped the little bag on the table in front of him, then picked something else out of his facial hair and flicked it on the floor.

'Anyone ever told you you're an arrogant little arsehole?' he said.

'Not once.'

They did the glance thing again. 'Certain you've done nothing wrong?' Nielsen said. His voice still hadn't lost the calmness. 'I like that.'

233

I smiled at him. 'Can I ask you another question?' I said.

'Hell, it's your house.'

I smiled. 'Say you wanted to ambush a car. Say you had a gun. Do you think the best way to get said car to remain stationary would be to point the gun at the driver, or at a passenger in the back seat?'

Nielsen shrugged. 'I couldn't comment. I've never ambushed a car.'

'Sorry. It's just — and I'm referring to an incident you were involved in about three years back — if I were planning to ambush a vehicle carrying two million bucks, I would have made damn sure it was the driver I took out first. Wouldn't you?'

Nielsen had creaked his chair so many times I had lost count. He reached up and felt the back of his neck, probing for stubble, then smoothed the front of his jacket again.

'You have a point you're trying to get across?' he said.

'Somebody pinched two million bucks out of a car you were driving. You don't seem to be aware of just how unusual the situation was.'

He glanced at Donald, looked back at me, somewhat bemused. 'I'm aware of how unusual it appears,' he said.

'I think most people would agree being confronted by an armed man while stopped at a traffic light is a pretty bizarre event. And I don't like what you're insinuating.'

'OK,' I said. 'Fine. I guess that makes two of us. But you can get out of my house, now. Come visiting again, you'd better have a damn good reason to do so, not half-cooked speculation based on amateur assumptions.'

■ TWENTY-FOUR

At midday I left Hale in sole charge of baby-sitting duties and drove in to the station to check in Fontaine's diary. I made a copy of the image of Emma Fontaine's shaven-headed companion, then headed down to Customs and parked in the vacant lot beside Heat.

Twenty past twelve in the afternoon, turnover was looking extremely healthy. The stools fronting the bar along the far wall were all occupied, and a good two-thirds of the tables in the room were unavailable. The clientele was mixed: labourers, businessmen, salespeople.

The woman with the espresso hairdo was the only one on duty; standing behind the bar, pouring lager on-tap with the kind of slightly detached, vacant look that suggested a change of scene would do her some good. I milled around amidst the throng a moment, then, when one of the blistered vinyl stools became available, I sat myself down and beckoned her over.

'Remember me?' I asked.

She had to think. 'Vaguely.'

I slid forward off the stool to remove the photocopy I had made from my trouser pocket. 'Do you remember this guy, too?'

She glanced down. 'No, but I remember the girl. She's the dead one.'

I nodded and took the photo back. 'Is Tyler in?'

'No, but he'll be in soon, I reckon.'

I pointed over her shoulder to the door marked *TOIL T.* 'When he gets in, tell him I said he needs to use the john.'

She gave me a strange look. 'OK . . .'

'I'll be down the back somewhere.'

She nodded. 'You're gonna have to order something, though.'

'What?'

She gestured around, threaded her hair behind her ears. 'It's busy, we can't let you just take up a seat.'

I looked at her. 'What *don't* you have on tap?'

'Corona.'

'One Corona, please.'

She reached under the counter and came out with a glass bottle full of golden liquid. She de-capped it, then set it on a napkin and slid it across the scoured wood to me. I passed her a ten and told her to keep the change.

I eased back through the crowd to the front of the room, found a table for two near the door then scraped a chair out and sat down. I didn't have to wait long. Tyler Mitchell arrived at twenty minutes before one. Jeans, T-shirt. That haircut. He walked straight up to the bar, exchanged a few words with the woman with the espresso hair, turned and fixed me with a long, hard stare, then made towards the restroom. I took my first and only pull of Corona then got up and excused myself past a woman in her twenties, and followed after Mitchell. I stepped behind the bar, pushed through the door to the toilet and found him in the process of using the urinal that occupied the far wall.

'I didn't mean for you to actually relieve yourself,' I said.

He twisted his head slightly and surveyed me in his periphery, but remained silent. There was a row of hand-basins against the left-hand wall, and toilet cubicles on the right. Everything was well set up to cope with the event of many people needing to purge themselves of large amounts of waste.

'What do you want?' he said eventually.

'I just want to show you a photograph.'

No answer.

'You seen a doctor lately?' I asked.

He did the slight twist of the head again. 'No, why?'

'Stream sounds a little weak. Prostate might need looking at.'

'I could come and piss on your shoes, then you'll be able to see how weak it is.'

I didn't reply. He leaned forward a fraction as if coaxing out the last few drops, then shook himself off, zipped up and turned around to face me. I held up the photo I had shown to the woman behind the bar.

'This the guy you saw?' I asked.

'When?'

'The night the girl was murdered.'

He squinted. 'Yeah.'

'You sure?'

'Yeah, that's the guy. He doesn't have a tattoo, though.'

I flipped the paper around and confirmed this observation for myself. 'Well spotted.'

'When I saw him, he had a swastika thingee next to his eye. I told you that.'

I didn't answer. I pocketed the image then turned and opened the door.

'Why the hell did you want me in here?' he asked.

'Worried you were going to make a spectacle, didn't want to turn away potential customers.'

He said nothing.

'Don't forget to wash your hands,' I said.

I drove over to Queen Street and bought cigarettes and a lighter from a little dairy just up from Britomart before heading back up to the station. Rain was beginning to fall; the drops were only intermittent, but the ones that did strike my windshield were the size of twenty-cent coins.

I left the Commodore in the garage and took the stairs up to my desk. The post-mortem report for Emma Fontaine was sitting front and centre. The toxicology report from the Environmental Science and Research Office was sitting beside it, and the scene examination courtesy of Mark Jameson was alongside that. I sat down and worked left to right. The post-mortem was simply a specialist's interpretation of what I had gathered for myself on first viewing Fontaine's corpse; cause of death was severe impact trauma to the frontal lobe as a result of a single, forceful strike from an elongated object. An examination had been performed to determine whether a sexual assault had occurred, but no evidence of such was discovered. Stomach contents were primarily liquid, somewhere in the region of three to three-and-a-half standard drinks, a fact backed up by the ESR's toxicology findings more or less stating that Fontaine had a moderate blood-alcohol reading. As per mandatory requirements, tests had been carried out for traces of a number of illegal drugs or known date-rape chemicals, but everything had come back negative. Interpretation: Fontaine hadn't ingested anything other than beer the night she was killed.

I didn't bother with the scene examination report. I'd been to the murder site and once was usually enough.

I waited at my desk until three o'clock ticked around, then I headed back downstairs, checked out the car and drove over to Carrie Jordan's concrete fortress in Epsom, parking ten metres shy of her front gate. I sat idle, watching smoke drift from chimneys and middle-aged housewives driving expensive European sedans pull into driveways, until ten minutes before four, when Carrie Jordan appeared in my rear-view mirror.

She had a coat over her uniform blazer for extra protection against the chill, and she'd eschewed the ponytail in favour of a plain black headband that trapped her hair back behind her ears. She was focused on something inside her satchel, so didn't notice me standing motionless beside the car until she was quite close. Again, my presence startled her, and again, she tried to make it look as if it hadn't.

'Got a minute?' I asked.

She abandoned her search of the bag and switched her full attention to my face. 'What for?'

'I need to show you a photograph of someone.'

After a moment she nodded, opened the passenger door and slid in. I dropped down beside her and closed my door. Even with the added layers I could tell she was cold, rubbing her hands to promote better circulation.

'Couldn't we just talk at the house?' she said.

'Your mother doesn't like me.'

A smile. 'She doesn't like anybody.'

I brought out the photograph for the third time that afternoon and passed it across the console to her.

'Know who that guy is?'

She said nothing. Trees shook and dumped leaves and a dusting of water on the path ahead. A Porsche coupé passed by my door too close and relocated a puddle onto my window.

'I've seen him,' she said.

'You know his name?'

'Emma said his name was Hendrik.'

She spelled it for me.

'He was seen with Emma the night she died,' I said.

She placed the photograph in her lap, then reached up and adjusted her headband.

'You know where that photo was taken?' I asked.

She nodded. 'Our rumpus room. It was a party I had last year, maybe October.'

'You invited that guy?'

'No, he was Emma's plus-one.'

'I see. You don't even know his full name?'

'Uh, no.'

I raised my eyebrows. She pulled the coat closer about herself and turned and looked at me. Pretty eyes. 'Haven't you ever been to a party?'

'Not in a while. I was a teenager once, though, I can assure you.'

The smile again, lips only. 'You get people turning up who are just, you know, randoms. People don't know their names, where they've come from, what they do. They just turn up with somebody to a party then take off and no one hears from them again.'

'You don't know anything about him?'

She leaned forward and glanced out of the windshield, then took a peep out of her side window. 'Not a thing.'

'How many times have you seen him, roughly?'

She thrummed her fingers on the top of the satchel while she thought. 'Maybe two or three times, I guess. Once at my place, obviously, then just, you know, around.'

'Were he and Emma an item?'

'I don't know.'

We both fell silent for several seconds. She swivelled in her seat and looked at me again. 'I've got to go soon, my mother will wonder where the hell I am.'

'Oh yeah, sure. Sorry.'

She made to open the door.

'How're you holding up?' I said.

She turned back, adjusted the coat, adjusted the headband. 'I'm OK. I guess I don't really find people dying all that sad, really. Do you know what I mean?'

I nodded. She went to open the door again, then stopped, fingers surrounding the handle, pulling it then letting go just before it caught. 'Do you like what you do?' she asked. 'I mean, all this murdery stuff?'

I shrugged. 'Yeah, I guess I do, in a way.'

'Did you have to go to university or anything?'

I shook my head. 'I did anyway, though.'

'What did you do?'

'BA in English.'

'So why are you doing this job? If you've got a degree or whatever.'

I didn't answer.

She smiled and this time managed to get the door right the way open. 'I guess it's just because you're a nice person.'

She slid out onto the path and slammed the door before walking away without further ado. I watched her all the way to her front gate, hair streaming, coat and satchel flapping as if they wanted to break free of her and find new owners. I sat for a moment, considering the nature of the world. I left a message on Claire Bennett's cell detailing my recent findings, then I lit a cigarette and drove back to town.

When I got home that evening it was pitch black and the air was still and cold and smelling of fresh rain. The marked patrol car was still present at the roadside. I parked behind Hale's Escort then went inside and found him sitting at the kitchen table with Grace. Grace looked strained, though composed. Her face was dry. I pulled out a chair and sat down at the head of the table. She inclined her head in my direction and gave me a smile that utilized the corners of her mouth only.

'How was the holiday?' I asked.

She shrugged and closed her eyes. 'It could have ended a little better, I guess.'

I didn't respond to that. She inhaled deeply then blinked and pressed a fist to her mouth to keep the emotion pinned down. 'Things like this shouldn't happen to normal people,' she said.

I gave her a moment. 'Where's Michael?'

She made a small gesture with her hand. There was a mug of coffee on the table in front of her. It wasn't steaming. 'He's back home. There's a police officer keeping him company. Do you think he's going to be all right?'

'Kids cope well,' I said. 'He'll bounce back. But Victim Support will be in touch.'

She nodded, and dropped the fist to her lap. 'You said there were two men?'

'That's right.'

She brought the fist back to her mouth and spoke through her knuckles. 'Where are they now?'

'Probably in an ICU, on a morphine drip.'

'Will they recover?'

'I don't know.'

'Who are they?'

'I don't know. I haven't heard anything since last night.'

She removed her hand and leaned back in her chair, gazing into her lap, hair falling down across her face. 'Would they have taken Michael with them?' she asked.

'Yes,' Hale said.

'Thank you for stopping them.'

I looked between the two of them and said nothing. I hadn't been expecting her to buy into Hale's personal brand of justice with such apparent complacency. Maybe in her eyes, threatening her family merited a totally different level of response which the normal course of authority didn't have the power to take. She raked her hair back behind her ears and looked up from her lap, and there was a renewed hardness and clarity to her eyes, something I sensed had been missing for a long time.

'Who would want to do something like that?' she asked.

'We don't know yet,' I said. 'Have you had friction with anyone? A dispute, any discord at all?'

She shook her head.

'I visited Michael's father's home,' I said. 'He wasn't there. It looked like he'd been away for some time.'

Grace didn't appear to react to this news. She was sitting in the same chair Alan Nielsen had used earlier, but when she moved, it didn't creak at all. 'Could it be something to do with him?'

'Potentially. Has he ever had a run-in with the law that you know of?'

She shook her head.

'Do you have a contact number for him? Like a cellphone, I mean.'

She nodded.

'When you get home, first thing you do, I need you to call him. If he doesn't answer, leave a message telling him to get in touch as soon as possible.'

She nodded a second time. I pushed my chair back, then went to the fridge and checked the contents before sitting back down again. 'Does the name Alan Nielsen mean anything to you?' I asked her.

'No.'

'Burke Donald?'

Head shake. 'Who are they?'

'It doesn't matter.'

She looked between the two of us a couple of times, then threaded her hair behind her ears and stood up from the table. 'Thank you for everything,' she said. 'I'm sorry, I don't know what else to say, but thank you. Thank you for protecting me, thank you for looking after my son.'

She did another quick glance around then clasped her

hands in front of her like an air-hostess and stared at the ground, self-conscious.

'You're very welcome,' I said.

She was barefoot, and I failed to hear her move as she crossed the kitchen and made her way down the corridor to the front door. I heard the security chain rattle, then the tongue catch as she stepped outside.

'Man, John, sometimes I can hardly shut you up.'

He still said nothing. He got up and gave the inside of the fridge a survey of his own, then, dissatisfied, stepped back to the table and sat down.

'I was thinking about ambushes,' he said.

'OK.'

'What would you need? Say if we were looking to take out a car carrying four guys? Maybe pinch a suitcase full of cash they were carrying?'

'Weapons, shooters, a getaway driver. Whoever took Alan Nielsen had a bike. For rush-hour traffic that's more or less ideal.'

He nodded. 'That's your skeleton crew. These days it's more complicated. You probably have backup sets of each, a dedicated team monitoring the cop radio frequency. But you also need to think about what happens afterwards — once the cash has been claimed, what you actually do

249

with it? You can't just deposit it. You try and cash a quarter-million dollars, even ten thousand, you're going to have the Financial Intelligence Unit breathing down your neck. If your income pattern suddenly spikes inexplicably, alarm bells are going to ring. The whole process needs to be handled highly meticulously. Company invoice records need to be modified to explain extra income, orders may have to be falsified. Basically, real slick laundering.'

I nodded. 'And your point?'

'Maybe Nielsen and Donald struck an agreement that would get them the money they were supposed to be transporting.'

'I'd considered that,' I said.

'Maybe they needed an accountant,' Hale replied.

I looked at him and smiled humourlessly. 'Elliot Treverne used to be an accountant.'

He nodded. 'He was an accountant, good with money. They could have had contact with him through work, it's plausible.'

'So why is he missing?' I said.

'If he was laundering stolen drug money, it doesn't take much imagination. Maybe he's being blackmailed, maybe he's blackmailing someone else, maybe he's just terrified shitless.'

'Maybe someone thought they'd kidnap his kid as an incentive to flush him out of hiding.'

Hale leaned back in his chair and inclined his face to the light so that his skin glowed yellow. 'It had crossed my mind.'

'Do me a favour, John?'

'Name it.'

'Find out everything you can on Elliot Treverne.'

'Okey doke,' he said.

■ TWENTY-FIVE

Hale left shortly after. I listened to the throb of the Escort's engine as he reversed out onto the street, then I got up and lit a cigarette, walked through to the living room and stared out into the blackness. The air had gone completely still; the road was quiet, there was nothing out there save the streetlights. The world looked shiny and replenished after the recent downpours. I blew smoke at the window and watched the plumes unravel and break, like pieces of stretched cotton. My cellphone buzzed in my pocket, and I removed it, pressing it to my ear.

'Sean, it's Grace.'

'Hi, what's up?'

'He didn't answer.'

I said nothing.

'Elliot,' she continued. 'Michael's father. I called him like you said, his phone was turned off. And someone just called to say a friend of ours is dead and I think it must somehow be related and—'

'Wait, slow down. Who's dead?'

'This—' her voice broke and she swallowed. 'This friend of ours from way back. Peter Mason, we've known him since high school. His brother just called to tell me somebody found him dead in his bath. Like, *murdered.*'

I moved back to the kitchen and extinguished the cigarette in the sink. 'Give me the address, I'll head over there now.'

She choked out the necessary details. The address was on Sandringham Road, just south of Eden Park Stadium.

'Sean, I'm really scared.'

'Relax. We've got a car out front keeping an eye on things. Just keep your door locked, don't panic.'

She hung up on me.

I headed out to the car and drove into the central city. I took Queen Street up to Ian McKinnon Drive and cruised south through easy traffic along Dominion Road through Mount Eden, then hopped west over to Sandringham. I didn't need the exact address for Peter Mason's residence;

his home was visible a mile away, marked by the presence of six blue-and-orange patrol cars, two unmarked detective's rides, an ambulance, and a Scene of Crime van. I drove past and parked in front of somebody's hedge three doors down, then got out, locked the car and walked back up the street.

Sandringham is a fairly typical, undistinguished middle-class area, characterized by twenty- and thirty-year-old family homes on close sections. Peter Mason's home was obscured nicely from the road by a head-high red brick wall. There was a neat little painted gate giving access onto a red brick patio, which fronted a white, single-storey structure with a garage bumped off to the right. A uniform was guarding the gate; I signed the attendance log, walked past a group of ambulance staff clustered on the patio, and went in through the open front door.

The layout of the interior was fairly simple. The kitchen left, living and dining right. I headed right through the dining area, then followed a group of Scene of Crime technicians clad in white coveralls down a short corridor towards a door at the rear of the house, leading to the bathroom. Straightforward design: bath against the far wall, loo on the left, basin on the right. There was a man in the bath. He wasn't washing himself. He was dead, completely naked, his body criss-crossed with knife marks, the walls of the tub painted red with his blood. The room stunk of a pungent cocktail of methane and faeces, and was crowded with crime-scene techs. In their full-body coveralls and masks, they looked like apparitions from some apocalyptic nightmare. The man in the bath made it all the more authentic.

One of the sets of coveralls turned around and lowered its mask, and I saw that it was Mark Jameson, the guy I had spoken to at the Fontaine crime scene on Saturday.

'You shouldn't be in here without a jumpsuit,' he said.

I glanced at him. 'It's at the drycleaner's.'

The man in the bath was in his early thirties, thin, with light brown hair buzzed close to his scalp. I noticed for the first time that his feet were still clad; a pair of tan leather boat-shoes, the laces still tied, soiled with blood.

'What happened?' I asked.

Jameson shrugged as if the scene didn't need an explanation. 'Injuries weren't self-inflicted, we found defensive wounds on his forearms. At a guess, I'd say somebody held him down, and somebody else cut him. Looks like he's been gone for a couple of days.'

'Christ.'

He bent down and retrieved a plastic zip-lock bag off

the tiled floor. It contained a crumpled sports sock. 'We found this stuffed into his mouth,' he said. 'Like they wanted to keep him quiet.' Murder works best when kept discreet.

I said nothing and stepped forward to clear the door, looking at the body again. There were probably twenty or twenty-five cuts in total, mostly to the torso and upper legs, some to the arms. I couldn't help but think what it would be like to die like that, pinned down and slowly butchered. Whether the mind can retain any sense of order or calm, or if it simply disappears beneath the rush of the moment. Swallowed up by the sound of heartbeats, like an overture for departure. Like abattoir music.

'Any evidence of forced entry?' I asked.

'Not on the front door. The ranch slider in the living room's locked from the inside.'

'He live alone?'

'I think so.'

'Any injuries besides the cuts?'

'None external, far as we can see.'

I said nothing for a moment. 'Did you find a murder weapon?'

'There's a set of knives in the sink in the kitchen, I think they could be a safe bet.'

I gave no reply, lost in personal queries.

'So what does it look like to you?' he asked.

I surveyed the damage to the corpse again; the depth and number of injuries, the volume of blood. 'Torture,' I said at length. 'Someone wanted information.'

He returned his mask to its original position, and I saw the skin around his eyes crinkle. 'I think if it was me I would have given it up,' he said.

'Not if you didn't have the information.'

He didn't have an answer to that. The floor of the bathroom was sticky from the biological residues the guy had been secreting for the past forty-eight hours, and I could hear the technicians' feet peeling off it as they moved.

'Have you come to help out or are you just interested?' Jameson said after a moment.

I glanced at him. 'My neighbour knew the victim.'

He said nothing.

'I had a break-in Tuesday night, they arrested two guys. Do me a favour and compare the prints they took off them to any recovered from this place, OK?'

'Yeah, but—'

My exit silenced him. I walked back out along the corridor, through the dining room then outside onto the patio, out the gate to the path. The street had been buffed to a shine by the weather, reflecting blue and red from the assortment of emergency vehicles occupying the roadside. I walked to my car, removing my cellphone and dialling Grace's number. She only took a moment to pick up.

'It's bad, Grace, I'm sorry.'

The phone was quiet. 'What did they do to him?' she asked at length.

I went for brutal honesty: 'He was in the bath, like you said. They'd used knives on him. I'm very sorry.'

Her breath started to come too quickly, rapid in her throat; the approach of panic. She started to cry, speaking fast and incoherently, her words lost under her emotion. I tried to speak over her, to tell her to be calm, but it was useless. Panic gains momentum like nothing else, and an empty voice across a telephone line does little to prevent it. I just stood there on the footpath with my eyes closed, listening to the rush of passing cars, waiting it out. It took a while, but eventually the rapidity of her breathing subsided, and her words were distinguishable again: 'Oh, shit,' and 'Oh, God,' repeated over and over and over again.

'Grace, listen to me.'

The chanting continued, but quietened.

'Take a breath, and listen to me. Calm down.'

She took a breath. Listened to me. Calmed down.

'I know it's scary,' I said. 'I think what's happened is that this man was tortured by someone wanting to know where Michael's father is. Do you understand?'

Silence. I assumed she was nodding.

'I think your son's father is in trouble with some very bad people, and they want to know where he is, for what reason I don't know, but I'm going to sort it out, OK?'

She snivelled. 'OK.'

'I'll suss out what's happening here, and I'll keep you safe. Promise.'

Another snivel, quieter. 'OK, Sean.'

'Repeat what I just said.'

She did so. On the street a car passed too quickly and showered me with groundwater. 'Do you want me to send John round?'

She thought about it. 'No, no, I'll be fine. Thanks, Sean, you're a good person.'

'So I've been told.'

■ TWENTY-SIX

I hung up, dialled Hale's cell and left a message detailing what had happened, then got into the car and set the heater running. The phone rang almost immediately and I answered in a hurry, thinking it was Hale calling me back, but it was Claire Bennett.

'Are you at home?' she asked when I answered.

'I wish.'

Quiet for a moment. 'I got a call regarding that picture you found,' she said at length. 'The one of the skinhead kid with Fontaine.'

My rear-view mirror was a mosaic of colour: red and blue from the cop cars immediately behind, backed by a softer yellow glow from Eden Park further north up the road. Raindrops on my windshield the colour of honey.

'And what's the issue?' I asked.

'Patrol unit in Manurewa just came across some guys planning to raid a dairy. They start taking details, one of them's called Hendrik Larsen. They recognize the first name from our bulletin, check the photo, bingo. They reckon it could be the kid seen with Fontaine.'

I started the engine. 'What's the location?'

'Group of shops ten minutes west of the southern motorway.' She went off the line a moment while she gathered the specifics, then relayed them to me.

'Tell them not to take anyone off-scene until I get there,' I said.

She laughed dryly. 'They're way understaffed. They couldn't move them all even if they wanted to.'

I hung up, found the motorway again and headed towards Manukau, through drizzle that grew in intensity the further south I headed. The scenery either side of State Highway One transformed gradually from clean, patterned concrete to rusted corrugated iron. Through the rain I could see everything from light industrial to cheap-rent caravan parks and derelict housing. Billboards at the roadside promised to cure my erection troubles.

I exited after ten minutes, heading west into the suburbs. The location Bennett had described was a long street-facing array of retail outlets set in the middle of a huge rectangle of asphalt, bordered by head-high wire fencing. General street appeal was low: the gutters were clogged with broken bottles and miscellaneous household rubbish, the wooden fences protecting many of the homes either side of the small shopping stretch were defaced with graffiti, and further up the street I could see a burnt-out Mini chocked up on cinder blocks, its doors and rear panel pockmarked with hammered dents, presumably made simply for the sake of inflicting damage. It was the sort of street where the nice folks locked themselves indoors and hoped the street gangs decided to take the day off.

The row of shops consisted of a bakery, a video store, a liquor place and, finally, a dairy. The parking lot was empty save for three patrol cars arranged in a loose triangle about a group of four dark sedans positioned outside the dairy. There were four cops in total, standing guard over a group of eight or ten young men, lying side-by-side in a line, hands cuffed behind their backs, illuminated by the headlamps of one of the patrol cars. I drove in through a gap in the wire fence and parked the car within close proximity of the little gathering, then got out and blipped the locks. As I did so a fifth cop exited the front of the dairy and walked towards me. He was a few years older than me, pushing forty, with hair and a face that had aged too soon. He was carrying a clipboard and wearing sergeant's stripes on his shoulders. I flipped my badge for him and he wiped rain off his brow and offered his hand. I took it.

'What's happening?' I asked.

He gestured behind me to one of the houses lining the opposite side of the street. 'Comms got a call a few minutes ago from a lady, reckoned a group of guys across here was planning on busting a shop. We send a unit along, find three cars full of blokes carrying hammers and bats. We run the licence plates, one of the cars is stolen, two out of the nine guys have outstanding arrest warrants for missed court appearances.'

'It's like Christmas come early.'

He winked. 'They're gonna double my office space and give me a coffee machine, I can feel it.'

I smiled. 'I heard you thought you had a person-of-interest in a homicide I've got.'

'Yeah, Comms said the name Hendrik came up on the general Wanted list, but take a look for yourself.'

I thanked him and headed towards the row of apprehended youths. Between fifteen and twenty-five, all male. Four of them were of Maori or Pacific Island descent, the other five were Caucasian. They were dressed in dark jeans and hooded jumpers, long since soaked by the descending mist and the oily puddles that had settled on the asphalt. Their cheeks were pressed flat against the uneven ground, eyes bright with the reflected glow of the headlights.

The guy at the far end was my man. Early twenties, six foot, lean. Head like a boiled egg. High cheekbones, prominent, almost gaunt features. I walked to the far end, then squatted down so I was level with the guy's head. I could feel the rain on the back of my neck, could see it settling on his hairless skull like pieces of ground crystal. He arched his neck and rotated his head in order to see me. His right cheek was patterned and inlaid with grit from where he'd had it pressed to the ground.

'I'm Sean Devereaux,' I said. 'Auckland Central CIB. Pleased to meet you.'

He said nothing. I gripped one of his cuffed wrists and frisked him quickly. He was carrying a wallet in his right trouser pocket. His driver's licence confirmed his name was Hendrik Larsen. He would be twenty-two in August. I slipped the wallet back into his pocket and glanced up, signalling to the sergeant I had spoken with a minute earlier. He hurried over, clipboard in hand.

'I need to have a chat with Mr Larsen,' I said. 'Is that going to be a problem?'

The guy shrugged. He was just a black silhouette, the way he was backlit by the cop car's flood-lamps. 'Go for it,' he said.

I gripped Larsen's bicep with one hand and raised him to his feet, then marched him out of the glare of the full-beams, over to my car. I unlocked it, then opened the rear door behind the driver's and lowered him onto the seat, my palm on his head so he didn't knock the roof, then shut him in, circled the rear bumper and climbed in beside.

Close proximity, he was emitting an odour: a vinegary funk from his armpits, mixed with what I thought might have been mud off his shoes. He kept his eyes dead ahead, ignoring me.

'Have you been advised of your rights?' I asked him.

He said nothing.

'All I need is a yes or a no.'

'Yes, then.' His voice was low, unhurried, unworried.

'You catch the news much?' I asked. 'Read the paper at all?'

Nothing in his expression. 'What do you want?'

I held my reply for a beat, watching the side of his face, but either he did not feel the need to observe me directly, or he was comfortable with the clarity of his peripheral vision. I said, 'On Saturday evening, a young girl was found beaten to death in Albert Park in Auckland. You were seen in her company only hours before she was killed.'

He clinked his cuffs behind him and his eyes shifted right, examining the view out of his window. 'That's a statement,' he said. 'Not a question.'

'It's a statement to which you are cordially invited to respond.'

His top lip fluttered at my pleasantry. 'I've provided my name and details to the guys over there, I'm not legally required to say anything.'

I smiled in an effort to present unfaltering calm, but it was pointless, he still hadn't turned to me. 'Right now,' I said, 'you're looking at a possession-of-an-offensive-weapon charge, and intent to commit robbery. I can promise you, they'll treat you a hell of a lot better over at lock-up if you manage to at least partially convince me you didn't murder someone within the last week.'

'I didn't kill anyone.'

His head moved towards me by a tenth of a degree, and

the shift in the light revealed, for the first time, a swastika, tattooed faintly, as if in pencil, beneath his left eye.

'So explain what happened,' I said. 'You were seen in Heat down on Customs Street with a girl named Emma Fontaine. Do you deny that?'

Silence in the car. He squirmed his butt on the seat, and the accompanying movement of his arms brought up a fresh wave of his stink.

'I don't have to speak to you. I can get a lawyer, I don't have to say a word.'

There was a smugness to his voice that I had to work hard not to punish physically. I badly wanted to strike him, to grab his head by the ears and smash his face against the window for his lack of concern for his situation.

'You're right,' I said at length. 'However, if you don't speak to me now, you're still going to have to submit to a formal interview, and that will be a lot worse than talking to me. For one, it will be video-recorded, so you'll have no opportunity to deny what you may have said at a later date, and secondly, the guys conducting the interview will be a hell of a lot tougher than I am. Bear that in mind.'

He bore that in mind, red and blue flicking in the whites of his eyes, and after a moment I said, 'Walk me through Friday afternoon. Emma said she was at a friend's place before she went out. Did you pick her up from there?'

I thought he was going to implement his right to silence as threatened, but he answered: 'I picked her up around five, I think.' His voice was louder in order to be audible above the rain on the roof.

'And then what?'

'We went to Heat,' he said, quieter again.

I smiled. 'Want to try that again?'

'I can't, she's dead.'

I shook my head. 'You didn't just pick her up then head into town to the bar. You didn't go in there until half past seven. Between you picking up Emma and entering the bar, there's a gap of two-and-a-half hours.'

The rain on the roof cut back, leaving the cabin of the car in silence for several seconds before the drizzle resumed. Hendrik Larsen made a little dismissive gesture, then massaged the bridge of his nose with his cuffed wrists, metal clinking delicately. 'We drove around,' he said. 'I got a new car, wanted to show it off to her, I guess. We went into town, then I brought her back because she wanted to take her own car to the bar, so we could leave separate if we wanted.'

'Did she lock her car?' I asked.

'What?'

'When you went to the bar. She left her car in the parking lot next door, is that right?'

'Yeah, we both did.'

'So when she got out, did she lock the car?'

He hesitated before responding. 'I got there a bit before she did. I saw the lights flash after she got out, like she'd used the remote or something.'

When Fontaine's car was found, it was unlocked. It had displayed no sign of forced entry.

I said, 'What was the relationship between the two of you? She your girlfriend?'

A brief pause, during which he shrugged again. I realized grimly that the last time I'd interviewed someone in a car, the interviewee had come out of it with a broken forearm.

'Girlfriend,' he said.

'You've known her long?'

'Couple of years. I met her at this party, started hanging out with her. Kind of secretive, she was real worried her mother would find out, Em said she probably wouldn't take too kindly to a guy like me.' A self-deprecating smile, despite the situation.

'What reason would anyone have to dislike you?' I said.

He said nothing.

'Is it because you deal drugs, Hendrik?'

'Up yours.'

'Do you?'

'I'm not admitting to anything. Whether or not I sell drugs is irrelevant.'

'Is it?'

'If you're telling me it's not, you're saying someone who sells a little weed from time to time is more likely to murder than someone who doesn't.'

His calmness reminded me of my encounter with Lionel Moss. There was no tension in his body, I could sense from his posture he was relaxed. He was either innocent; or, failing that, a veteran of back-seat chats with police officers. I said, 'So you took her for a drive, for two-and-a-half hours?'

'Two hours. We spent a while up at Long Bay Beach on the Shore, then drove back down to her place so she could pick up her car. After that we went to Heat.'

I nodded. 'OK, show me your vehicle.'

For a moment he made no indication he had even heard the question, before he leaned forward and rested his head on the headrest in front of him, and looked through the windscreen to one of the dark sedans surrounded by the triangle of patrol cars.

'Lancer Evo,' he said. 'Full body kit. Turbocharger, I had a cold air box fitted the other day.'

I looked in the direction he was pointing. His Lancer was an indigo four-door with a spoiler mounted on the boot lid. There were skirts attached beneath the front and rear bumpers and the doors, only one or two inches clear of the ground.

'What did you do at Heat?'

He shrugged, and made a face at the headrest. He still hadn't turned to look at me. 'We drank.'

'What?'

The shrug again. 'I had a couple of Steinlagers, couple of cocktails.'

'And Emma?'

'Couple of lagers, don't really remember.'

'What were you talking to Tyler about?'

'Who?'

'Tyler Mitchell, the owner.'

'Oh, this and that,' he said. He raised his wrists off the headrest and rubbed at the swastika.

'What time did you leave?'

'Some time after eight, I think. Like, quarter-past. Em

said she'd had too many to drive, so I took her in my car. We cruised for a bit, then I dropped her home about ten, then I went home.'

I watched the side of his face for any sign of a lie, a flicker beneath his eye, a quiver of the lip. But his face was empty.

'What do you mean, *we cruised for a bit*?'

He shrugged, like the phrase was self-explanatory. 'I just drove around. It's fun, you should try it.'

'We checked for witnesses in her street,' I said. 'Nobody saw you drop her home.'

He shrugged again. Then, 'If I was going to kill her,' he said, 'why would I leave her somewhere so obvious?'

I paused. I was still hoping he might turn and look at me, but he didn't. 'I can't answer that,' I said. 'I've never killed anyone. As much as I try to understand people who take innocent lives, I always come up short.'

■ TWENTY-SEVEN

I left him in the car and went to talk to my sergeant friend with the clipboard again.

'When you searched the vehicles, did you find anything in the black Lancer?' I asked.

He turned and looked back over his shoulder, identifying the vehicle I was referring to. 'A softball bat,' he said.

'No crowbar?'

He pursed his lips and shook his head. 'Why?'

'Forget it. Is it OK if one of your guys carts him over to Central? I really need to hang on to him.'

He looked at me as if he thought I might have been joking. 'You can take the lot of them if you want, we sure as hell don't need them down here.'

I thanked him and shook his hand, and watched one of the patrol officers remove Hendrik Larsen from the back of my Commodore. I headed over and slid into the driver's seat, radioing Comms to request a tow truck be sent to collect Larsen's vehicle.

Claire Bennett answered on the third ring when I dialled her cell.

'Larsen says Fontaine locked her car,' I said.

No reply. I heard bedsprings squeal. 'What?'

'When the patrol found Fontaine's car, it was unlocked. But Larsen just told me when Fontaine left her vehicle on Friday night, she locked it. If he's telling the truth, at some point Fontaine's car keys made it back to her car and disengaged the locks.'

'OK,' she said.

'He also says he dropped Fontaine home late evening; she was still alive when he left her.'

'Do you believe him?'

'I'm reserving my conclusions. The implications, however, are that Fontaine made it home safe and sound, then for some reason headed back to her car on Customs Street and unlocked it.'

'Why?'

'It's possible she could have forgotten something.'

'Something so important she had to fetch it at two a.m. on a Saturday?'

I said nothing.

'Forensics didn't find anything around the car. It was clean for blood.'

'The ground there's just loose aggregate. It'd been raining.'

She exhaled. 'I'll call you tomorrow,' she said. 'Go to bed.'

Thursday, John Hale reached his office off High Street in central Auckland at five minutes after four in the morning. Pre-eight-a.m. starts were not standard practice for Hale; it was restlessness that had brought him in. Insomnia visited often in times of tension. In the absence of sleep, productivity would suffice.

He locked the door behind him as he entered the secretarial pen and flicked the lights on; crisp shadows cutting the floor where the glare of the bulb was shielded by the reception counter. He let himself into his office, leaving the door open to allow the glow to filter through, threaded behind the two chairs set out for prospective clients, and sat down at his desk, cushion springs disrupting the silence. At this hour the walls were lit a cool purple that he found soothing, and the window in the right-hand wall which gave out over lower High Street offered nothing but an occasional fractured glimpse of light. He liked it at this time of day. The emptiness calmed him, and it was sometimes enough to help a troubled man ignore all pressing issues. Though perhaps not tonight.

He raised the handset on his telephone and dialled in the access code for his voicemail service. He had two unanswered messages. The first related to the condition of the two men he had encountered Tuesday night. Neither had regained consciousness yet; one had required surgery to relieve cranial pressure due to swelling of the brain. Hale let the message run, then hit three for delete. The second message pertained to Elliot Treverne. Relatively trivial details, in his mind, but he'd pass them on regardless. He let the recording play out and listened to the polite automated voice inform him his inbox was empty, then lowered the handset and rose from his seat. The quiet times were a mixed blessing on occasion; the silences, the long periods of inactivity, though mostly therapeutic, served as triggers for memory. The ugliest of his experiences would always visit spontaneously, without purposeful recollection, bringing echoes of crime scenes, images of the fallen innocent he did not wish to reexamine. Thankfully, music proved a powerful narcotic. He got up from the desk, stepped through a cut of yellow from the door and powered up the stereo unit standing on a low shelf against the opposite wall. The Mutton Birds' *Envy of Angels* had been pre-loaded. He stood there in the dark and heard out 'Like This Train'. The magic of that track never dulled for him, regardless of revisits. He ran 'Train' a second time, then cycled the disk tray to Grant Lee Buffalo's *Copperopolis* and advanced to 'Armchair'. Anguish in those lyrics; he didn't know what brought him back to it. The melancholy fitted the hour.

He powered the unit down at half past four. He went to his desk and removed from a drawer the set of car keys he had claimed from the pocket of one of the men he had rendered unconscious, then took the stairs down to the garage bay where his Escort was parked. There was no other sound in the building save his footfalls; this early in the morning those working late had long since gone, those working early hadn't yet mustered the courage to brave the cold.

He put the Escort out onto High, drove south and turned west on Victoria, then north on Queen and headed down to Quay Street. Traffic was minimal, and it was safe enough for him to run the reds. With his lights off, the Escort's paintwork melted away into the wet morning like a shadow or a wobbly glimpse of mirage. His window was down, and the passing air smelled of wet tarseal and cold exhaust.

He wound his way east along the waterfront, past the ancient red-painted fence separating the docks from the public, through Mechanics Bay, and on towards Mission Bay. He turned right off Tamaki Drive shortly after. He crested a rise and pulled to a stop at the end of Devereaux's street, lights laid out before him in a perfect corridor of sodium yellow amidst the gloom.

He worked the set of confiscated car keys from his pocket and set them in his lap. He had already reconnoitred the area once for a vehicle, but without a specific model or body shape to look for, his search had been fruitless. He sat at the kerb with his engine off for a moment, and felt a silence descend which was so profound, it made him wonder where it had been earlier when he'd shut his eyes and tried to sleep.

He understood basically what he was looking for. A Toyota, obviously; that much was written across the remote fob on the keys. Something compact, efficient, unobtrusive. Almost certainly not an SUV. A sedan most likely. Mid-sized, dark. He twisted the ignition and felt the engine shudder to life before moving away down the road, slowly. He held the blond guy's keys in his right hand and draped his arm out over the top of the door. He blipped the remote fob intermittently as he drove, watching for the telltale orange flare of tail-lights amongst the blackness. He figured the vehicle couldn't be more than a couple of minutes' walk from Devereaux's home. If they'd been planning on abducting a child, proximity to the getaway car would have been paramount. He reached an intersection and dabbed the brake, looking both ways. The road was well-lit, stretching away in a straight black ribbon either side of him. No parked cars. He drove on through, his thumb continuing to depress the unlock button on the fob as he went. Lights were beginning to come on behind windows now. The dawn parade, as he liked to think of it. The shift workers; the posties and bus drivers and hospital staff, or people who worked further from home than they should. He kept the speedo at a steady twenty-five and continued along the road for another two minutes, and when his constant remote-clicking still hadn't rewarded him, he turned around and went back the way he had come.

Rolling down to Tamaki Drive, he turned left and drove up the street which paralleled Devereaux's to the west, but saw nothing. The area was generally up-market; large-scale three- and four-bedroom homes for people on large-scale incomes, and he imagined a late-model Toyota sedan parked at the kerb wouldn't be too much of an unusual sight. Certainly it wouldn't be likely to stand out.

He repeated the process on the street immediately to the east, but found nothing. He passed plenty of Toyotas; none, however, responded to the discrete frequency emitted by his particular unit. It was irritating, but not overly so. In total he had twelve years' military and police experience, and he was used to things taking longer than preferred. He knew that in the end his patience would prevail. In his mind the possibility that there was no car at all was a non-issue. There was a vehicle, there was a finite number of locations that vehicle could be stored — eventually he would find it.

He worked the brake again and saw the road behind glow red in his rear-vision mirror, then pulled a neat U-turn and felt the air rush in as he changed direction and headed back along the street. He pushed the Escort hard now, revving it to within the red line, cleaning out the cylinders. He hung a right at the intersection he had paused at earlier, dropped his speed back, and resumed his clicking regime with renewed vigour. He followed the road one hundred and fifty metres, and when he saw nothing he swung across the road and backtracked, arm extended beyond the car, the blond guy's key held out like a blade.

He saw an orange glow in the darkness twenty metres before he reached the intersection with Devereaux's street. He was surprised. He had noted earlier that the street was empty; he had covered the stretch simply for the sake of conforming to a pre-ordained itinerary. Which therefore meant the car was parked in someone's property.

He pulled the Escort over, got out and blipped the lock button on the confiscated keys, just to get a better bearing on the other vehicle's location. He saw the orange glow again; harsh and instantaneous, illuminating the surrounding features of the street the way a flare might before it is suddenly extinguished. He jogged across the street and saw the car was a black Toyota Camry. It was parked beneath an open car shelter which consisted of only a roof supported by four vertical wooden beams. The shelter was positioned next to a small brick pensioner's flat. The front lawn was longer than Hale generally preferred. There was a for-sale sign erected on the grass verge beside the footpath.

Hale stood and looked at the back end of the car, and, after a moment, turned and headed back to the Escort and drove away.

■ TWENTY-EIGHT

I slept poorly that night; my mind filled with images of dead people in bathtubs, and Hendrik Larsen, a scarlet swastika tattooed across his face, leering at me out of the dark.

I rose at seven and made myself coffee and toast for breakfast, eating it at the kitchen table. The wind was up; I could hear branches squealing against the roofing iron. Rain was falling in grey, vertical sheets. July.

At quarter past seven I called Grace. Michael answered.

'How are you doing?' I asked.

'Pretty good.'

'No break-ins?'

'Nuh-uh.'

'How's Mum?'

The line went quiet. 'I could hear her crying last night. I think she's sad.'

His tone was flat. I imagined he was probably experiencing a follow-through effect from Tuesday evening. 'I think she's just really stressed out, kiddo. She's worried because of what happened to you. You have to look after her, OK?'

Wind gusted and sent the rain sideways, washing in against the window.

'All right.'

'Think you can manage?'

'Yeah.'

I said goodbye and ended the call. I left my breakfast dishes in the sink, then drove into town to the station.

Hendrik Larsen was still on my mind. As far as suspects went, he was convenient. He had a tattoo of a swastika, and hung out in dingy bars. Forensically and statistically speaking he was also a match. I had been told on Saturday when I first viewed the crime scene that the perpetrator was most likely a tall male. Add that to the fact most young women who fall victim to murder are killed by either a spouse or a blood relation, and things were looking tidy.

If only it was as easy as fitting a typecast.

When I reached my desk I opened the Fontaine

investigation file and turned to the witness-interview section. It was an insubstantial collection near the back totalling maybe ten or twelve pages. I skimmed everything briefly, but found every statement to be more or less identical, in that they were each simply a variation of the same message: nobody had seen or heard a thing on Emma Fontaine's street the night she was killed. In other terms, nobody had seen her dropped home, as Hendrik Larsen had told me he had done.

The last page of the interview section was a map of Fontaine's neighbourhood. Her street dead-ended in a cul-de-sac only a hundred or so metres beyond her front gate. Twenty-four houses in total; twelve to a side. Whether or not a house had been surveyed was indicated with either a tick or a cross. I counted three crosses. Three locations where knocks had gone unanswered.

The Fontaines' place was located approximately half-way down the street, allowing me to disregard two of the crosses corresponding to homes on the far side of the cul-de-sac — unlikely anything of use had been witnessed from that distance. However, the third cross was located across the street from the Fontaines', on a shallow diagonal. The map had been printed from a software package indicating property boundaries. The place was within close proximity to the road; a view of houses directly opposite would most likely be unobstructed.

I called Claire Bennett's office.

'Did anybody go back to double-check witnesses on Fontaine's street?' I said when she answered.

'I'm sorry?'

'I was wondering whether anybody had gone back to check on the place across the road from her.'

I heard heavy paperwork being shifted as she searched for her own copy of the file. 'You realize I'm just down the hall, you can actually come and speak to me in person.'

'I like the phone better. It lets me do rude faces while I'm talking.'

She grunted. 'The copy I've got here was up-to-date as of midnight. The place diagonally opposite Fontaine is crossed, which I guess means nobody's bothered to check up.'

I ended the call and booted up my computer, then brought up the Habitation Index and fed the address through the database. Early morning the server must have been relatively inactive, and the software responded quickly: one occupant only. *Paula Webb*. I brought up a reverse directory and obtained a telephone number for the address, and dialled it on my cell.

A young woman answered after only the second ring, with a slightly curt hello, which led me to think she was unaccustomed to being disturbed at such an hour.

'Is that Paula Webb?' I asked.

'No,' the woman said. 'It's her daughter. May I ask who's calling?'

'My name's Sean Devereaux, I'm a police detective.'

'You're not doing a recruiting run are you?' she said dryly.

I laughed politely. 'No, but if Ms Webb is in, I was hoping to be able to come and speak with her about an issue I'm looking into, sometime this morning.'

The woman paused, then said 'Oh,' and I got the impression she knew the nature of the issue I wished to discuss. 'Mum's in hospital right now, I don't think she's going to be in any real state to speak to anyone.'

I hesitated. 'OK, sure, but could you tell me whether or not she was at home, Friday evening? It's a funny question, I know.'

'This Friday just been?'

'Yeah.'

'Yes, she was in.'

'Do you think it would be possible for me to see her at some stage?'

The woman sighed. I pictured a hand raking through hair. 'She's on dialysis.'

'I appreciate speaking with me could be an effort, but it is important. I'm sorry.'

I heard her breath on the line. 'Is it about the girl who died?'

'Yes,' I said. 'It is.'

'She's in Ellerslie Meadowcare,' the woman said. 'Visiting hours are between ten and two. Don't go today, she won't be well enough. And take some ID with you, or they probably won't admit you.'

I told her to have a lovely day, and ended the call.

■ TWENTY-NINE

I went and made myself a cup of coffee, and when I got back to my desk my phone was ringing. It was Hale.

'I can't take personal calls at work,' I said. 'You'll get me in trouble.'

'Don't worry, it's a law-enforcement issue,' he said. 'Related to Elliot Treverne.'

I didn't reply.

'Nineteen-ninety-six, Treverne was with patrol in Rotorua, also worked on-call for the Armed Offenders Squad.'

'OK.'

'Ninety-four through to ninety-seven, Alan Nielsen and Burke Donald were Rotorua CIB, but Nielsen also ran the local branch of AOS. So if you're looking for a link between Nielsen and Treverne, you've got one dating back at least fifteen years.'

'Well, bingo.'

'Yeah,' he said. 'I've been busy. I also found the car.'

'What car?'

'The one the guys from Tuesday night used. Black Toyota Camry, hidden in a shelter just past the first intersection from your place.'

'Where are you?'

'Guard duty, your place. The patrol unit they've got posted doesn't strike me as particularly vigilant.'

I glanced down at my cup of coffee. Only a quarter done, but the remainder was going to have to be sacrificed in the name of criminal investigation. 'Give me twenty minutes,' I said.

I ended the call and took the stairs down to the garage, logged out my car and threaded north through town to Quay Street, turning east towards home. Winter keeps Tamaki Drive relatively quiet: bikers prefer calm weather so the cycle lane was close to empty, and because restaurants and cafés tend to do best business during summery climes many of the eateries that line the southern side of the road were pushed in terms of clientele. If it kept the traffic to a minimum, it didn't bother me.

I turned into my drive moments later and found Hale's Escort parked beneath the Norfolk pine for shelter against the weather, its body beaded with water. I pulled to a stop behind it, went inside and found him seated at the kitchen table drinking a Heineken.

'I thought I'd left the house locked,' I said.

'You did.'

'Any more beer?'

'Your supplies were critical, I bought you a six-pack.'

I opened the fridge door, removed a bottle from the cardboard carton he'd brought with him, de-capped it, then sat down next to him at the table. I thought he appeared somewhat deflated; his shoulders were rounded and he was cupping the bottle in front of him in a manner making it seem he was gaining comfort from it.

'Have you checked next door?' I asked him at length.

He drained the last of his bottle in three long swallows and placed it down on the table, licking his lips. He was wearing a T-shirt, and I could see his arms still hadn't recovered from the blows he'd been dealt two days before.

'The boy was in bed when I called, but I spoke to him; he seemed OK.'

'And what about her?'

He smiled faintly. 'She seemed fairly reassured that

justice was going to prevail eventually. She said she'd spoken to you on the phone, that you'd told her you were going to fix things.'

I nodded. The bottle was sweating, moisture slick against my palms. 'That's the plan,' I said.

Hale didn't reply. He pushed his chair back along the lino and took his empty bottle to the sink, rinsing it under the tap; water from the tap loud against the steel. He raised his face to the window and gave a grimace, as if he was displeased by what he saw.

The car Hale had located was parked under a shelter attached to a small brick unit twenty metres west of the first intersection beyond my home. It was a matt black Toyota Camry Sportiva. An unexciting, middle-of-the-pack sedan, the sort of vehicle rental companies like to purchase in bulk. It was sitting on top of a grey concrete pad that had fractured with time, allowing weeds to penetrate. That, together with the real estate sign at the end of the driveway, the curtained-over windows, and the foot-long lawn, suggested the place had been uninhabited for quite some time.

Hale stopped the Escort on a clear stretch of kerb ten metres down the street and the pair of us got out into the cold greyness and walked back towards the abandoned Camry. In its current location, nobody would pay it the slightest regard, unless they were specifically looking for it. A car left unattended at the roadside might attract attention, but one left under shelter on private property almost never will.

'How did you find it?' I asked.

A smile broke his lips. 'With great difficulty.'

I didn't reply, allowing him to relish the memory of his great discovery. The surface of the driveway was slicked with furry moss, and as I drew closer, I saw the underside of the roof was sagging with rot and tinged green with mildew. I glanced at the house then reached into my pocket and removed a pair of disposable gloves I had taken from my kitchen, snapping them on, the stretch of rubber loud in the quiet.

'What's our cover story if we get made?' Hale said.

'Nothing. Beckon them over, then knock them unconscious and put them in the boot.'

He said nothing, but his mouth remained curled. He circled the car once, searching for what, I wasn't sure, then removed a set of car keys from his pocket, clicked a remote button, and a beat later the indicator lights on the Camry flared bright and there was a ragged quadruple thunk as the locks disengaged. He walked to the passenger door and held it open, bent at the waist, beckoning to me like a chauffeur.

'You're the cop,' he said, 'you can do the breaking-and-entering.'

I didn't argue with him. I stepped forward and lowered myself down onto the seat, awkward without the use of my hands. The interior of the car smelled like a mix of air freshener and cough drops and aftershave. Pristine, though; nothing in the foot wells, no loose paper or food containers. No mud transfers from dirty shoes. I opened the glove box. It was empty save for a set of printed documents; a rental agreement from Hertz. The lease on the vehicle had become active the previous Thursday. It was due to expire two days from now. The header at the top of the page stated that the car had been collected from Auckland International Airport, and the signature at the bottom had been written hurriedly but legibly: M Smith.

'It's a rental,' I said. 'They picked it up from the airport.'

He grunted, maybe in disinterest, maybe because he'd guessed as much already. I leaned forward and checked the map pocket in the door, then ran a hand along the lower edge of the seat squab. Nothing but dust.

I said, 'I don't think they would've been dense enough

to leave something potentially inflammatory behind.'

He glanced down at me, his attention momentarily pulled from the street. 'You want me to keep my fingers crossed anyway?'

'You're a riot.'

I checked the glove compartment a second time for the sake of thoroughness, then opened the CD holder in the central console. There was a cellular telephone, and a key attached to a plain plastic luggage tag arranged neatly inside, one on top of the other. I reached in gingerly with my thumb and first finger and removed the key by its tag, angling it towards the light from the open door. The key itself was completely unremarkable, but the plastic attachment bonded to it with a length of twine bore the words *Hideaway Palms* in clear uppercase vivid marker across one side. I raised it for Hale to see.

'That's the universe getting even with you,' he said. 'Punishing you for your pessimism.'

'Or rewarding me for my unrelenting thoroughness.'

I passed the card to him, reached back in for the cellphone and began my inspection. It was a silver Nokia, a couple of years old, recent enough to have a camera lens built into the rear face. The keys were so small and spaced so tightly, a person with wide fingers could potentially depress all of them at once. I powered the thing up and navigated through the menu screens until I located CONTACTS. The directory was empty. I found my way back to the main screen and punched the key for redial, but was rewarded with nothing other than a message informing me the phone's physical memory had been purged.

'Anything?' Hale said.

I shook my head. 'They left it sterile.'

He cupped the key in two hands and tapped the luggage label absent-mindedly against the top of the doorframe. 'What's Hideaway Palms?'

I placed the phone back in the compartment and closed the lid. 'Accommodation, most likely.'

'Hotel?'

'Sounds more like a tacky motor lodge.'

I leaned across the console and popped the boot-release lever, then climbed out and walked around to the rear of the vehicle and lifted the lid. The space inside was occupied by a pair of leather duffel bags, one large and one small, pushed tight against the rear wall.

'I think I found their luggage,' I said.

The sound of the door closing and feet on the concrete then Hale was beside me, leaning into the recess. He pulled the large duffel towards him across the carpet and opened the zip, gripping the metal tab through the material of his shirt. He paused a brief second, then pulled the flaps wide, tilting the opening towards me so the objects inside were clearly visible: The bag was full of guns.

'I guess they were expecting someone to fight back,' I said.

Hale made no response. He reached inside and sifted gently through the contents, using the backs of his hands so as not to deposit a fingerprint, heavy polished metal chiming faintly.

'Serial numbers have been burned off,' he said.

'What are they?'

He stretched the aperture wider and bent closer. 'Couple of pistols; a Glock and an SIG, two cut-down shotguns.'

I leaned forward and slid the smaller duffel towards me then hefted it onto the drive at my feet and unzipped it. It was an expensive piece, carefully segregated by internal pockets. I checked each of them and discovered close to ten thousand dollars in mixed bills, two Australian passports, and two creased black leather wallets. I checked the passports first. They informed me that the short blond man who had visited my home was named Shaun Rayner, and his tall bald companion Lee Thoms. I checked the wallets and recovered Australian driver's licences which reinforced the first conclusion.

A truck passed and Hale's eyes flicked back to the street. 'The IDs are fakes,' he said. 'The passports are probably genuine serial numbers registered with the government, made to false names. Very elaborate.'

'Any thoughts?'

'I think I took out a pair of contract killers.'

I closed the bag and dropped it back in the boot, slamming the lid. 'Got a phone book with you?'

We returned the Camry to the state we had found it in then walked back to the Escort and slid inside. Hale brought up the Yellow Pages website on his cellphone.

'Two listings,' he said, after a minute of hushed searching. 'There's a Hideaway Palms in Newmarket and also on Great South Road.'

I nodded. Clouds were low on the horizon; their undersides blurred by rainfall. 'They picked the car up in Mangere,' I said. 'It's likely they flew in, grabbed the car, looked for somewhere to lay up.'

'Which would make the place on Great South Road

the most obvious choice, in terms of convenience.'

'Have they listed a description?' I said.

'No, just the name, and the phone number.'

I said nothing. He pocketed his phone, then turned and looked at me before placing a hand on the ignition. 'To Great South Road, then?'

'Take it away.'

The Hideaway Palms motel turned out to be a somewhat appealing single-level establishment located on a side road branching west off Great South Road in Manukau. We arrived there at a little before eleven in the morning, after a brief journey through light traffic watched over by heavy clouds which, thankfully, only went as far as threatening to disgorge their contents.

The street was a mix of residential and commercial development: there was a Mobil station located directly opposite the motel, with a bakery occupying the adjacent unit. The remainder of the street was housing; drab and unexciting, largely in demand of basic maintenance.

The Hideaway Palms was marked at the roadside by a large square billboard elevated on a power pole, and Hale turned into the mouth of the driveway beneath it, coasting in neutral onto the property. The motel building itself was a simple, rectangular structure of about twenty or twenty-five rooms, oriented perpendicular to the road, floating amidst half a hectare of tarmac. Reception was housed in the nearest unit, its location announced by a simple placard hanging from the guttering. I counted a grand total of five cars, all of which were parked outside rooms in the closer half of the building. A sandwich board erected just beyond reception's door advertised vacancies.

Hale cut the engine and brought us to a halt with the Escort's grille just short of the sandwich board, and ratcheted the brake. The Reception door stood open invitingly, and we slid out and trooped across the little concrete porch and went inside. It was a small space, large for a hotel bathroom maybe, but tiny by anything else's standards. The air smelled of aerosol freshener, and the floor was lino. A pair of threadbare armchairs were situated to the right, an old Sony CRT television to the left and a desk directly ahead with a bored-looking young man of about twenty-five seated behind it. He had a sheaf of paperwork and an open can of Diet Coke in front of him. His weight was forward on his elbows, and he looked up as we entered, his head rising slowly, as if our presence was an intrusion. He could probably tell we weren't interested in a room. He had dark hair reaching his shoulders, and wore a faded T-shirt with a picture of Neil Young plastered across the front. He remained silent as we approached the desk, clearly preferring that either Hale or I initiate the conversation.

I brought out my badge from my coat pocket and opened it long enough for it to register with him, and when he still chose to remain quiet, I took the key out of my trouser pocket and laid it in front of him, next to the Coke can.

'I found this,' I said. 'I think it's yours.'

He made a face, contorting his nose, inhaling wetly through one nostril. His eyes dropped to the desk, then swivelled vertically and found mine, then shifted to Hale. There was an open door behind him which might have led into an adjoining office. 'No,' he said, with a wry smile, 'I think it belongs to the motel.'

'You work for the motel, it's yours by association. It was issued to two guys who checked in sometime late last week.'

His expression remained flat, neither denying nor confirming my statement. He picked up the stack of papers in front of him, held them upright and tapped them gently on his lap to get them square, before depositing them in a desk drawer that was invisible from our side of the room.

He looked at me benignly and raised his eyebrows.

'And?' he said.

'Excuse me?'

'Obviously you want to know something about them.' There was boredom in his voice. Not a tone I was unfamiliar with. People think a show of boredom presents an image of rebellion. Police officers get rebellion a lot.

'When did they check in?' I said.

He gave a shrug, reached across his chest with his right arm and pulled at the seam of his shirt, making Neil Young's face warp. 'I don't know.'

'Can you check the register?'

His eyes left mine and went to Hale's, then back to mine. He raised the Coke can and inverted it above his open mouth, one eye staying with me as he drank. He swallowed audibly then placed the can down slowly, calling flatly, 'Michelle, come here a sec.'

There was a brief silence, then from the adjoining room came the sound of a chair spring slowly decompressing, before a young woman clutching a baby to her chest emerged through the open doorway and shuffled towards the desk. She was perhaps twenty-eight or twenty-nine, but the lines in her face meant she could have been mistaken for a lot older. She was wearing a faded Nike T-shirt which was too big for her, and jeans she probably had to struggle to get into. The guy with the Coke twisted in his seat and looked up at her, and she gave him an apologetic expression and tried to offer him the child.

'Sorry, Owen, could you take him?'

He turned back to the desk, disgust in his face. 'Hell, no. It's probably carrying something.'

He laughed once and glanced at me, seeking my approval, but didn't find it. Hale stepped forward and reached across the counter.

'I'll take him,' he said.

The woman called Michelle shot him a thankful look, her cheeks blushing, then passed the infant quickly to him. 'He has to be held,' she said. 'If somebody's not hanging on to him, he just cries and cries.'

Hale smiled. The child turned his head towards him, mouth ajar, eyes wide, marvelling at the unfamiliar face, then grasped Hale's neck, tucking his head beneath his chin. Michelle blew an errant strand of air off her face then bent low and slid something dense off a shelf below the desk, placing a buff register on the counter.

'Sorry,' she said. 'Normally the records are all on computer, but the program's been giving me hell, we have to use a book.'

'That's fine,' I said.

She turned, seemingly noticing me for the first time. 'Who were you after?' she asked.

'Two guys,' I said. 'Mid-thirties, one very small, the other very tall.'

She'd been in the process of opening the ledger, but she left it alone following my description.

'They checked in Monday,' she said.

'You're sure?'

She nodded. 'Tall bald guy, short guy with a blond ponytail.'

'Have you seen them since they arrived?'

'I don't think so. I think they left Tuesday morning.'

'How did they pay?'

'Cash. When they checked in.'

'Is the room still vacant?' Hale asked.

The man called Owen looked up and said, 'What is this, twenty questions?'

Hale said nothing. The child squirmed slightly against his grip and resettled in his arms, but didn't cry. The woman's cheeks turned a deeper shade of red, embarrassed by her colleague's behaviour, and looked between Hale and me. 'No, sorry,' she said. 'It's re-allocated. It's the only one with a working Sky receiver.'

303

'Did they leave anything in the room?' I asked.

She shook her head. I looked at Owen. 'Did you take anything from the room?'

He flicked his head to clear his hair off his face. 'Get lost,' he said.

'Yes or no, or I'll make you eat the book.'

'No, then. Jeez.'

He drank from the can again, still keeping one eye on me as he did so. I looked at the woman. 'Were any calls made from the room?'

She opened the register, standing side-on to the desk so that her hip wasn't in contact with Owen's arm, turning pages vigorously, running fingers down neat columns of printed text. Her inner forearms were webbed with a network of long-since-healed scar tissue. She paused a brief moment then flipped to the last page; a clear plastic protector. She removed a single sheet of A4 paper and laid it on the countertop, rotating it under her fingers so that the data printed across it was legible from where I stood. Her nails were long and pink and perfectly rounded; probably false.

'Computer registered one incoming call, at seven on Tuesday morning,' she said. 'Nineteen seconds long, didn't bill for it though. We only do outgoing.'

Her nail slid to the base of the page, to a line where a single set of nine digits, constituting a mobile phone number, was typed.

'Can I keep this?' I asked.

'No,' Owen said.

She took her hand back and smiled shyly. 'Yeah, sure.'

I folded the paper once and pocketed it, and Hale raised the small child off his chest and passed him delicately across the counter back to the woman named Michelle. He gave her a wink and exited the room then walked back across the porch to the Escort and climbed in. Owen watched him, then raised the Coke can, took a sip and placed it back in front of him on the desk. I pointed to it.

'That finished?' I asked.

He glanced up. 'No.'

I picked it up and drained the contents on his head then tossed the empty can in his lap and headed out the door.

■ THIRTY

We drove out of the neighbourhood onto Great South Road, and when we found the motorway and turned north I said, 'I need you to check that number for me.'

He inspected his reflection in the mirror, his face speckled by settled water on the windshield. 'You can't do it yourself?'

'I'd rather stay under the radar for now.'

He touched his chin contemplatively. 'You're not going to report the car?'

'Not just yet.'

He shot me a glance, removed his phone from his pocket and dialled a pre-programmed number. I passed him the document I had been given and he trapped the phone with his shoulder and read the page quickly, eyes darting between it and the road. He delivered a set of short, barely audible instructions then hung up and tossed the phone to me.

'The guy at work's on it,' he said. 'It's a database job, no more than ten minutes.'

'Less if he's not slacked off and has his computer on already.'

He passed back the paper. 'Longer than eleven minutes, I'll tell him he's fired.'

As it turned out though, the guy's job was saved: nine minutes from the time Hale ended the call to when his phone buzzed in my lap. I answered it myself.

'Give me good news.'

There was a short silence, either because the guy had been surprised by the unfamiliar voice, or he wasn't quite sure what would constitute good news.

'The number's private,' he said. 'I got it through the Telecom database.'

'Did you find a name?'

'Stephen Hyam,' the guy said.

'I'll throw in some extra brownie points if you've found specifics.'

'Land Information reckons he's got a place in Westfield.' He gave me the street address.

'OK.'

'Like, between Mount Wellington Highway and the southern motorway.'

I thanked him and hung up. Hale glanced at me.

'Any luck?' he said.

I nodded. 'Get off at the next exit.'

Stephen Hyam's address was found after ten minutes' travel in the opposite direction. The neighbourhood was shabby, unimaginative and claustrophobic. Roofing was damaged, weeds were sprouting, the remains of a bonfire served as the centrepiece of the cul-de-sac where the road truncated ten metres short of State Highway One. There was a construction site further west; acres of naked yellow earth, stacks of bound timber, prefabricated concrete-wall structures. No activity though. Development seemed to have halted. Maybe financial backing had dwindled.

The address we had been given corresponded to a plain, double-level unit two doors shy of the bonfire remnants. It was essentially a glorified cube: the upper storey was drab green with a pair of windows, while half the lower level was occupied by a garage to the left, the right-hand side shielded by a head-high wooden fence.

The door on the garage was up, and there were two

men in their late twenties working on the stripped-down chassis of what had once been a Mazda RX-7.

Hale paused at the kerb and put the Escort in neutral. Two heads turned our way. Grey above us, mist on the windscreen.

'What do you want to do?' he said.

I didn't reply for a beat. 'Which one do you think is Stephen Hyam?'

Silence for a long moment before he replied. 'Neither of them.'

I glanced at him questioningly.

'They both look familiar,' he said. 'Bells are ringing, from way back.'

I turned back to the garage. Neither of the men was engaged in his previous task, and the general vibe I was receiving wasn't a positive one. Both were clad in jeans and T-shirts. I could see tattoos indicating prison time.

'Were you all in the same church choir?' I asked.

He shook his head. 'The phrase *breaking-and-entering* springs to mind.'

'Pull into the driveway,' I said. 'We need to make an impression. Find out where our buddy Stephen might be.'

He put the car back in gear and let the brake off.

'They look hard-case,' I said.

He swung in past the letterbox and stopped the car three metres short of the Mazda's rear bumper. 'That's all right. So do we.'

He turned the engine off and pushed open his door; I waited a brief second and climbed out into the mist. No hello from the two guys. They eased around the body of the Mazda with the sort of confident fluidity bouncers display, and stood shoulder-to-shoulder in front of its rear bumper, arms folded, as if they'd been told that one day trouble would come knocking, and that they'd better be ready. Disregarding the obvious similarities presented by their attire, they were both vaguely alike. They had that lean, slightly drawn and rangy look underfed rodents sometimes exhibit. The guy to the left had a picture of Bruce Springsteen on his shirt, while his friend's bore the slogan *If you take a swing, I'll take one, too.* Springsteen surveyed us both with interest, but the guy on the right had eyes only for Hale. His mouth fractured at the corners, then pulled back into a grin of complete recognition.

'Shit,' he said. 'John Hale?'

'How you doing, Sally?' Hale said.

The man called Sally shrugged and glanced at Springsteen. 'We're getting by, John, we're getting by.' He nodded at the Escort. 'What is that, an eighty-one?'

Hale smiled. 'Seventy-nine, Sally,' he said.

'Seventy-nine,' Sally breathed, and shook his head. Springsteen smiled.

'Who's your buddy, John?' Sally said. 'He a cop, too?'

Hale smiled again. 'I'm not a cop anymore, Sally.'

'Well, shit. You're outta the life, John?'

'I'm outta the life, Sally. Who's your buddy? I think we may have met.'

'His real name's Chris, but most of us just call him Springsteen. Can you guess why, John?'

'I can speculate, Sally.'

Sally shared a look with his companion and his smile extended, displaying a rather mismatched dental structure, then looked skywards into the grey coolness with the sort of appreciation that made me think he thought it was just grand to be alive. He waited for an old Bongo van laden down with scrap steel to cruise to the end of the cul-de-sac and back before he said, 'What can I help you with?'

'We're looking for a cellphone,' I said.

Sally's gaze dropped to me. 'I'm talking to John. Don't open your mouth again, kiddo.'

I stared at him evenly, hoping my calm would in some way unsettle him, but his expression was empty.

'We're looking for a cellphone, Sally,' Hale said.

Sally glanced at him, apparently surprised. 'Is that so, John?'

Hale nodded. 'The phone belongs to a chap named Stephen Hyam,' he said. 'I know this is his address. Sally, you don't think you could tell me whether or not Stephen is in, could you?'

Sally dropped his arms to his sides, then folded them again, exhaled and looked sideways at his companion before bending slightly at the knees, turning and calling back towards the open garage: 'Steve, are you in?'

There was a lengthy pause. Silence out on the drive. Sally held his position, an expression of hopeful anticipation pasted on his face. Then, the word 'no' was heard quite clearly, shouted from within the depths of the lower storey.

Sally turned back to us. He spread his arms wide, apology in his eyes. 'Look, sorry, John, he's unavailable. Why don't you try back some other time?'

Hale paused. He looked at Sally, looked at Springsteen, looked in at the garage. The car was chocked up off its tyres, power tools and wrenches and plastic extension cords scattered on the concrete floor beneath it. Against the walls were built-in metal storage units supporting plastic boxes of screws and woodworking saws and a half-dozen or so vehicle licence plates.

'This is important, Sally,' he said.

'I'm sure it is, John, but this really isn't a good time.' He kept at the smile. 'You got a problem, kiddo?' Question directed at me.

I waited. 'I was wondering if your mum could make me a T-shirt like that, too.'

He made no reply, just stepped forward and raised his foot and kicked out the front right headlight on the Escort. Heavy steel-capped boot, light plastic shielding, instant result.

He stepped back.

'I told you not to open your mouth,' he said. 'I guess that makes for a good lesson though, doesn't it? Sorry about the car, John.'

Hale said nothing. His eyes were moving; the rest of him was still like lake water. 'Let us in, Sally,' he said at length. Quieter than dust settling. 'Or there's going to be fucking hell to pay.'

John Hale doesn't swear very often.

Sally seemed to consider that. He glanced at Springsteen, as if weighing up what Hale had just told him. 'No,' he said eventually. 'John, I think you can piss off. If you

313

could move that piece of shit off the drive it'd be great, too. I'm about to give my beast a fresh coat of the red.'

Hale looked at him a moment longer and said nothing. Then he glanced down at the shards of plastic on the concrete beside him and turned and climbed back into the Escort and started the engine. I waited a beat then slid in beside him and he backed the car out on to the street.

Hale didn't speak to me until we were stationary again. He rolled along the cul-de-sac, swung behind the dead bonfire and shut the engine off then coasted for a few metres, bringing us to a halt in a position slightly south-east of the property we had just visited. Springsteen and Sally stood watching us for a minute, and when they turned and went back inside the garage, Hale took the keys out of the ignition and pocketed them then sank back in his seat as if in retrospective contemplation of recent events.

'Sorry about the light,' I said.

'Don't worry about it. The universe gets even. It prefers equilibrium.'

'It's constantly expanding. It can't be in equilibrium.'

'If you take the geometrical centre as a datum, the net motion is approximately zero.'

I didn't reply. He stretched forward suddenly and

removed something from beneath his seat and pocketed it. 'The guy's definitely on-site,' he said.

'I know. But we're not.'

He looked across at me and opened his door and winked. 'Move on my signal,' he said.

'What?'

And then he slid out and slammed his door, removing his cellphone and dialling as he did so.

Hale jogged until he was clear of the target address. He was happy for them to believe he was parked at the kerb across the street, idly watching, but he didn't want what he was truly intending to become evident.

The call he placed lasted only half a minute. He closed his phone, pocketed it and walked easy, just watching, observing the rhythm of the neighbourhood. Not that there was a rhythm. Noon on a weekday, not much for him to observe. Conversely, not much to observe him, either. Which was always a benefit. There was a handful of parked cars, no one else to share the footpath with. He glanced left and right as he walked, but as far as he could determine, he attracted no attention. Nothing inherently curious about a man passing by on the street. Just a mundane suburban scene. Nobody was going to think twice about him.

At a brisk walk, he soon reached the construction site and came to a casual halt. He could hear the constant mechanical hush of cars moving north and south, away to the east. The breeze was gentle, hesitant about causing discomfort. He turned slowly where he stood and examined the temporary roadside fencing. Thick, greasy automobile tracks streaked beneath it, connecting tarseal with barren clay. Clearly this had been an access point. Vehicle entry was facilitated by a gated section in the wire fencing, secured by a long length of heavy-duty chain locked with a bronzed padlock. The padlock was branded proudly across its face: *ABUS*. A frequent nemesis. Hale was used to keyless entry. He removed the pouch from his pocket, selected a hairpin, and kept his attention around him as he worked on freeing the mechanism.

He left the chain and lock in a neat little pile then lifted the gate off its support bracket and swung it squeaking back in a wide arc. The hinge had been designed in such a manner that the gate could open a full one-hundred-and-eighty degrees, leaving a gap almost four metres wide.

He wiped his hands across the front of his shirt to clear the moisture he had picked up off the metal, rubbed down the metallic surfaces he had touched with his sleeve, and moved onto the site with as much authority and nonchalance as he could muster. First conclusion was that the place was a shambles. It struck him that development had been started with decisiveness and rigour, then suddenly postponed. Or abandoned. To his right was a cluster of three control offices. Temporary rectangular structures trucked in to serve as on-site management facilities for foremen or engineers or developers, or whoever it was that oversaw general labour.

Dead ahead of him was where the bulk of the activity had taken place: a twenty-metre square of smooth grey concrete, boxed in with plywood support and thick columnar pieces of steel sunk into the yellow earth.

To the left was where the heavy machinery had been left. Front-end loaders, a concrete mixer, a grader, three dump-trucks. The concrete mixer appealed to him. It had bull bars. A printed notice above the right front wheel dictated that the gross laden weight should not exceed 13.9 tonnes. It bore the name of a large, well-known, financially secure construction firm, whose logo was also present on the centremost of the three site offices. He knew the firm was financially secure to the extent that a stolen concrete truck would not represent too great a financial deficit. Big firms have insurance.

He walked to the mixer, stretched up and tried the

door handle, lifting it with the backs of his fingers so as not to leave a print. Locked. For it to be open would have been too convenient. He stepped away and moved across the scalloped earth to the temporary office. The twin windows either side of the entrance were shielded by cages of steel rebar; the front door was the only feasible option as far as access was concerned. He pushed down on the handle with the back of his fist, but it didn't yield. He delved into his pocket again and removed the pouch. Heavier lock this time, the hairpin would be outclassed: he chose a fine flat-head screwdriver and a dental scaler.

Lock-picking is simple in practice: a lock opens when the half-dozen or so pins or tumblers oriented vertically within the barrel arrange themselves in such a manner as to allow the inner section of the lock to rotate within its housing. Alignment of the tumblers is achieved via careful application of a long, thin instrument, such as a dental scaler. The torque necessary to provide the rotation can be achieved with a flat-head screwdriver.

Hale had the lock open inside four minutes. He was wary of the fact there could be internal motion sensors, but figured that even if someone was dispatched to investigate his presence, he would be long gone before they arrived. He pushed the door back, returned his tools to his pocket and peered inside. The smell of the place suggested it hadn't been exposed to fresh air for several days Weeks, perhaps. There was a desk running along the adjacent wall, littered with paper. Topographic maps, geo-technical reports. Documentation generally associated with the process of building something. There was a squat little fridge at the left end of the opposite wall, with a filing cabinet beside it.

He found the keys to the mixer on a pegboard above the desk. They were attached to a large plastic tag bearing the truck's licence-plate number in bold vivid marker. Convenient, as far as thievery was concerned.

He pulled the door of the office closed behind him as he exited and strolled easily back to the mixer. He unlocked the door, hauled himself up into the driver's seat and shut himself in. He had driven trucks in the army. The process was not unfamiliar. He jiggled the stick into neutral, inserted the key in the ignition and twisted it once, feeling the cold motor turn over twice, then a third time, then catch on the fourth try. The dash lit up and a little graphic informed him he had half a tank of diesel. He smiled. More than sufficient for a trip to the end of the street, even if the thing did weigh fourteen tonnes.

■ THIRTY-ONE

I saw the concrete truck swing out onto the road. It was an immense vehicle. I could virtually feel the reverberation of the turbo, even across a couple of hundred metres of bitumen. It straightened up in the approaching lane and accelerated, a thick black stream of carcinogenic smoke vomiting up from the exhaust. I knew Hale was driving. I had seen him enter the site. The logic leap was not great.

Sally and Springsteen had jacked the Mazda down off its blocks and rolled it out into the driveway. Now it was just parked there, red and naked and vulnerable. Springsteen and Sally were inside the garage. From where I was sitting, the angle was too sharp to see them.

Hale was driving slowly. It took him nearly half a minute to close the distance. He swung the truck out into the centre of the road to open his approach angle. The big vehicle listed under the cornering force, engine roaring in protest at the choice of low gear.

Concrete mixers and other heavy vehicles are instinctively regarded as cumbersome, clumsy machines, but for all their brutish inelegance, this truck hopped the kerb into the front of Stephen Hyam's property with surprising grace. It was probably doing thirty-five when it broadsided the RX-7 with a near supersonic smack, but speed alone is not what dictates the outcome of automobile impacts. Generally speaking, momentum is of most interest. Numerically, it's a simple quantity to obtain: mass times velocity. The truck wasn't going all that quick, but it weighed a lot. Hence, the resulting contact was considerable.

The mixer accelerated the Mazda to twenty in about half a second. It took maybe another two-and-a-half to skid it sideways across the concrete and bordering strip of lawn then through the fence and into the front yard. At some point the friction acting laterally on the RX-7's tyres reached a critical peak, resulting in the red sports car flipping onto its roof. I heard a series of sequential crunches which were probably windows exploding.

I wasted maybe a second-and-a-half sitting idle in

surprise. It was hard not to. Fast action often proves difficult after sudden catastrophe. I was quick to recover, though.

I climbed out of the car and ran across the street, just as Springsteen and Sally were emerging from the garage. Emotionally, they were still at the disbelief stage. A concrete truck appearing in the middle of your front yard and taking half your fence is a rare event. I don't think they even noticed me.

I ducked into the garage. There was a doorway built into the right-hand wall, providing access to the main house. I stepped through it into a short entry area and came face-to-face with a short, heavy man of about my age. He had been in the process of opening the front door, but when he saw me he stopped completely. Surprise in his face initially, followed quickly by confusion. The prospect of an uninvited guest surprises most people, but when the uninvited guest is wearing a suit, it gives them pause. It's all very well beating the shit out of an intruder, but a phenomenal waste of effort if it's only a Jehovah's Witness on a local recruiting effort.

I took advantage of the guy's hesitation to check the area: the front door he had been about to pass through was to my immediate right, a set of stairs led up to the left, beyond it the corridor extended out of sight.

'Stephen Hyam?' I said.

'Yeah, who are you?' He was wearing a pair of dark-blue swimming trunks that reached his mid-thigh, and a threadbare blue-and-green rugby jersey of a team I didn't recognize.

'Police,' I said.

He frowned. The skin on his forehead was soft, and the resulting creases looked like a street map of central Paris. 'You can't just—'

I got between him and the door and gave him a gentle push in the chest that got him sitting down on the bottom step of the stairs.

His breath left him quickly and he glared up at me with the same expression he probably used on people who cut in front of him at the Lotto counter. 'Did you just push me?'

'I did. I'm sorry we couldn't just have a civilized chat, but Sally wouldn't let me in.'

He stared up at me, irritation being forced out by confusion. I took the document I had obtained at the motel out of my coat pocket, smoothed it and passed it to him. He accepted it, kept his eyes with me.

'I need to make this quick, Steve,' I said. 'There's a

concrete mixer parked on your lawn, so I'd really like to skedaddle before too long, if you catch my drift.'

He just looked up at me, comprehension evading him.

'Read the paper,' I said.

He looked down and read the paper.

'You recognize that number, Steve?'

'Yeah, I—'

'Is it yours?'

His eyes flicked across the page a couple of times and the creases in his brow grew in number so that they looked more like downtown Manhattan. 'Did you say there's a concrete mixer outside?'

'Stephen, is the number yours?'

'Yeah, but I—'

'Tell me why you dialled that motel, Stephen.'

'I didn't!'

'You just told me it was your number!'

'It is, but I don't have the phone.'

I looked down at him without saying anything. Outside it was curiously quiet. I worked hard to keep my voice level.

'And the dog used to eat your homework a lot, too, did it, Stephen?'

'What the hell, man? I told you I don't have it.'

He thought about trying to stand up, but saw the look on my face and decided against it.

'So who does have it, Stephen? Who the *fuck* has been making calls on it?'

'I don't know! Who *are* you?'

I stepped forward and snatched the paper back from him. 'Why don't you have the phone, Stephen?'

'Because it was *taken*!' His eyebrows raised in exasperation and his brow rippled.

'By who?'

'Jesus, I dunno. Cops. It was like, a search warrant. They took stuff—'

'What?'

I could hear shouting outside in the yard. I wondered irrelevantly whether the truck had been carrying a payload.

'This is like two weeks ago,' he said. 'They had paperwork, they took a whole pile of shit off me, said it was evidence or something, they took my phone.'

'Do you have the receipt?'

'What?'

'They would have given you an inventory of everything they took. The inventory would have been signed by a police officer. I need the police officer's name.'

He shook his head. 'I don't have anything like that.'

'Heavens above. So what was the cop's name, Stephen?'

'Shit, I dunno.'

'Think!' I hissed.

He looked around, panicky, like the answer was hanging in the air somewhere. Then recollection dawned in his eyes, followed quickly by the relief that maybe he'd be OK after all. 'The guy's name was Donald,' he said. 'Yeah, Christ, it was Burke Donald. He pinched my phone.'

■ THIRTY-TWO

I didn't waste any further time. I walked straight out the front door and onto the drive. Springsteen and Sally were in the yard, backs to me. They were still pondering the oddity presented by the mixer. Sally was pondering in a more exasperated fashion. Both his hands were linked behind his head. Springsteen was on the receiving end of some colourful language. Through the gap in the fence I could see the driver's door of the mixer hanging open. No Hale.

I stepped out into the street and saw him in the Escort, waiting patiently at the roadside forty metres west. I closed the distance at a sprint, leapt in beside him and he was off before my door was even closed.

'Shit, John,' I said.

327

He didn't answer. He just drove. Quickly.

'We could be in trouble,' I said. 'There could be comeback.'

'There won't be. I made a call.'

'You made a call?'

'They had a stack of licence plates in the garage. At least one of them is stolen.'

'Well golly, that's OK, then.'

'They won't want anyone taking too close a look at whatever they're doing there.'

I said nothing. I hoped his logic would stand up. Hale braked for a turn and swung hard and opened the throttle again. 'So what happened?' he said.

'The guy had no knowledge of the call,' I said. 'Because Burke Donald had his phone. Burke Donald called the men who tried to kidnap Grace's boy.'

Hale made no reply to that. He was tense all the way back to the motorway.

We were back at my place just before two in the afternoon. Light rain, though the cloud had receded to the point where blue sky was actually partly visible. Hale left the Escort under the Norfolk pine and we went inside to the kitchen where I flicked on the stove for warmth. Hale went to the fridge and took out another beer.

'You drink like a fish,' I said.

He stood leaning against the edge of the sink, the same position he had adopted when Nielsen and Donald had visited, and inclined the bottle towards me. 'Hydrates you faster. And nothing beats a Heineken.'

I pulled out a chair and sat down, the table bridging the gap between us. He rolled open a drawer, removed a bottle opener and popped the cap on the beer so it fell free and clattered into the sink.

'You're going to need a face-lift one day,' he said.

I nodded my admission, consciously un-furrowing my brow. 'Give me a reason why a police detective would want to have my neighbour's son kidnapped.'

He took a pull, swilled the liquid around in his cheeks like mouthwash before swallowing. 'Money,' he said simply. 'It's the ultimate motive for everything.'

'Thanks, you've made things so much clearer.'

He put the bottle down again but said nothing. I pushed my chair back, but didn't get to my feet. I pressed my hands to my face and exhaled into my palms. The skin across my cheeks was hot and throbbing gently. 'Alan Nielsen won't get off my case,' I said. 'I can't help but think he must be up to his elbows in shit, too.'

He said nothing.

I lowered my hands and looked at him. Behind him the window was showing uninterrupted blue. I got up and took a pack of cigarettes from the cutlery drawer, lit one, then used my cell to call Leon Ross.

'Leon, it's Sean Devereaux,' I said when he answered. 'Do you owe me any favours?'

I could sense him trying to think. 'Not that I'm aware of. I could be good for one, though.'

'I need you to cross-reference the name Burke Donald with Lionel Moss.'

A pause. 'In case-records?'

'In whatever, yeah.'

The pause again. I blew smoke at the window, watching the plumes unravel. 'It could take me a while,' he said.

'That's fine, but I do need you to look. Is that OK?'

Quiet from his end. 'What's going on, Sean?'

'Two guys tried to kidnap my neighbour's son. I think Donald asked them to.'

A soft release of breath from his end. 'Give me until morning.'

No questions, no disbelief. Complete and immediate acceptance.

'Thanks, man.'

'Don't mention it.'

I put the phone down and looked at Hale. He was nearly done with the beer

'A penny for your thoughts?' he said.

I blew a smoke ring across the room. It was poorly formed, dissolving halfway across the table. 'Moss and the two guys who visited on Tuesday are part of the same thing: someone, probably Burke Donald, according to the phone record we just recovered, recruited them to snatch Michael.'

He offered no response, and as always, it was impossible to decide whether this implied he agreed with my reasoning, or whether he saw some glaring and potentially debilitating flaw. I looked at him a second longer, then I walked outside to finish my smoke.

I called the desk at Auckland Central and obtained Donald's address from the duty guy. I told him I needed it because I was dropping off golf clubs. Not strictly true. We set out for his home at five p.m. dead, when the city to the west was a myriad of yellow lights and the darkening greyness above was webbed with lightning, returning the world to daylight for glimpses at a time.

We drove into town and took Nelson Street down to

Wellington then linked up with Williamson Avenue, which we followed all the way southwest into the suburbs.

Burke Donald lived on a wide, secluded street lined with elm trees and five-year-old BMWs. The houses were on thin elongated sites and were predominantly two- and three-bedroom villas, some of which had probably seen better days, but I knew the proximity to town would mean anything in the area would come with a hefty price tag. Donald's home was a well-kept post war design with a porch and a pitched tile roof. The south wall facing the street consisted of a large bay window with a front door tucked in beside it. His property was narrow, barely wide enough to accommodate the width of the driveway which reached up from the roadside to a simple open-end carport. There was a battered red Saab parked inside and a light was on behind the bay window.

Hale drove past once then pulled a U-turn further up the street and cruised back, parking on the opposite side of the road beneath a streetlight, raindrops swirling yellow around us.

'You just want to walk up and knock on his door?' he said.

I twisted against my belt, just as the clouds above were

split by a sheet of electricity. 'Were you considering an alternative method of entry?'

He said nothing and looked out through his window at the house across the street. The trees along the footpaths looked skeletal without leaf coverage; emaciated shadows traced against the road. I opened my door, pulled my collar up against the wet and walked across the street, Hale following a moment later. The bay window to the left of the front door was curtained over from behind, and the light wasn't powerful enough to cast a shadow if anyone was moving. There was a cast-iron weather vane, a rooster, rotating slowly inside a steel collar bolted to the roofline. It made a squeal like a fingernail on aluminium. I stopped still a moment and stood in the driveway, hoping to be able to hear something above the rainfall, but I caught nothing. A moment later I sensed Hale at my shoulder.

'Window's broken,' he said.

'What?'

'Rear window on the car, it's cracked.'

I looked as he'd directed, at the rear windshield on the red Saab parked beneath the shelter. In the poor light, it was barely noticeable that it was webbed with fractures; I was amazed he'd managed to pick up on it at all. We

333

moved closer, me sending regular glances in the direction of the lit window in an attempt to catch movement. The Saab was a well-used vehicle; low on its suspension, with dented bodywork and tyres that were partially deflated. The paint was chipped and one of the tail-lights had been shattered at some stage. It had a peeling green bumper sticker slicked next to the tow bar which read: *GE FREE NZ!* Its rear window was damaged because somebody had shot at it with a firearm. There were six bullet holes clustered in the top right-hand corner; slightly burred, with an elaborate network of fissures spreading across the entirety of the glass. I was speculating on how recent they were when I saw Burke Donald, slumped in the driver's seat.

I moved into the carport, raised my arms and eased down through cobwebs that clawed at my clothing, until I was level with the driver's door. I cupped my hands to the glass, but the glow from the streetlights was insufficient to provide a detailed view of the inside.

I called out to Hale: 'Got a torch?'

'Is he dead?'

'He's not asleep.'

'Hold on.'

I stood poised beside the battered red sedan, breathing

334

the musty odour of wood left to decompose, waiting for Hale to locate a torch. He returned a minute later and handed me a heavy plastic unit the size of a softball bat. I switched it on and directed the beam in through the window. Burke Donald hadn't anticipated the arrival of his death. He hadn't been trying to escape his car; he didn't appear to be scrabbling for his door handle or attempting to free a gun of his own. On the contrary, the keys were still in the ignition, his seatbelt was still fastened. It looked as if he'd turned in off the street, pulled to a stop, then somebody had stepped out of hiding and shot him. His eyes were wide, shining in the torch beam, and his mouth was slightly ajar, his moustache obscuring his top lip. The blood coating the seat behind him hadn't yet coagulated. He couldn't have been dead for more than thirty minutes. My head began to throb and I could feel my heart palpitating solidly.

I sidled out into the gloom and gave the torch back to Hale.

'He hasn't been dead long,' I said. 'I need you to check the area, in case whoever did him decided to hang around.'

'What are you going to do?'

'Look inside.'

His eyes went to the window, then back to my face. 'You need lock picks?'

'I'll break the door if it's locked.'

He turned wordlessly and started jogging towards the road. I watched him dissolve into the black, then flicked water out of my hair and walked towards the house, treading as lightly as I could. By now I was reasonably sure there was nobody inside, but it would be stupid not to be cautious. I stepped up onto his porch, wincing at the creak of the boards, hoping my roaring circulatory system was audible only to me. I sensed my breath coming shorter than it should have, and I inhaled deeply to try to calm down, then pulled my hand inside my sleeve and turned the handle on the front door.

It was unlocked.

I released it and toed the door fully open, slipping back into the gloom for a moment, confirming nobody was about to leap out and grab me, then stepped inside. Out on the street I heard the Escort's motor start as Hale pulled away from the kerb.

I checked the room behind the bay window first. It was a living area. Chairs, television, bookcase. Nothing turned over or thrown about; everything seemed undisturbed. There were paintings on his wall, mostly prints of work by Michael Smither. No photographs of family. Nothing really indicative of the presence of a wife or kids in his life. No toys or Barney DVDs or the smell of perfume.

I backtracked into the entry hall and moved through to his kitchen. Breakfast dishes in the sink, newspapers on the table. Nothing suggestive of the possibility he had orchestrated a plot to kidnap a ten-year-old boy. I checked his cupboards briefly, then did a quick walk-through of the bedroom and bathroom. Nothing appeared to be out of place. If whoever had killed Burke Donald had searched his home, he or she had done so with a degree of expertise, without leaving a trace.

I walked outside onto the porch and dialled Claire Bennett's cell number.

'I've got a dead one,' I said.

Quiet for a second. The sky cracked sharply. 'Who and where?'

'A cop named Burke Donald, at his home.' I gave her the street address. 'Are you still at the office?' I asked.

'Yeah, I'll send someone out.'

'I need you to come.'

My blood pressure thundered in the brief quiet.

'I'll be there shortly.'

337

I ended the call, stepped off the porch and walked down to the roadside to wait for the first of the patrol cars to arrive. I closed my eyes and squeezed my hands into fists, trying to counteract the shakes which inevitably follow an overdose of adrenaline.

The air was dense with the cold, and the wind was gusting a firm nor'easterly, which meant the first of the sirens carried to me while they were still minutes away. The first on scene was a blue-and-yellow Highway Patrol unit driven by a young guy in his early twenties. He slewed into the driveway so that his high-beams put the Saab in stark illumination, and climbed out without so much as a glance in my direction, heading inside the carport. He reappeared moments later, face pale, and I was certain his knees were unlocking slightly as he walked. He pulled his fluorescent yellow raincoat closer about himself, more I thought in an effort to rid himself of mental images than the cold, and stepped towards me.

'You made the call?' he said. There was a quaver to his voice, but I didn't think the cold was doing that either.

'Yeah.' I fumbled my badge out and held it up for him. 'I'm CIB.'

He nodded vacantly, then looked away over my shoulder as Hale's Escort reclaimed its spot at the kerb.

338

More patrol cars turned in at the eastern end of the road and halted in various places.

I said, 'The inside's secure, but I need you to do a loop of the outside, just check everything's OK. Set up a street cordon, start canvassing neighbours.'

'Who put you in charge?'

I ignored the question and stepped past him to his car and climbed into the back seat. The air-con was set to sauna and there was a takeaway bag of McDonald's resting on the passenger seat. Maybe I should consider swapping to Highway. The opposite door opened up and Hale slid inside, followed by a gust of chill.

'Anything?' I asked.

'Nothing. You?'

I shook my head.

'So what do you think?'

I gave a shrug. 'I think he came home and someone shot him in the back of the head before he had time to get out of his car.'

He nodded, his head turned away from me, watching the light in the drops on his window. I checked his hands, but they showed no sign of even a mild tremor. Calm. 'Weapon looked small-calibre,' he said. 'Not more than a point-two-two, probably the same gun used on Moss.'

'Did you see a shell casing?'

'No, I think they'll be lucky to find one.'

Silently, I agreed with him. We sat in the back of the patrol car watching the various crime-scene procedures gradually administered. The street was cordoned twenty metres east and west of the driveway, and emergency tape was strung across the mouth of the carport. Phone calls were made, and through the radio console mounted to the dash I heard a request for an ambulance and a Scene of Crime team, and finally, specialist technicians from Environmental Science and Research. Thirty minutes after I'd placed the call to Claire Bennett, the first people in suits showed up. Five minutes after that, Bennett herself emerged behind us on the driveway, hair plastered to her head as if she'd just stepped out of the shower. She exchanged a few words with the Highway cop in the raincoat, then walked up to the passenger door of our car and dropped inside, thumping the door closed.

She sat face-forward for a bit, perhaps gathering the necessary energy to engage the pair of us in conversation. At length she swivelled in her seat and pushed hair out of her eyes, producing a thin smile her eyes weren't a part of.

'How you doing, John?'

'Getting there,' Hale said. 'And yourself, Claire?'

Either she didn't hear the question, or chose to ignore it. She raised a drenched coat sleeve and wiped water off the tip of her nose. 'What have we got this time, Ranger?' she said to me, and there was a dry humour to her tone.

'Ranger?'

'You know. The Lone Ranger, and Tonto.'

'Cute.'

I gave her the situation as concisely as I could manage: Burke Donald, red Saab, shot through the head. Dead.

She looked at me a long moment, nothing in her face, as if her brain had simply decided it couldn't be bothered processing the details. At length she glanced away and wiped at her nose again then shook her head violently as if she was trying to clear water from her ear canals. 'You just turned up here on a whim?'

I looked at Hale, but his attention was elsewhere. The interior of the patrol car had turned stroboscopic, lit red and blue by so many different pairs of emergency lights it was almost a discomfort not to close my eyes.

I said, 'We followed a lead. He'd placed a call to the two men who attempted to abduct my neighbour's child the other night.'

She wiped her nose a third time and tried to involve Hale in the conversation by looking at him, but his consciousness was a long way away. She raised her hands to her face and rubbed her eyes and said quietly, 'Oh, shit, Sean. Start from the beginning.'

I did. I went right the way back to Saturday evening, when Grace had first visited me, and related her problem involving a man who later proved to be Lionel Moss. I told her of the unsuccessful attempts by two men to kidnap her son, after he'd been left in my care. I told her about finding the abandoned Camry, and the key it had contained, which led to the discovery of Burke Donald's home number through the motel records.

When I was finished she closed her eyes and took a breath. 'Run that past me again.'

I did.

She shook her head and opened her eyes. 'If you discover information pertaining to an active criminal investigation,' she said carefully, 'you surrender it to whoever's running the case. You don't act on it yourself.'

I said nothing.

'How did you gain access to the car?'

'One of the guys was carrying keys. We found falsified identification in the boot of their vehicle and a stockpile of guns.'

She said nothing. The right side of her face was

342

alternating blue and red. She had deep-set eyes, and they were cast in black shadow. With her lank wet hair, her head seemed almost haggard. She gestured out her window.

'Have you contaminated the scene?'

I said, 'Donald had only just arrived home, but his lights were on, so I figured whoever topped him broke in and searched the place.'

Her face didn't waver. 'Searched for what?'

'I don't know, I didn't find anything. I figure they just flicked the lights on to make everything look normal.'

She said nothing.

'Alan Nielsen's part of this too,' I said.

'What?'

'The guy who visited me the other morning. Ever since we ran into Moss on Sunday, he and Donald have been giving us shit. Nielsen wove me some junk story about how Moss was an informant and they have to protect him, but the only reason he was so interested in what was going on was because he'd assigned him to watch my neighbour.'

She gave me a disbelieving look.

'John and I warned Moss off on Sunday, right?' I said. 'Monday morning, Nielsen was waiting for me at my desk, pissed off because he realized Moss had been made. So he had him killed on Monday night, and replaced him with the two guys who broke in on Tuesday.'

'Why on earth would he have any interest in you?'

'It's not me he's interested in, it's my neighbour's son.'

Quiet in the car. If Hale was even aware there was a debate taking place, he didn't show it.

Bennett said, 'I don't want you pursuing this.'

'Speak with Nielsen.'

She didn't answer. She turned in her seat and looked away from me. I got out of the car and walked across the street, hoping Hale would regain consciousness in due course and drive me home.

■ THIRTY-THREE

We escaped the neighbourhood a little before midnight. We drove northeast back towards town then turned onto Quay Street and headed along the waterfront. Traffic was non-existent. Hale pulled up at the end of my drive at dead on twelve.

'You want me to hang around?' he said.

'No, it's fine.'

'I might need to be on hand to thwart any more attempted kidnappings.' I couldn't tell if he was serious or not.

'It's fine, John, thanks.'

I got out of the car and stood and watched him drive away, rooster tails of red ground water thrown up behind his rear wheels. The air was chilled and carried the heavy organic scent of rotting pine needles and sodden grass. I was alone on the street, and tree cover made me feel reasonably secluded, so I held my arms straight out, fingers extended, to check if I was still shaking. There was a slight wobble. I was still aware of the beating of my heart. I took a long breath to quell my nerves and dropped my hands to my sides. Whether by coincidence or from a subconscious sense of responsibility, I was looking directly at Grace's home. It was probably twenty years newer than mine, and in slightly better condition. I could see a light on in the living-room window beside the front door. I pictured her sitting in there, racked with worry. It was difficult to imagine what a woman would be thinking, after learning her son had nearly been kidnapped, her ex-partner was missing and a close friend had been found murdered in a bathtub. I wondered briefly whether she had close family, or friends even. I couldn't help but think that if she did have, it might have been them she confided her problems to on Saturday evening, instead of me.

I turned into her driveway and walked up onto the low deck area fronting the house, then knocked on her front door. There were painted clay pots containing various shrubs placed against the house, and Michael's bike leaning against the roller door on her garage at the top of her driveway. I heard the dull thud of feet on flooring, then the door arced back and Grace stood framed in its void.

Her red hair was loose, down across her shoulders. She was wearing faded blue Levis and, although it couldn't have been more than six or seven degrees outside, a sleeveless top. Her face went blank for a moment when she saw me, then it crumpled as she rushed forwards and pulled me into a hug, burying her face in my shoulder. She'd caught me unprepared, and nearly pushed me off-balance, but somehow I managed to retain my footing. I started to say something, before I realized she was crying. Quietly at first, then deep heaving sobs I could feel through the material of my jacket. She was mumbling, but I couldn't understand what she was saying. I moved her gently inside, then pushed the door closed behind us. She had me around the neck, and the skin on her arms was freezing. By the smell of her I could tell she'd been drinking.

We stood in the entry hall for a while until she'd regained her composure, then I eased her back and looked at her.

'What's the matter?'

She seemed to see some irony in that, because she smiled and choked out a laugh and looked up at the ceiling.

'What *isn't* the matter?'

'Let's sit down,' I said.

Without waiting for her to move, I brushed past her and made a right into her living room. It was small, but that didn't detract from the space. A pair of soft leather couches faced each other across a low coffee table, and I sat down in one of them and waited for Grace to enter the room and settle herself in the other. She gazed at the carpet for a spell, gripped by self-consciousness after her emotional outpouring, and I looked around the room for a moment to allow her to fully regain her composure. There was a fireplace on the right-hand wall which had been sealed off years ago and replaced with a gas heater. The original mantel was still intact, though, and displayed a series of framed photographs, most depicting either herself or Michael. Her television was in the corner to my left; a plain black box topped with dust.

'Where's Michael?' I asked gently.

She sniffed, pushed her hair back behind her ears and cleared her eyes with the heels of her hands. 'In bed.'

'You been drinking?'

The ironic laugh again. 'A little, yeah.'

'What?'

'Shots of gin.'

'Don't.'

She looked up, surprised at the hardness in my tone, but said nothing.

'Kids don't like seeing parents drunk,' I said.

She looked at me a long moment, and I glanced away. I could feel residual vibrations in my fingertips. I glanced up in time to see her nod once, then blink rapidly and lean back into her chair.

'He's a good boy,' she said quietly.

'I know. And you have to look after him. Sitting around at night getting pissed isn't the way to do it.'

She nodded. 'Why did you come here?' she asked.

'Hale and I caught a break,' I said.

Her lips were pressed hard together, blue from either fear or cold.

'You might not remember,' I said. 'I asked you if the name Burke Donald sounded familiar.'

She made no reply.

'Donald's a cop,' I said. 'We found out he'd been in contact with the two men sent to take Michael on Tuesday night. We went to speak to him, and found him dead.'

Nothing. I could see tears starting again, though.

'Are you sure the name means nothing to you?' I asked quietly.

She nodded. 'Why is he dead?'

'I think he might have been involved with the men who tried to take Michael. I think there was somebody working with him. I think that person murdered him because they were scared of him becoming a liability.'

She twisted on the seat cushion and looked towards the door, like she was afraid we were being overheard. She turned back to me at length, and her eyes were wide, pupils dilated. 'How?'

'He was shot, pulling into his driveway, probably sometime this afternoon.'

Her hands went to her face and she jiggled her knees up and down, so that her feet pattered against the floor. I could hear her beginning to hyperventilate. I got up and stepped around the coffee table then sat down next to her and put my arm around her, waiting until she'd calmed down. Nothing else I could do. I felt very awkward. I could obviously sympathize with her, but not really empathize. I had no family of my own, my parents had disappeared from my life before I was old enough to recall them. Concern for the well-being of someone close was not a sensation I had really felt before. I looked over my shoulder every so often to make sure Michael hadn't poked his head in the door. After thirty seconds of sustained crying, the tears halted and she lowered her hands and gripped her knees, turning her head away from me so that her fringe hid her face.

'I never wanted to be caught up in all this terrible stuff,' she said.

I gave her back a pat, then took my hand back. 'I know. But you can't just decide you're not going to have anything go wrong in your life. Sometimes shit just happens, and you have to grin and bear it.'

She nodded, fringe swaying. Bearing it. She didn't grin, though.

'Will they try again?' she said. Her voice was hoarse. The smell of booze seemed stronger.

'Try what?'

'To take Michael.'

'Hale and I are watching, don't worry.'

She nodded slowly, but didn't seem entirely convinced. 'He's a strange man,' she said.

'Who, John?'

'Yeah.'

I laughed. 'A little odd, I admit.'

'So what's his story?'

I shrugged. 'He went into the army when he was eighteen, after that he joined the cops. He left them a couple of years ago and set up his own PI business. That's the extent of him, really.'

'Where did he grow up?'

'Somewhere, evidently. He doesn't like to talk about it much, so I don't really know. You should ask him, if you're interested.'

She pushed her hair behind her ear and turned so I could face her. She exhaled, and I caught a load of sour alcohol breath. There was a subtle smile curling at her top lip. 'Make sure you keep your promise, won't you?'

'What promise?'

'That you'll keep us safe.'

I patted her knee gently. 'I have no intention of breaking it,' I said.

The smile grew and her mouth parted as she leaned towards me. Her lips were moist and smooth. I put a hand on her arm and pushed her away gently and stood up.

'Stay with me,' she said quietly. 'Tonight, please.'

I looked down at her, pathetic and tear-streaked, her life and perception of security in tatters, completely vulnerable. 'Not when you're like this.'

She didn't reply. I left her there alone on her living-room sofa, with nothing for comfort but the thought that I might be able to protect her.

■ THIRTY-FOUR

Friday morning, I woke up comparatively late at eight a.m., left for work at half past, and was at the station by ten minutes before nine.

My email and voicemail were showing eight and twelve new messages respectively, which I took as all the more reason not to embark on checking through them.

But Leon Ross had come through for me, apparently. He'd sent me a package: three files. Prohibited photocopies, delivered courtesy of FedEx. That Leon.

I went and made myself coffee then returned to my desk and pulled the collection of paperwork towards me. The first file covered information I was already reasonably familiar with: it was the case file for the investigation following the ambush of Alan Nielsen's two million dollars of drug money. I flicked through it for form's sake, familiarizing myself with the particulars again: Quay Street, men on motorbike, money gone. I pushed the file aside, drank some coffee and opened the second folder.

I had never read it before, but I was nevertheless familiar with the information it contained. The reports it held were all dated July and August of 2000, and related to an aggravated assault on a woman named Lauren Pietersen, committed by one Lionel Moss. My attending officer's report was near the front, relating the steps which had led Hale and me to the parking garage where we found Pietersen bleeding from a stab wound.

I tossed the two files back into my in-tray and picked up the third. It was a case file. The last report contributed was dated November of 1992. Again, the subject of the file was Lionel Moss. It was a chronological record of an investigation eventually leading to the imprisonment of Moss and two other men for assaulting a pizza delivery man.

The officer in charge of the investigation was listed as Detective Sergeant Burke Donald.

I closed the file and dropped it in my lap, and put away the rest of the coffee much quicker than a liquid of that temperature should ever be drunk. The pain was masked by my sense of accomplishment though: I had hard proof of interaction between Donald and Moss reaching back more than fifteen years. The possibility that he had recruited Moss for a job within the last month seemed increasingly feasible.

I left the file on my desk and headed down the stairs to my car.

The woman I had spoken to the previous day had told me that visiting hours at the hospital Paula Webb was admitted to were between ten and two, so I thought it best to get in early. I looked up the address for Ellerslie Meadowcare Hospital in a phone book I carry with me in the car, which indicated the hospital was located on a street I knew was not far from the Fontaines' home.

I fed Neil Young's *Sleeps with Angels* into the Commodore's stereo, drove west across town and caught the motorway south to Epsom, heading into the suburbs. Travel was easy; rush-hour traffic was heading in the opposite direction, but it still took me longer than expected to find my destination. The hospital consisted of a cluster of low, red brick buildings seated comfortably amidst expensive homes fronted by expensive cars, ten minutes beyond the motorway. The property was marked at the street by a smooth waist-high concrete wall, in place more for aesthetic appeal than to keep anybody out. It was broken midway to accommodate a wide tarsealed driveway, which expanded into a rectangular parking area out front of a reception area reminding me of a primary school admin office. The rest of the facility was separated into two wings stretching back either side of reception. There was a separate lane for emergency vehicles which disappeared from view of the street. It was nice though, I'd grant it that. The hedge bordering the drive was cut so crisply it was almost perfectly square, and there were enough flowerbeds to ensure the sick and dying at least had something pretty to look at.

I parked in a free space beside an ambulance, got out and walked in through the front entry. It was set out like a hotel. The floor was cream carpet and the desk was polished wood panelling with a mirror-like granite top. Seated behind it was a young woman with a smile like porcelain. I took my badge out of my pocket and opened it on the countertop in front of her.

'How may I help?' she asked. She had the politeness of a bank teller.

'I was wanting to speak with Mrs Webb.'

'Visiting hours are at ten, sir.'

'It's nine-fifty. It's not a personal visit, I'm investigating a crime.'

She fluttered her eyebrows and gave an understanding little nod, as if that changed things. She picked up a telephone handset and rolled away from the desk a fraction, so that the conversation that ensued was not audible to me. After not much more than a minute, a male nurse dressed in a white uniform emerged from a door beside the desk. He was a thin guy of about forty, with gold-rimmed glasses and a receding hairline that had left him with a pronounced widow's peak. He chose not to introduce himself and instead just raised his eyebrows.

'I'm here to see Paula Webb,' I said.

He checked his watch. 'Visiting hours are from ten.'

'It's nine-fifty.'

The receptionist said, 'It's not a personal visit, Craig. He's investigating a crime.'

Craig adjusted the glasses. 'Are you with the police?'

'I am.'

He touched his glasses and beckoned to me. I followed him down a windowless corridor floored with grey linoleum. The doors we passed were windowless; some announced access into semi-restricted areas, others were ajar and revealed storage cupboards containing first-aid

357

kits, IV bags and packaged defibrillators on wheeled metal trolleys. The hallway dog-legged shallowly, and when we reached the end of it, Craig stopped and used an electronic swipe key to admit us through a door reading *SENIOR CARE*. I followed him along more grey lino until we reached a doorway I imagined must have been at the very far extremity of the left-hand wing of the hospital.

We stopped outside, and he looked me in the eye, key-card raised above the electronic lock, as if poised to deliver instructions before allowing me inside. His face was an oddity; his nose was thin and almost flush against his face, and I got the feeling his eyes didn't focus in unison.

'Don't be long,' he warned. 'She's not well.'

'OK.'

'She's hooked up to an IV, so she could be drowsy.'

'All right.'

'When you want to leave, there's a buzzer next to the bed, I'll come and walk you back.'

'Thanks.'

He appraised me silently for a second, then pushed the door open and stepped back, allowing me to move past him into the room.

The floor space within was little more than could be expected from a prison cell; not in excess of eighteen or twenty metres square. It lacked the charm and warmth of the reception area: same grey lino as the corridor, the walls a shade of yellow something akin to mustard. That smell only hospitals have. There was a bed, its headboard flush against the far wall, with heart and blood-pressure monitors and intravenous-fluid stands occupying the spaces either side. There was a window directly above, curtained over, so that the lighting was tinged grey. The bedclothes were draped over the form of an elderly woman, hiding everything except her head. Her fingertips gripped the blankets either side of her chin, giving the almost comical impression of somebody peeking over a wall.

I closed the door gently behind me, took a step forward and hovered near the foot of the bed. I was unsure of the proper etiquette. I didn't know whether the woman had been told I was coming, I had no indication of her temperament, other than what Craig had told me. She was awake and watching me, dark eyes holding my face, but she waited for me to initiate the greeting.

'Mrs Webb?'

Her face registered no change and I was uncertain as to whether she had heard me, before her eyelids drooped and she made a little shape with her mouth and said, 'Ms Webb, yes. That's what I go by.'

'Ma'am, I'm a police detective, I was hoping to ask you a few questions. I don't know whether you're aware, a girl living across the road from you was murdered.'

'Yes, I read the news.' There was energy to her voice, in contradiction to her physical state. I figured her for about seventy-five.

'Can I just ask to begin with, were you at home on Friday evening?'

The smell of the air became more pronounced as I spoke; a heavy disinfectant stink.

Her eyes left my face and she freed an arm from the blankets and rested it atop the covers, enabling me to notice the clear plastic tubes snaking in beneath her wrists. She followed the line of my gaze, taking in the sight of her withered arm, then switched her attention back to me. I looked at the blood-pressure monitor to avoid her. The graphic display was showing a steady, periodically spiked line. There was a text window above it reading 121/79.

'Here's a piece of advice,' she said. 'Don't get diabetes.'

I didn't answer her.

'And if you *do* get it, look after yourself.' She raised the arm, letting me see the tubes again. 'I've had a double-figure HBA1c for ten years. I got retinopathy, and my kidneys have given up the ghost. I've got to have my blood filtered by a machine now.'

Her tone was neutral. Just a bland factual report. I made no comment. I was hoping she'd come back to my original question.

'You shouldn't smoke, either,' she said.

'I don't.'

She waved her arm dismissively, and the lines clacked softly. 'I was speaking in general terms. *People* shouldn't smoke. But you do, don't you?'

I just looked at her. A wryness had come into her eye that I found disconcerting. 'Lying's almost as bad,' she said.

'Do you mind if we come back to the original question?' I asked.

She smiled and batted her eyelids. 'Remind me.'

'Were you at home Friday evening?'

She nodded. 'Absolutely, yes I was.'

'OK. I guess, all I was wanting to know was, whether or not you heard or saw anything out on the street that evening.'

She rolled her eyes and lolled her head back on her pillow and looked at her monitor screens. 'That's a bad question,' she said. Purely observational, no irritability to her tone.

'In what way?' I asked.

She turned her head the other way on the pillow and checked the remaining monitors and muttered to herself. Her skin had a faint yellow tinge to it. 'You haven't given me any sort of time-frame,' she said. 'No indication of what it is I might have noticed that could be of use to you.'

'Well,' I said, 'to rephrase, I guess what I'm asking is, did you happen to see or hear any activity on your street between the hours of ten p.m. and three a.m.?'

'Yes,' she said, 'I did.' No hesitation, no pause to quietly reflect.

I swallowed and felt my breath grow shallower and the pit of my stomach chill. 'You heard something, or you saw something?'

She touched one of the IV lines absent-mindedly. 'The *first* time, I heard something,' she said.

'I'm sorry, the *first* time?'

She frowned and nodded at me as if I was slow. 'Yes, at about ten o'clock, I heard a car stop across the street, then later at about midnight I saw—'

'Sorry, hang on. Start with what you heard.'

I moved away from the bed, leaned back against the door and took a breath, held it and let it out. She watched me, her mouth curled at one corner, curious as to my reaction.

'You heard a car at ten o'clock on Friday night?' I asked.

'That's what I said.'

'Across the street from your home?'

She nodded, grey hair bunching against the pillow. 'I was in bed, it was quiet, I could hear quite well. It was a loud car, like one of those hoonish young men drive. One of those modified sports cars or what-have-you. I heard it stop.'

A loud, modified sports car. Like Hendrik Larsen's Mitsubishi Lancer Evo.

'And then what happened?' I asked.

She frowned then yawned widely, strings of saliva in her mouth extending and snapping as she did so. 'Don't you people normally use notebooks?'

'I have a good memory. What happened after you heard the car? Was there anything else?'

Quiet while she considered the question. I needed to know if she'd heard a door open, but didn't want to be too suggestive and provoke her into fictionalizing something. I looked at the monitor and saw her blood pressure had jumped to 132/81. At length she shook her head, but offered no explanatory comment.

I gave in: 'No door?' I prompted.

'No, just the engine. Waiting for a little bit, then driving away. There might have been a door, but it was too quiet for me to hear.'

'OK, so tell me about the second incident.'

She swallowed down another yawn and directed her focus at the floor beside the bed, as if she'd decided to withdraw from the conversation. A pattering began against the roof, hopefully a sun-shower as opposed to something more permanent.

'You said you saw something,' I prompted.

Her eyes shifted towards me, pale and flecked with red. 'I had low blood sugar,' she said. 'The Protaphane I take at dinner tends to peak around midnight, I get two-point-fours, two-point-sixes all the time.'

I nodded.

'I went to the kitchen to get fruit juice,' she said. Her attention went back to the floor, then to the ceiling, eyes wandering as she siphoned the contents of her memory. 'It's painful these days. I get aches in my legs, and in my kidneys. My feet aren't too fond of walking, either.'

I smiled sympathetically. She paused to catch her breath.

'Anyway,' she said, 'I got myself some juice, and then I

went and sat in my big chair by the window. It's a specially designed one, orthopaedic or what-have-you, supposed to be good for posture, maintaining bone structure, you know what I mean?'

'Yes, absolutely.'

I saw the BP reading drop to 125/78, as if my understanding was a source of relief to her. The rain on the roof cut back to a soft hush.

'It's difficult not to see across the street from there,' she said. 'Just because of the angle, I can see the end of the driveway and everything.'

I didn't respond, hoping she'd take it as an indication to press on.

She said, 'I saw a car drive out.'

I tried to keep my tone level: 'What did it look like?'

She frowned slightly and closed her eyes, looking irritated, as if the question had disrupted the flow of her narrative. 'It's the one that's usually parked there,' she said.

My heart stumbled in its rhythm. 'Christ, you mean the VW?'

She eyed me sternly. 'Never say His name in vain, you'll end down there.' She gave a nod. 'Yes, it was the blue one, the VW. A Beetle, I think it's called.'

■ THIRTY-FIVE

I found the call buzzer on a table next to Paula Webb's bed, and Craig opened the door so quickly I was convinced he'd been standing outside, attempting to eavesdrop. I wasn't worried about that, though. Right then, amongst the greater scheme of things, nosy male nurses didn't really rate.

I walked back out to the car through light mist and climbed in, but didn't start the motor. I didn't feel I could dedicate the necessary cognitive capacity to driving. I looped my thumbs through the bottom lip of the wheel and leaned my head back against the rest. The Fontaine case was nearly a week old, Saturday to Friday. It was just unfortunate the greatest lead so far had arisen so late in the game. I stuck my keys in the ignition so I could set the wipers going and rid the windshield of water, in case visual clarity in some way corresponded to mental acuity.

Mark Jameson had told me on Saturday that Emma Fontaine had not been killed in Albert Park; the primary crime scene was somewhere else. Six days later I had gathered two further pieces of information. Firstly, Emma had quite likely been dropped home on Friday evening, as Hendrik Larsen had told me when I interviewed him. And secondly, although Elizabeth Fontaine's official statement had made clear she had not been home the night her daughter passed, somebody had taken her car for a drive early on Saturday morning.

I leaned forward and cranked the heater up, then started the engine and backed out of the space, accelerating towards the exit. It was a short drive to the Fontaine home, and the streets were quiet, early on a Friday. There was a sense of serenity hanging over the place that almost made my presence as a homicide investigator completely inexplicable.

I turned into the Fontaine driveway and followed the basalt ribbon up to the turning circle, parking in the space normally occupied by the VW. I hoped she was in. If any of the flowers left against the house and along the driveway had been brought inside, I couldn't tell.

I climbed out and walked over to the front door, the smell of wood smoke greeting me as I inhaled. I brushed mist from my hair and knocked three times on the door, the acoustics insignificant in the morning stillness. Elizabeth Fontaine clearly heard though. She opened up for me after barely half a minute's pause. Her hair was pulled back and she was smiling. She was wearing a knitted jersey and a pair of black track pants. Her expression was radiant.

'How are you?' she asked.

I was half-turned from her, and pretended I'd missed her greeting. 'Why haven't you cleared the flowers?' I asked.

She didn't respond immediately; I thought it was quite possible she didn't actually know the answer to that herself. She started to say something, then stopped, then began again. 'I don't know. I guess, looking at them would sort of confirm it all to me. I don't think I'm quite ready for that yet.'

I nodded. 'May I come in?'

There was a beat during which the smile dwindled a fraction, but then she stepped aside to allow me to enter.

She led me through to the small living room. I was sure we were alone in the house, but as she ushered me in she pulled the door closed behind us, the tongue ticking against the latch, making the space seem more confined. Like our meeting was in some way conspiratorial. I sat down in the same couch and Elizabeth sat down opposite me, the coffee table at knee-height between us.

She leaned back and folded her right leg across her left, leaving her slip-on shoe dangling precariously off her toes. 'What can I do for you?' she asked.

I watched her face, but tried do so without appearing obvious. There was no tension to her whatsoever. I said, 'I just wanted to update you, primarily.'

She smiled and bounced the folded leg, and the slip-on shoe fell to the floor and rolled onto its back. It was well-worn and the sole was smooth. 'You're making progress then?'

'I spoke to a neighbour,' I said. 'Actually, a lady who lives opposite you.'

'Paula?'

'Yeah.'

'She's a lovely woman. Did she have anything to offer?'

Her hands were held loosely in her lap; the tendons weren't pronounced, she wasn't anxious.

'She thought she may have heard a car outside your home on Friday evening,' I said. 'She raised the possibility that Emma had been home.'

She shook her head and frowned. 'Very unlikely. She didn't leave any sign she'd been inside again.'

'Was that your conclusion when you arrived home on Saturday?' I asked.

She nodded. Still relaxed. There was a small vase of flowers on the table between us, positioned to the right so my view of her was unobstructed.

I said, 'Ms Webb says she saw your car leave the property at approximately one o'clock in the morning.'

Elizabeth Fontaine made no reply to that statement. I could tell she considered it unusual, but it didn't bother her to the extent that she objected. I let it hang between us for a good moment before continuing.

I said, 'Ma'am, I don't mean to offend, but I need you to tell me exactly where you were on Friday evening.'

Her head cocked to the side by a minute angle and her demeanour transformed in an instant; placidity to anger, just like that. She leaned forward and her fringe fell across her face, and when she spoke her voice lacked its prior steadiness.

'I hope you're not implying I may have had some involvement in my daughter's death.'

'Please just answer the question.'

'Are you suggesting that my daughter was killed *here*? For heaven's sake. And then what? Just carted off?'

I didn't answer her.

She clenched her jaws hard and the sinew in her cheeks pulsed and her eyes swam. 'Idiot!' she hissed. 'Arsehole! My presence was accounted for all night, about two dozen people can back me up on that. I can only assume a better detective might have checked up on such detail before . . . insulting me, and . . . certainly making himself look like an ignorant twit!'

She shouted the final word, but with the dryness of her throat combined with the closed door, I didn't think the sound would have penetrated far.

'So can you explain who was driving your vehicle?'

She stood up suddenly and came around the table, leaning towards me, her whole face red and contorted, and streaked with moisture, and for a moment I was scared she was going to strike me. 'My car was with me all *fucking* night, you little prick! How should I have a clue who was driving it around here?' She was shouting; saliva flicking free of her mouth to the floor.

I said nothing, hoping she'd calm. She didn't.

'What car did the woman see?' she demanded.

'A blue VW Beetle.'

The anger in her expression dwindled somewhat and was replaced by confusion, and in that same heartbeat I felt a cool wash of realization hit me that made my head dizzy and sent my vision out of focus. Elizabeth Fontaine looked at me and swallowed as she straightened up and sat down again, beside me now, collapsing against the couch cushions. I was certain I could feel the vibration of her heart reaching me — unless of course, it was simply my own.

'That's not my car,' she whispered. 'That's Ruth's.'

■ THIRTY-SIX

We sat side-by-side on the couch for what seemed like a long time. No doubt the sensation was misleading, the speed at which I was thinking probably extended my perception of time.

'It's Ruth's car?' I asked.

In my periphery I saw her nod. She raised a hand and threaded her fringe behind her ear.

'Does she have a key?'

She turned and looked at me, and her face was a mess. 'What?'

'A key to the house?'

She nodded, and the movement was very slow.

'I need you to tell me her address,' I said.

She got up and retrieved her shoe from where it had

fallen, not replying until she had sat back down and replaced it on her foot. 'It's the dark-brown two-storeyed place,' she said. Her voice was empty.

'Where is it?'

'At the end of the street.'

I got up and left her there alone on the couch. Her posture was sagged; head forwards, legs and arms as limp as if filled with putty. She looked like a mannequin somebody had just dumped there.

I opened the door and left the house. The driveway was strewn with wilted petals, moulded into the basalt by the passage of feet like some dead mosaic of discarded sympathy. I knew it was only a short trip up to the end of the street, but I drove anyway. Elizabeth Fontaine's description had been brief but sufficient. The house at the far end of the cul-de-sac was a two-storey place clad in mahogany-coloured panelling. It was essentially a cube, with the front door positioned halfway along the lower level. I got out of the car and rang the bell. The wind was up and I could hear the roofing material flexing under the force of it.

I pressed the bell again, heard the muted chime from inside the house, and a moment later the door opened to reveal a small round woman with curly red hair smiling up at me.

'Hi,' she began, 'not a very nice morn—'

'Is Ruth in?'

She hesitated, probably put out by being cut off mid-sentence.

'Why, who are you?'

'I'm a police detective. Are you a relation?'

'Yes, I'm her mother.'

'Is Ruth in?' I said again.

She placed her hands on her hips. Authoritative. 'I think I'd better ask for some ID or something.'

I obliged and showed her my badge. She frowned, as most people are inclined to when police officers come around flashing identification and requesting on-the-spot interviews. She glanced past me at the weather and pursed her lips, making a little tutting noise, and said, 'You'd better come in, I guess.'

I followed her in to the entry area. The air was warm and smelled of mince pie. The floor was cedar panelling a few shades lighter than the exterior cladding, and the walls were a subdued tone of off-white. There was a staircase to the left, and the woman took a step towards it and called up.

'Ruth? Ruth, there's a guy here to see you!'

No sound from upstairs. The woman turned and made

a gesture for me to follow, then started up towards the second level, feet clomping against the panelling, calling as she moved.

The stairs led up to a hallway adorned with much the same décor as downstairs: wood on the floor, off-white on the walls. The woman turned a sharp left to a door set into the near side of the corridor. She called her daughter's name again, then leaned forward, weight on one foot, putting her ear close to the jamb and knocked.

'Ruth?'

The door opened almost immediately. There was a brief silence, then a creak, before Ruth emerged into the hallway, closing the door softly behind her as if she was afraid of someone discovering what lay beyond it. She did not look surprised to see me and seemed barely aware we had even met before. She was dressed casually in jeans and a T-shirt, and, excluding an initial glance my way, directed her attention to her mother. She kept her hands at the small of her back, holding the door handle.

'Ruth,' the woman said, 'this man wants to talk to you.'

There was no real sense of intrigue or worry in her tone. She wasn't concerned at the possibility her daughter could be in trouble.

'Ruth, we need to have a chat,' I said. 'Would you come downstairs?'

There was a sadness to her face. She was still holding the door handle. 'No, I can't. Sorry.'

I tried to catch her eye, to draw her focus, but she was everywhere except with me.

'Please,' I said.

Her mother placed her hands on her hips, the possibility that her daughter could be in strife looking more likely now. 'Why do you want to see her?' she said. It was more of a demand than a question.

'I'd prefer to discuss that with your daughter,' I said.

Her mother turned and looked up at me, then back to her daughter, suspicious there was something going on beyond her level of understanding.

'Ruth,' I said. 'I really need you to come downstairs and have a talk with me. Can you do that?'

She closed her eyes and shook her head. 'No, I can't. I'm really very, very sorry.'

I got the impression the apology wasn't intended for me.

'Why not?' I asked gently.

There was a pause during which she looked at me with an expression of complete and utter tranquillity, then she turned, opened the door again and disappeared. I heard footsteps, rapid across a hard floor, followed by a tremendous shattering of glass so sudden and forceful I could almost physically feel it.

I threw the door aside and ran across the room, a bedroom, to a large window now cragged with massive fractured shards. I looked out over the sill, down onto the driveway. The girl I had spoken to not ten seconds earlier was lying on the damp concrete in a pool of her own blood, the shocking realization of what she had just done forcing her eyes wide, even as her life left her.

I couldn't have saved her. She had dived through the window head-first, which meant gravity had rotated her just enough to cause her skull to take the brunt of the impact as she landed. She had raised her arm at the last instant, but mid-air is too late for a change of heart when it's a suicide plunge. She was dead within a minute.

I didn't call for backup for another three or four minutes, because I had to try to stop her mother from screaming. I detained her on the concrete beyond the front door. I have never heard anyone scream so loud. She fought me, but ultimately all she succeeded in doing was summoning the neighbours. The first of them approached with genuine concern; it was likely they knew the family, understandably shocked at what had happened. The next waves of people were brought more by voyeurism than worry. In the end I shooed away all of them and threatened to arrest anyone who came within fifty metres.

I left the woman downstairs in the living room then used my cellphone to call Claire Bennett. I found a sheet in a linen closet and draped it over the corpse. I did not go back inside. I did not want to have to deal with other people's misery. I just stood on the footpath and watched the end of the road, waiting for the sirens.

I believed I had answered the question of who killed Emma Fontaine, but I felt no real satisfaction. I had always lived with the idea that the best possible result to a problem was to discover the answer. Yes, I had a suspect, a person on whom to pin blame, but I had no real understanding of motive. No hard evidence to tell me in plain terms why two people had lost their lives. There was nothing liberating in causing another death.

The ambulance crew was the first to arrive. The paramedics lifted the sheet, checked pulses and shone lights in eyes. A time of death was recorded. Two of them went inside to tend to the girl's mother, while the rest of them returned the sheet to its original position and went back to their ambulance. There was nothing further for them to do. None of them looked particularly traumatized, though. No signs of discomfort. I guessed suicides committed by young women were something they saw often enough.

It was almost eleven-thirty by the time Claire Bennett showed up. I saw her park behind my Commodore, get out and walk along the path towards me. She was content not to go and look under the sheet. She'd seen dead people before. She just stood mute at my shoulder, expecting me to get the conversation started. She was out of luck. I wasn't in the mood for talking.

Eventually she said, 'So what happened?'

No genuine intrigue; the scene was self-evident.

'I had reason to believe she may have had involvement in Fontaine's death. I came here to question her, she jumped out her bedroom window.' I was strangely aware of the tone of my own voice, like listening to a played-back recording.

'What was her name?' she asked.

'Ruth Morgan.'

Bennett looked around through crinkled eyes, taking in the street as a prospective home-buyer might. She was wearing a grey skirt, and a blue denim jacket over a white blouse. Wisps of her hair were in her face. 'We'd better talk in the car, Ranger,' she said.

She turned without waiting for me and led me over to her Commodore, unlocking it with the remote fob. She climbed into the back seat and slid across to the far side, and I got in next to her.

'Déjà vu,' she said.

I didn't answer.

'Your two friends from Tuesday night have woken up,' she said. 'By that, I mean they were momentarily conscious. We ran their prints through Interpol, both have prior charges for assault. We've charged them with the attempted kidnapping at your place, but we don't yet have enough to put anything else on them.'

I nodded. She shrugged and spread her arms slightly in an invitation to say something. 'So take it from the top,' she said. 'What have you been up to this morning?'

I took her back one-and-a-half hours, to when I had met with Paula Webb. I explained how Webb had heard sounds late on Friday evening, indicating the possibility Emma Fontaine had in fact been dropped home. When the woman had told me she'd observed the VW leaving the Fontaine property, my first instinctive thought was

381

that it had been Emma Fontaine's mother who had taken her life; waiting for her daughter to arrive home, then killing her and putting her into the car to transport her. When I learned the vehicle did not belong to Elizabeth Fontaine, I realized it was almost certainly someone else who had killed her.

Bennett nodded in response to all this then arched her neck to catch a glimpse of herself in the rear-view mirror, propping her elbow on the sill and thrumming her lip gently with her index finger. 'And from that you decided it was her, then?' She nodded in the direction of the sheet on the drive.

'Not for sure. All I knew was that Emma had arrived home, and was seen driving away shortly after that. Obvious next step was to talk to her.'

She played with her lip again and angled her gaze out of the window, as if her next question was suspended somewhere amidst the fabric of the air.

'We should take the suicide as an admission of guilt,' she said. 'Do you agree?'

I nodded. 'For now.'

'So in retrospect,' she said, 'what happened?'

I shrugged. 'Ruth was waiting for Emma when she arrived home on Friday evening. She attacked her, causing an injury severe enough to kill her, then used her car to transport the body to Albert Park.'

'Forensics combed the house, didn't find anything to suggest that.'

'If she was attacked on the driveway it's plausible. The head injury would have bled, but not so much that the evidence couldn't drain away with the rain. Emma was physically small, I think Ruth would have been quite capable of moving her.'

'Have you come up with a reason yet?'

I shrugged. 'The inherent frailty of the human spirit. Complex social dynamics.'

She kept her eyes out of the window, but left her lip alone. 'And in layman's terms?'

I shrugged. 'People just do stuff.' I paused. 'I don't know. I think as much as we like to try and force a frame of logic on crime, sometimes you can't. Sometimes people just do stuff, and it can't be labelled with an explanation that makes sense. She wanted to kill someone, you know? That's it.'

Bennett made no reply to that.

'The day I visited,' I said, 'I checked through Emma's desk, but didn't find anything. When her mother eventually came across the diary, though, that's where it was. She said she'd found it in a drawer. I think Ruth might have put it back in there after I left.'

'You think she'd been wanting it as a memento?'

'I don't know. Pages had been torn out of it. She might have decided to remove anything incriminating, then put it back in the hope it would lead us on to someone else. It's likely after she killed Emma, she used her keys to access her car and grab what she wanted. Mementos, I don't know.'

Bennett smiled, but there was no humour or satisfaction in it. She turned to me and said, 'You know what my father used to say?'

I shook my head.

'He used to say, "Girls, who'd have 'em?"'

I didn't offer her my thoughts.

'At the end of the day,' she continued, 'We've got two dead girls in the space of one week.'

I nodded, but it was more for the sake of feeling myself move than to pass opinion. Bennett took her elbow off the sill, spread her fingers wide and pushed her hand back through her hair, the skin of her forehead stretched taught like latex as she did so.

■ THIRTY-SEVEN

The driver of the grey station wagon let the hand-brake off and coasted gently until he was only one hundred metres east of the target address. Conditions were favourable. Intermittent traffic, no pedestrians. The Norfolk pine in the adjacent property limited visibility somewhat but that wasn't too much of a setback. He ratcheted the brake again, very quietly, halting the big vehicle. There was a patrol car parked opposite the mouth of the driveway, but the cop inside didn't seem the observant type; he seemed restless — perhaps aware his shift was about to end. He seemed to be considering the possibility of leaving his post twenty or thirty minutes ahead of time, before his replacement arrived, just to make it home a bit earlier.

The driver of the grey station wagon hoped the policeman would depart soon. It would leave the street unguarded, the target address unwatched, the person of interest residing inside completely vulnerable to whoever might wish to pop by and say hello.

I left the scene at a little before two.

I drove slowly. The tremors had returned, and I didn't want to risk an accident. The weather had closed in, and the clouds above looked like lumps of steel wool. I took the motorway up to town then found Customs Street and stopped on a yellow line outside a dairy on the corner of Anzac Avenue to buy a pack of cigarettes. I drove on up to Symonds, then hopped across to Princes Street and pulled up outside the University Clock Tower, directly opposite Albert Park.

I got out and locked the car then crossed to follow the black wrought-iron fence to the nearest entry, tracing the network of red concrete paths towards the central fountain. Maintenance crews had been through since I last visited a week ago, and the fountain itself was gone, leaving only a rusted cast-iron pedestal in the middle of a huge, empty white basin. I sat down on one of the wooden benches that form concentric rings around the water feature and tore the plastic wrapping from the cigarettes, placing a cigarette in my mouth and lighting it. The atmosphere hadn't changed at all during the past six days; it was grey overhead, I could hear droplets clicking amongst the trees. Far off there was thunder. It was very mood-appropriate. I was disheartened though. The pursuit of truth was meant to be wholly enlightening. It was never meant to be ugly. Whatever I discovered or brought about, whichever way you want to look at it, wasn't meant to be something to shy away from. It wasn't supposed to make you consider whether or not you should have become involved in the first place.

The surface of the path in front of me was uneven, and pools were forming, their skins dimpled as more and more raindrops fell. I sat and sucked on the cigarette and watched the weather swallow the horizon.

I'd left my cellphone on the passenger seat of the car, and when I got back I was greeted with a message informing me I had four missed calls. One from an unknown number, three from John Hale. There was a text from Hale, too: *Call me ASAP*. Not particularly encouraging.

I dialled his cell. He answered immediately. I could hear the tone of the Escort in the background.

'What's up?' I said.

'The boy's gone.'

I waited for him to continue, but clearly elaboration would require prompting.

'*Gone*? What, you mean someone's just—'

'Yeah. She thinks someone's taken him.'

My stomach washed cold. 'What, kidnapped?'

'Apparently.' In the same tone he'd use if he lost his car keys.

'She's sure he's gone?'

'She's positive. She called me, completely hysterical, said she'd tried you a couple of minutes earlier, but you didn't pick up.'

I felt my head start to throb. Water on the windows had distorted the view to the extent that almost nothing was distinguishable. 'There's a unit posted at her doorstep, for God's sake.'

'It went off-shift early, there was a twenty-minute window when nobody was watching.'

'Ah, fuck,' I said.

He didn't answer, and I was left with my own echo.

'Did she see anything?' I said.

'No, he just vanished. No sign. The police are there apparently, and they haven't found anything, either.'

'Oh shit. So where are you?'

'I was at the office, but I'm heading to your place, now, I'm only a minute or two away.'

'OK, good. I'll meet you there.'

'Where are we going?'

'I'll tell you in a minute.'

Access to my street was prevented by red-and-white emergency tape. Hale had parked the Escort fifteen metres further on, and when I pulled up beside him he climbed out and jumped into the passenger seat beside me, whereupon I took off back towards Tamaki Drive, tachometer touching red.

'You'd better put your belt on,' I said.

I heard the latch click home. 'Where are you taking me?'

'Don't sound so frightened.'

I turned onto Tamaki and floored it west through mid-afternoon traffic, chin to the wheel, wincing at a sun that had somehow penetrated the cloud cover.

'Whoever fucking snatched him thinks Grace is in contact with her husband,' I said.

'She isn't.'

'Apparently whoever took her son doesn't know that.'

He looked at me. I ventured out across the median and honked my way past a truck.

'He's been kidnapped because of Treverne,' I said. 'They think if they take Michael, Grace will panic, relay the information to her ex, force him out of hiding.'

'I think they're counting on him finding out by himself. If they thought Grace knew where he was, they'd just ask her.'

I hit an uneven patch in the road and the suspension bottomed out, jolting us in our seats.

'Where are we going?' Hale said.

'Back to Treverne's house. They want him out of hiding, first thing he'll do if he goes with that is to check in at home. My guess is they're waiting there so they can cash his chips in.'

'*Cash his chips in?*'

'Don't think it'll catch on?'

'If I had to hazard a guess, I'd say not.'

Before long, Tamaki ended and we were through onto Quay. I set the grille lights and the siren going, blew through red light after red light, all the way to the Viaduct, then hung a fast left and hit the ramp access through to Fanshawe. City driving is tough without the aid of official status. I think the day I make it all the way along Fanshawe Street without hitting a single red light will be the same day the Pope gives up Catholicism. Today was no exception, with traffic halted at the lights just past the Air NZ building. Congestion was bad, and we were forced to stop.

'We can't just break down the door on our own,' Hale said.

'No, not with that attitude.'

He freed the radio handset from its cradle and passed it to me. 'Call backup.'

■ THIRTY-EIGHT

He'd left the boy downstairs in the kitchen. He could hear him crying, quite audible despite the gag. He slung the shotgun over his shoulder, checked the load in the pistol then stepped into the master bedroom. There was a window directly opposite the bed providing a view out onto the driveway. With the blinds across, he could stand just inside the door and look out without risk of being observed.

He'd left a radio scanner on the night table beside the bed. Its reports had been mostly unremarkable, but as he stood looking out towards the street, listening to the boy blubbing, he heard a police detective identify himself by code and request backup for a check of a property on Chequers Avenue.

He smiled and removed his badge wallet from his pocket, tossing it on the bed. It didn't seem right to continue carrying it, given the circumstances. He slipped out of the room and touched the butt of the shotgun to stop it sliding off his shoulder. Tomorrow, for the first time, he was going to be headline news. Print, television and radio.

We got off the motorway at Tristram and took Wairau Road down to Archers, following it past auto repairers and hardware shops, all the way to the lights at Chartwell Avenue, then turned right on a red light.

'Your driving's a real concern,' Hale said.

'Thanks. Have you got a gun?'

He strained against his belt and freed a silvered Colt .45 automatic from his trouser pocket, laying it in his lap.

'Shit, are you licensed for that?'

'Sort of.'

The kerbs were lined with parked vehicles on either side, and at eighty an hour I had to float near the middle to avoid clipping wing mirrors. The radio chirped and a patrol constable requested we update our current position. Hale picked up the mic.

'We're two minutes away,' he said.

He heard the latest status report from the detective's car, then heard the patrol unit reply they were still twenty minutes away. He shut the radio unit off. He wondered what they were planning to do. He had been cautious about bringing the kid inside, but was confident he hadn't been seen. If Treverne had been reported missing, it was entirely possible a unit had been dispatched to check his home. Sending a patrol car and a detective seemed a little excessive, though.

He collected his badge and the radio scanner as well as the mail he had taken from Treverne's letterbox and stashed them in a duffel bag he'd left in the corridor, then hurried downstairs and checked the ground floor. He'd drawn the curtains in all of the rooms save the lounge and duct-taped the edges to contain the glow at night. Not ideal, but sufficient for now. He checked the ranch slider outlook. No problems. The boy was still in the kitchen. He headed back up the stairs.

Along with the pistol and shotgun, he had a Remington .22 hunting rifle which he'd brought up from the car and stored in the bathroom. He retrieved this now and brought it through to the bedroom, setting it down on the floor inside the door. He stepped to the window and drew the blind back, then freed the latch on the right-hand aluminium frame, sliding it in behind the left to form a metre-square gap free of obstruction. He moved back to the door and picked up the rifle then stepped up onto the bed, crouched and sighted down the length of the barrel towards the street.

His firearms training had been extensive. Direct shot from the bed to the roadside must be thirty, forty metres. Not excessive. The bed creaked beneath his weight and downstairs he heard the boy whimper. He adjusted the focus on the Remington's Nikon scope until the letterbox was etched crisp in the lens, then chambered a round, feeling the silence return.

The house was unchanged as far as I could tell. I stopped the car short of the driveway, shut the engine and my blood pressure filled the quiet. When I had last visited, cars had choked the kerbside, but today the street was clear. Risk of collateral damage was minimal.

'Are we going to wait for backup?' Hale said.

'If they're twenty minutes away I'm not waiting,' I said. 'I need a vest.'

He dropped flat against the mattress as he heard the car pull up, then slowly, after hearing a door open, arched his neck so he could see above the sill.

The detective was Sean Devereaux. He had John Hale with him. Hale appeared to be watching the house; elbow propped on the doorframe, a knuckle pressed to his lip.

He took his weight on his arms and inched his head higher, feeling his neck throb with pressure, and watched Devereaux climb out of the car and drape his suit jacket over the roof before raising the rear lid, removing a bulletproof vest from the boot and shrugging into it. He thumped the lid shut and when he emerged around the near side of the car he was carrying a Glock 17 pistol in his right hand.

Hale slid out. He was carrying what looked like a 1911-model Colt .45. Taking a round from that would be like getting struck by a torpedo. The two of them stood together beside the car's bumper, eyes on the house, conferring.

He smiled to himself. Their last conversation held among the living would be concerning which door they should enter through. He wouldn't have long. They would see him as soon as he rose to fire. He rehearsed the process in his mind. *Raise, shoot Devereaux, swing to Hale. Devereaux, Hale; Devereaux, Hale.*

With the window open the curtains acted as a

windsock. They hung there limp and lifeless, like the butterfly-soft skin of some long-since-expired creature. The men moved along the path towards the letterbox, guns held down along their thighs. He lowered his head and shifted his weight, gripping the rifle with both hands, ready to thrust up. He exhaled, felt the rhythm of his heart slow, like the gradually decelerating *whop* of a rotor as its momentum ebbs away.

He heard their feet on the driveway. The boy cried out, louder this time, as if he sensed rescue might be near.

He rose to one knee and brought the rifle scope to his eye in one fluid motion; saw Devereaux's head float to the intersection of the crosshairs, and pulled the trigger.

■ THIRTY-NINE

When we reached the driveway, a number of things happened at once. First, I noticed someone had cleared the letterbox. Second, I saw the wind catch the curtains at the right-hand end of the upstairs bedroom window.

Then Hale crash-tackled me.

We fell right and I felt something tick my earlobe, before a rifle shot reached my ears.

We crashed to the concrete, but even as we hit the ground Hale was pulling me up again.

'Run, run, run!' he roared at me.

I stumbled forward and he pushed me again between the shoulder blades — the next shot exploded the pane out of the bedroom window and shards of glass blew out onto the drive. I could feel blood running down my neck, seeping into my collar; I could hear glass crunching beneath my feet, and strangely, the sound of bedsprings compressing.

Hale swerved in front of me, and when we reached the door, he raised his foot and struck it on the handle, busting the lock. Both panes of frosted glass cracked and fell, the frame buckled and sagged, and next thing I knew he was pulling me inside.

The shot must have missed killing him by only four or five centimetres. Hale had seen him as soon as he raised himself, pushing Devereaux off his line.

He fired again, but they were out of sight, and all he succeeded in doing was shattering the window. The sound was massive in the small space. He dropped the rifle and picked up the shotgun. It was a Mossberg 500 twelve-gauge pump-action, fitted with a seven-round magazine. He raised the butt to his shoulder and stepped out of the room, making his way to the top of the stairs.

With all the doors leading off it closed, the entrance hall was dark and claustrophobic. Hale covered the stairs and I ducked left, opening the living-room door.

'Clear,' I hissed.

'Keep your goddamn gun up, for Christ's sake!'

I ignored him and opened the door to the right leading to the kitchen. I saw Michael. He had been wrapped in duct-tape, his body enswathed in so many black lengths he looked mummified. The tape covered his torso, was wrapped around his neck, secured his wrists at the small of his back, and trapped his ankles together. A sock had been stuffed in his mouth, held in place by more tape encircling his jaw and lower skull. His eyes bulged and flared red when he saw me.

'Shit, I've found him, I've found him.'

I rushed into the room and Hale backed in after me, gun levelled at chest-height towards the door. I pushed the table aside and knelt, seeing my own blood run freely to the floor, dark red and fluid, splashing gently as it hit the lino.

The wall exploded.

The effect was deafening. A half-metre-square section of drywall separating the kitchen from the hall blew into the room, the table split in half from buckshot and the air filled with white dust. The sound expanded to fill the space so completely I felt we and everything else would surely be vaporized.

I fell on the boy and saw Hale crouch and shield his face with his forearm, then the explosion came again. It was so loud you wouldn't have heard yourself scream. I flattened myself against the mound of tape as another section of panelling disappeared, reappearing in powder form, and shotgun pellets tore the floor with numerous tiny clicks almost lost beneath the roar.

And then again. And again, a fourth time, so that another section of wall flew towards us. The cavities were progressing towards the doorway in a diagonal fashion, as if the source of the assault was descending from the top of the stairs. The linoleum was completely shredded, the floor thick with desiccated segments of plaster and timber and wallpaper like confetti. The air was heavy with gun smoke and white dust finer than flour.

On the fifth explosion, Hale went down. He fell to the floor gripping his left knee, red immediately welling between his fingers. His jaw was clenched, lips pulled back from teeth which seemed dull in a face powdered white by dust.

I raised the Glock and fired to the right of the door, aiming for the base of the stairs. The report sounded minuscule in comparison to what we'd just experienced. I saw the round punch a neat ring in the wall, a thin puff of dust spitting free as it did so.

I fired again, and then again and again and again. The Glock's mechanism locked on the sixth round. I dropped it and scrabbled frantically, raised Hale's .45 and aimed for the open door.

No one emerged. Hush descended, eerie in the way silence is after traumatic noise. I got to one knee then slowly stood, the sights at the end of the gun trembling from the pressure in my wrist. I made it to the door. I was shaking. I inched the barrel of the gun around the frame and peered out.

Leon Ross sat slumped at the base of the stairs, his left calf in ragged bleeding tatters, his face pressed to the wall.

I didn't pause to consider the implications of his presence, ponder the logistics of it all. I slipped my cuffs off the back of my belt and locked his wrists together behind him. A shotgun had fallen to the floor at his feet, and I picked it up by the barrel, stepped into the kitchen and slid it across the lino to the far wall.

Hale was lying in a foetal position near the remains of the table, his clothes rimed with white dirt, both hands clutched to his knee. My fingers were greasy with the blood from my ear, clumsy as I unbuckled my belt and whipped it out through the loops. I moved over to Hale, knelt and slipped the belt under the top of his thigh, buckling it firmly. The floor beneath his lower half was stained bright red. He didn't look at me. Michael was silent. Or, if he made a noise, my ears were ringing too severely to tell.

I abandoned the Glock on the kitchen floor and made my way outside through the tatters of the door. The split ring with the two spare keys attached was as I had left it, trapped beneath a plant pot near the edge of the deck. My hands shook as I inserted the second key into the lock on the garage door.

The hinges squealed as I pushed the door back. I clambered across the bonnet of the Pajero, streaking blood on the paintwork. I pulled the acetylene cutting-torch down off the workbench. It consisted of two large steel tanks bolted in parallel to a sturdy aluminium frame, coupled to a pair of hoses, topped with regulator valves. The entire assembly was heavy and awkward to transport, but I managed to drag it out past the deck and up the step to the house. I manoeuvred it past Ross in the hall and got it into the kitchen, setting the thing down next to Hale. His cheek was against the floor and his eyes were closed. His hands were drenched scarlet, wave after greasy wave of redness roiling out beneath his grip. Michael was unmoving.

'I'm going to cauterize the wound,' I said.

He nodded, cheek rubbing the lino. I reached up and turned the valves on the top of each bottle. There was an audible hiss as I opened the acetylene wheel.

I freed my lighter from my pocket and held it to the torch nozzle and thumbed the wheel.

'You're lucky I'm a smoker.'

There was a spark, then the gas caught, flaring brilliantly, cutting an orange streak almost a quarter-metre long. I opened the oxygen valve on the torch handle, changing the flame to blue.

'You'll feel this, John.'

He did, too. I held the flame to his skin and his face contorted, his breath quickened and came as a wild hiss through his teeth as the wicked heat slowly dried up the flow. The blood around the ragged wound and on the floor turned brown under the intense glow, and I could smell his flesh slowly cooking. He drew his hands away as the flow dwindled and pressed his clenched fists into his eyes against the burning, but it was not until the fissure beside his knee no longer ran red that I eased off on the torch. I closed the valves off and the flame died immediately, robbed of its fuel, the metal outlet smoking gently. I propped it against the remains of the table, then collapsed to the floor, removed my cellphone from my pocket and pressed one — three times.

▪ FORTY

Four days later, on a fine Tuesday afternoon when the air was still and remarkably mild for winter, Claire Bennett stopped her car in my driveway and knocked on my front door.

'You could have just called,' I said when I answered the door.

She smiled. She was clad in jeans and a denim jacket and her hair was pulled back into a bun that was taut enough to iron out some of the lines in her forehead.

'I thought you could do with the company,' she said.

'I've only been off two days.'

She said nothing, brushed past me to the corridor and walked down to the kitchen. I closed the door and followed her. I had left a lit cigarette on the table, and when she saw it she picked it up and took it to the sink, extinguishing it under the tap. She dropped it in the basin and dusted off her hands as if she had been handling something noxious, then turned and leaned against the edge of the bench top.

'How's Tonto?' she asked.

'You mean John?'

She nodded. 'If you're the Ranger, he's gotta be Tonto.'

I smiled. 'He'll recover. He's been shot before.'

She said nothing. I pulled out a chair and sat down at the table. My ear was bandaged quite extensively, and still throbbed following any sudden movement. I had been told the entire lobe was now gone.

'So are you managing to scrape by without me?' I asked.

She smiled. 'Just barely. Tying up loose bits, you know how it is.'

'You've got everything knotted?'

'More or less. We searched Ruth Morgan's room, found an album full of photographs of Fontaine she'd taken covertly over a period of about six or eight months.'

My hand searched for the absconded cigarette, but of course came up empty.

'How?'

'Camera.'

'From where?'

407

'They were close-ups, primarily. Probably shot with a cellphone camera.'

'Infatuation or jealousy?'

'I don't know. Maybe infatuation. Maybe there was a sexual element. Her mother was adamant there wasn't. Apparently there've been boyfriends in the past.' She looked down at the cigarette she'd doused. 'I don't know,' she repeated. 'I suspect it was just jealousy. Who knows.'

'A photo album dating back eight months is pretty extreme. That's obsessive. That's a personality disorder.'

'A personality disorder nobody picked up on. You'd think an eight-month photo album would go hand-in-hand with other behaviour people would notice. But nobody did.'

'Which suggests she was an average person who just developed a craving to kill somebody. She probably identified Fontaine as a potential victim, for one reason or other, whether it was jealousy or lust, and intended the album as a sort of souvenir.'

She shrugged, made a face like she wanted to discard the notion. 'Murder weapon was a crowbar. She'd buried it in her backyard. We think she lay in wait in Fontaine's house until she turned up on Friday night, then ambushed her.'

I nodded. 'The driveway's basalt. If she'd killed her outside, any residue left would've drained through and then been rinsed by the rain.'

'Yeah. Probably. They found blood and fibre traces in the car. She must have driven the body back into town, then used Fontaine's keys to access her vehicle and take her diary, like you said. The premeditation was thorough. She would have always had the intention of misdirecting suspicion. She would have known Fontaine had been out with Hendrik Larsen, which made dumping her body in Albert Park seem sensible, if the murder was supposed to look like the result of a boyfriend losing his rag.'

'How are they taking it?'

She looked at me, not understanding. 'Who do you mean?'

I shrugged at her. 'Everyone. Fontaine's mother, Ruth Morgan's family.'

She made a face. 'Morgan's mother took it hard, but Elizabeth Fontaine is cut from sterner stuff. She'll recover. People always do. Normality always creeps back, even if it takes years.'

She smiled suddenly, almost embarrassed by her insight, and cast her gaze around my kitchen as if she was looking at a quaint replica of something from another age.

'We liaised with Queensland Police,' she said at length. 'They found a Brisbane landline registered to one of the guys who tried to abduct your neighbour's kid last Tuesday. We checked Ross's cell records, he'd dialled the line maybe a dozen times. He had a bin liner buried in his vegetable patch with a twenty-two Ruger pistol inside. We had ballistics tests done, it's almost certainly the same weapon used to kill Lionel Moss and Burke Donald. There was cash in there as well, close to ten grand.'

'And what's the official consensus at this stage?' I said.

She looked at me. 'We still can't find Elliot Treverne.'

'Then he's dead.'

She looked at me silently.

'Leon Ross's name has already hit the papers; if he was hiding from him, he would have popped his head up by now.'

She let that hang between us for a moment before she said anything further. She ran the tap again, like she was trying to drown the remnants of my cigarette.

'I think Ross and Donald were blackmailing him,' she replied after a moment. 'Whether Donald got cold feet or greedy, I don't know, but for some reason, Ross decided Donald needed killing.'

'Has Ross said anything?'

'He's lawyered up, hasn't said a word.'

We both fell quiet for a beat.

'I thought it was Alan Nielsen,' I said eventually. 'The day Michael disappeared, I was convinced it must have been Nielsen who'd taken him.'

She shook her head, half-turned and looked at the dead cigarette. 'His interest in Lionel Moss was legitimate,' she said. 'He'd been using him as an ongoing source of information for about six months.'

'OK,' I said. 'So I need to find Elliot Treverne.'

■ FORTY-ONE

I pulled up outside the pharmacy at the bottom of Elliot Treverne's street the following day shortly before one in the afternoon. It was an odd little establishment, positioned at the far right of a ten- or fifteen-shop row of outlets, as if it had been attached as an afterthought to supplement the general practice further along.

Most of the front wall of the place was glass; bordered above and below by a three-quarter-metre strip of cracked weatherboard, interrupted dead centre by the shape of the front door, which was propped open.

I had to wade through shelves supporting colourful little displays of shampoo and body lotion to reach the counter at the rear of the room. There was a woman of about sixty seated behind it, pricing packets of glucose tablets. She smiled at me primly, gave my ear a concerned frown.

'You should see the other guy,' I said.

'May I help you?'

Her hair was arranged in a tight perm, and she was wearing a lime-green cardigan over a purple blouse. To the left of the desk was an open door leading to what was probably the dispensary. A sign on the wall said *Pharmacist on Duty: Madeleine*.

I produced my badge for her. 'I understand you had a break-in recently, about three weeks back.'

'Yes, we did. Have you come across something?'

It sounded like a good euphemism for *Have you arrested the bastard?*

'No,' I said. 'I'm afraid not, this is just a follow-up, to clarify one or two things.'

She glanced around quickly, but there was nobody else in the store. 'OK,' she said.

'I only looked at the details of everything quite recently,' I said. 'I saw some photographs, they showed some blood smears that had been left.'

She nodded. 'He left blood on the light in the back room. And on the fire exit.' She pointed at a door to my right as if to validate the assertion. 'And also in the staff sink.'

She delivered this last line in a hushed whisper, as if the staff sink were sacrosanct.

'Yeah,' I said. 'I think there was a floor-tile as well, and a desk drawer.'

'I don't think anything was stolen,' she said. 'He might have used some plasters and gauze and our scissors, and that was it.'

'You're probably right,' I said. 'I was interested in the drawer, though, do you know which one it was?'

'Nothing was stolen.'

'You're probably right,' I repeated. 'But do you know which one it was, anyway?'

She tapped the countertop. 'One of these,' she said. 'Though I forget which one.'

I moved in behind the counter beside her, and she edged out of the way. There were two cupboards, two four-high columns of drawers, a possible eight handles he could have touched.

I started snooping. I found cardboard boxes full of ball-point pens and vivid markers, boxes of protein bars and nasal spray and A4 sheets of adhesive-backed barcode tags. In the second-to-bottom drawer of the second column I tried, I found a copy of the Auckland White Pages. I picked it up and dumped it on the counter in front of me.

The woman watched me with interest. I winked at her.

'Detection as you watch,' I said.

Her eyebrows raised in acknowledgement. I began flipping through the phone book. It appeared to have had frequent use; the cover was dog-eared, the pages bore a dark discoloration down the depth of the long edge. I held it by the spine and fanned the pages with my thumb, front to back.

A page had been torn out.

The paper was so thin its absence could easily have gone unnoticed. It had been ripped free, top to bottom, leaving a ragged concertinaed strip near the bottom of the binding.

I closed the book and returned it to the drawer.

'Thanks for your time,' I said. 'Is there a payphone around here, do you know?'

'Yeah, right down the opposite end. You need to call someone?'

'No, it's fine.'

I could sense her watching me as I walked to the door.

The fruit shop three doors down was kind enough to lend me their copy of the White Pages. I brought it back to the car and identified the page missing from the

415

pharmacy's copy. It listed surnames beginning 'Br—'.

In the glove box I had a photocopy of Sergeant McKay's list of cars passing the camera at the intersection at the end of the road. Sixty licence-plate numbers, sixty vehicle makes, sixty names, sixty phone numbers, sixty time stamps. Thirteen of the listed names began with 'B'. Three began 'Br.' One of them wasn't present on the page of interest. One of them wasn't present on any page at all.

The third name I looked at was.

The third name was Charles Brannon. He had a slot near the top of the page. *Brannon, C N.* The time stamp read 12:58. Mr Brannon had been driving a light-green Ford Courier ute. His home address was a place on Commerce Street, central Auckland.

I returned the list to the glove box. Half past twelve on a morning more than three weeks ago, Elliot Treverne had torn a page out of a phone book in a pharmacy, presumably with the intention of placing a call. Thirty minutes later a man listed on that page was recorded driving not one-hundred-and-fifty metres away down the road. Probably not a coincidence.

Commerce Street branches south off Customs, a block east of Queen. It's not an appealing stretch of road. The eastern side is occupied by a dump of a brown low-rise at the north corner, and the two-storey buildings further down arc home to a porno retailer, a couple of bars and some low-rent flats. The opposite side is fairly similar, the presence of a Wilson-administered parking building being the only major point of difference.

Charles Brannon lived on the upper floor of the double-level housing the porno place. At the left-hand end was a neon XXX sign jutting out over the tarsealed pavement, and further right a door giving access to the rooms above.

The carpet on the staircase was yellow and mottled and smelled of damp as I made my way up, and the floor of the corridor I emerged into had decayed to the extent where large patches of particle-board were visible. Naked bulbs hung from insulated electrical cord dangling from the ceiling, casting the hallway a dirty yellow.

There were four doors on the left-hand wall of the corridor; Charles Brannon's flat the third. The brass number had been removed from the door at some stage; burred screw holes the only evidence it had ever been there.

His door was unlocked. I swung it back and smelled rotten eggs. I looked down and saw a man lying on the ground with his throat cut.

The door opened into a hall, boxed in on two sides by cream plasterboard. The dead man was lying on his back across the threshold between the hall and a small living area, arms spread in a last hopeless prayer for mercy, eyes and mouth and carotid agape. He was about my age, but small and doughy. The floor beneath him was black with his fluids, and the fetid stink of it was horrific even from three metres away. The curtains across the windows had been pulled, and I got the impression the odour had saturated everything.

I cupped my hand over my nose and mouth and entered the flat. I glanced into the living room and found another man sprawled on his stomach in front of a small television, a red gash across the base of his skull. The blood around him was sufficient that I didn't bother checking for a pulse. I gathered from the fact that his face somewhat resembled Michael's that this was Elliot Treverne, suggesting the other guy was probably Charles Brannon.

Treverne and Brannon, murdered. Nothing like a happy ending.

I walked back out to the corridor and called Comms on my cell.

■ EPILOGUE

'Thanks for seeing me.'

Ross looked up as I entered the interview room, but chose to say nothing. There was a rectangular section of one-way glass in the wall adjacent to the square table he was seated behind, and he glanced sideways at it, assessing his profile. Beneath the table, I could see his left leg was heavily bandaged.

'Did I really have any choice in the matter?' he asked.

I shrugged and sat down in the chair opposite him. He looked drained. Scared, even. Not of me, but of what inevitably lay ahead for him. His fringe hung across his forehead, the cuffs of the long-sleeved shirt he wore were unbuttoned, hanging limply from his wrists, which were resting against the edge of the steel tabletop. He had two days' growth on his jaw.

'They told me you weren't talking,' I said. 'I guess this is a step in the right direction.'

He held me with red eyes. His mouth parted, as if about to form a question, then closed again. He said, 'Is the camera on?'

I glanced to my right, to the lens mounted where the wall met the ceiling. 'You've conducted interviews before, Leon,' I said. 'What do you think?'

His mouth curled humourlessly. *Of course it's on.* 'What do you want, Sean?'

'To chat.'

He leaned back in his chair and looked at the mirrored glass. It must have been disconcerting, not knowing whether anyone stood behind it. 'Chat?' he asked.

I nodded. 'More like Q and A. I think you probably know how it goes. You've played it before, only from this side of the table.'

He touched a cuff, making as if to button it, then let it hang. 'If you're going to get cute with me, maybe I'll keep quiet, just to piss you off.'

I shook my head. 'You won't do that, Leon. If you were going to keep quiet, you would have done so from the second I stepped in here. But you didn't. You aren't.

You've kept your mouth closed for too long and you're just dying to tell me everything.'

He smirked.

'I'll start things off by letting you know you had me fooled,' I said.

'I know I did.'

'That night you and I had a beer,' I said. 'The story of how you pissed your pants in Alan Nielsen's car. It was well done.'

He didn't respond. He raised a hand and raked his fringe off his face. His eyes flicked to the window, so fast I almost missed it.

'It was unpleasant,' I continued. 'I pitied you. It set you up as a victim. Ensured any suspicion I may have had of you evaporated.'

He just looked at me.

'I know you took the money, Leon.'

He pushed his sleeves to his elbows and leaned forward, linking his fingers on the table between us. His hair fell down across his face again.

'You misdirected me perfectly. You misdirected every-one perfectly. Surely the guy who'd had a gun stuffed in his face and lost bladder control as a result couldn't be in any way involved with the theft?'

The room was almost silent for a long time. The fluorescent tubes fixed to the ceiling hummed faintly.

'They think you were blackmailing Treverne, Leon,' I said. 'But I know you weren't.'

He looked up at me. His stubble was like sand stuck to his skin. He ran a hand across it absent-mindedly.

'Come on,' I said. 'Speak.'

He looked around, just his eyes, no movement of his head. His fingers were still at his chin. He smiled, somewhat ironically.

'He kept wanting more,' he said simply. A film of moisture across his eyes.

'More what, Leon? Come on, talk to me.'

He leaned away from me and dropped his eyes to the floor somewhere off to my right, like a petulant child.

'Donald and I set up the grab,' he said.

'You and Burke Donald arranged to have the money stolen?' I asked.

He nodded. 'Yes. Donald had gang contacts, he was going to have a crew stop us when we moved the cash.'

'OK. And what about Elliot Treverne?'

'What about him?'

'Tell me why he's dead.'

He shrugged, still not looking at me. 'He came into the

picture afterwards. We knew him through work. He had background with financial crime units. He knew how shit was done. We needed him for the banking side of things, to filter the cash into accounts, make it seem normal. The grab guys were gang-affiliated, they wanted someone to wash the cash through companies they used for laundering before it got to them.'

'You gave him a cut in exchange?'

'Yeah.'

'But he wanted more.'

'More and more, yeah.'

'And you refused?'

'Yeah, we said no.'

'So then Treverne went on the run?'

'He fucking vanished. We thought, shit, he's gone into witness protection, something like that. He'd just gone. We could have faked warrants, checked to see whether his credit cards were still active, but it wouldn't have been legit.' He broke off and looked around, massaging his left wrist absent-mindedly; echo of a handcuff burn.

I made no reply, hoping he'd feel compelled to fill the silence. He said, 'Donald wanted to use this drug snitch he had called Moss to scare the shit out of Treverne's ex-wife, make the guy think maybe it wasn't such a good idea to muck us about, get him out of hiding. But these gang guys he'd roped in were getting edgy, called in a special team who owed them a favour, some shit like that. Like top-shelf, ex-military. Called "the twins". After you got to Moss, Moss was supposed to be gotten rid of, they were meant to take over.'

I looked at him. His eyes rose off the floor and found mine. 'You shot Lionel Moss?' I said.

'I'm not confessing to murder, Sean.'

I made a small gesture, as if whether he did or didn't was of minimal consequence. 'Tell me about the twins,' I said.

'The accountant had a kid. They were meant to snatch him, just so the accountant got the message. It was Donald's idea.'

I smiled. Piling the blame on the dead guy.

'Who are these gang contacts of Donald's?' I said.

'You'd have to ask him.'

'I can't, he's dead.'

Nothing in his face. Nothing on his mind, either, apparently, because he said nothing.

'Someone killed Treverne,' I said. 'I'd kinda like to know who did it.'

He took a laboured breath. 'Asian guys, like Triad

connections. They were wrapped up in the original drug-ring thing we were looking into that got us the money to begin with.'

'You don't know exactly who they are?'

He shook his head.

'You're very vague.'

'You're very fucking annoying,' he said calmly.

'Why'd they kill him?' I asked.

He shrugged again. 'They probably didn't like the fact he was on the run, wanting more money. He was a liability, easiest way to deal with him was to pull his plug.'

I said, 'Did you kill Burke Donald?'

He swept a hand idly across the table, as if clearing it of detritus. 'What do you think?'

'I think when I called you and asked you to cross-reference his name with Lionel Moss, you panicked, realized I was onto something, and shot him.'

He made no reaction. No denial, no confirmation either. He glanced one last time at the mirrored glass, swivelled in his chair and looked up at the camera.

'Do you blame me, Sean?' he said.

I didn't answer.

He looked at me steadily. 'I don't blame myself,' he said in answer to his own question. 'Like, I didn't want to just live my life as I was, and then wake up one day and realize I was old, and I'd wasted the last thirty, forty years for no reward.'

I didn't reply.

'It'll be you one day,' he said. 'That'll be you. You'll get up one morning and be midway through your shave and you'll think to yourself, "What have I spent my life doing?" And you'll answer, "Shit all, essentially." Because you've made no headway, you didn't play some integral, indispensable role. You're just another nobody. Nobody will thank you when you've gone, nobody will remember you.' He smirked. 'Nobody will shed a tear for Sean Devereaux.'

He looked at me, waiting for my defence, but it never came.

'Am I going to hell, Sean?' he said.

I shrugged. 'I hope not. I don't want you for company.'

He laughed dryly. 'You won't end up down there. You're a good bloke. You're a man of principle.' He raised a clenched fist. 'You're a crusader for the fallen innocent.'

'You're a man of principle, too. Just different principles from mine.'

I let that sit between us for a good moment, like a verbal offering for him to respond to. When he said nothing, I added, 'Regardless of where you go when you die, I figure you've still got another thirty years of living to get through. And with what you've done, I think I'd find the prospect of that hellish enough without continuing it into eternity.'

He said nothing further. Maybe my comment had resonated with him on some level he found saddening. I got up from my seat and knocked once on the door to be let out.

Grace was out when I knocked on her door at three o'clock that afternoon; I left the letter I had written for Michael, along with a small present I had wrapped neatly, in her mailbox. The letter was brief but I knew he'd get a smile out of it:

Hey Dude,
Sorry I haven't come to visit you, but I'm scared of hospitals (yeah, truly). I hope you're feeling OK, though.
I've given you a couple of CDs from my collection. One is Neil Young's Greatest Hits, the other is Up by R.E.M. They're both good. Listen to 'Walk Unafraid' on Up. I think I mentioned it to you, it's one of my favourites. It's good to listen to when you're not feeling all that flash,

because it makes you keep soldiering on. Remember to have it up really loud. Sorry I had to use Christmas wrapping paper.

When you get better come round to my house and we'll play snakes and ladders. I'm way better than John.

All the best from your mate
Sean

Grace answered her cell when I tried it.

'Where are you?' I asked.

'Oh.' She laughed, and it sounded strained. Like she'd had to cope with ten years' worth of stress and anxiety within the space of two or three hours. 'I'm visiting Mike.'

Mike. I'd never heard her call him that before.

'Are you all right? Is he all right?'

'Well, yeah. He'll get there.' She paused and gave me the strained laugh again. 'I've never been more relieved in my whole life. Just so, you know, grateful for everything.'

'I know what you mean.'

Silence.

'So what are you going to do?' I said.

The question was vague but she knew exactly what I meant.

'I'm starting anew,' she said. 'I've called a real-estate agent, we're getting out. All I want to do is just scratch it from memory. Just scratch everything.'

Quiet again.

'Well, I'm glad you're OK,' I said.

'Thanks.'

'Let me buy you a drink sometime. Or just pop over for coffee. You know I make a pretty mean cup.'

Her laugh this time was easier. 'OK,' she said. But there was something in her voice that told me she wasn't going to take me up on the offer.

Scratch everything. Does that mean scratch everyone?

I said goodbye to her and wished her all the best and she ended the call.

By half past five it was well on the way to full dark as I put the car out into the hush of the street and rolled down to Tamaki Drive, winding my way along a yellow-lit waterfront towards town. I was travelling against the rush-hour flow, and reached Quay Street after no more than ten minutes. The skyline to the right above Mechanics Bay was dominated by hulking stacks of cargo containers, halogen lamps beneath casting their edges white against the space beyond like some gift from above.

I turned up Gore Street to Customs and stopped at the light on the corner of Queen.

It's odd that this city appeals to me. It's grimy, disconnected, impersonal, frantic, and the traffic's a nightmare. But despite it all I love it. I love the constant transience you observe in a city. I love the little niches of classiness interrupting the sprawl: the bars along Vulcan Lane brimming with easy laughter and the hiss of pull-tabs; the too-expensive clothing retailers that dot High Street, and their pompous, coiffed clientele; the restaurants along the waterfront smelling of rotisserie chicken and chilled champagne and sea spray all at the same time. I love the fact I can sit at an intersection I frequent on an almost daily basis, and not find any of the hundred and fifty or so people waiting to cross in any way familiar. It's the nature of any metropolis, but to me, this is my city to a T. But the multitude of strange faces was what kept me in a job: you pick a score of people at random from any city environment and almost certainly one of them is a criminal. One of them is a sex offender, one of them has committed a serious assault, one of them is mulling over the possibility of fraud.

The light turned green and I hung a left onto Queen, accelerating past the Dilworth Building, then Louis

Vuitton further south. The footpaths either side of me were choked. This was the central artery of the city; five to six was occlusion hour. Traffic was slow.

I believed what Leon Ross had told me. I was aware one day I would wake up and ask myself what I had devoted the last forty years of my life to. And whether it had been worth it. The answer didn't bother me though. Consider that random number of urbanites I just mentioned. The idle, disconnected soldiers of the workforce, waiting for the lights to change. Sure, some of them are criminals. Logic would indicate, however, that an equal number are victims. I think the victims are what make the job worth it in the end. The thought of them is what brings you back, day after day. The memory of them is what keeps you awake after the sky turns dark, and gets you up even before it has cracked blue again.

I followed Queen up to Wellesley and turned left. Homeless Maori men, clad in filth, camped beneath the eaves of the Civic Theatre watched my passage. Five metres away, oblivious white men in suits waited for buses. I drove up to Symonds and stopped again at the lights. The world beyond the window was a spectacle of bright colour. It puts on a good ruse, does the city. Tourists probably think it's trouble-free.

I wound my window down and breathed in a chill that burned my nostrils. I thought I might head up to the hospital, treat John Hale to a beer with an old friend, then go home and sit and do nothing except indulge in the pleasantry of music.

Not for too long, though. I had work in the morning.